Champion of Valdeor

Book 1 in the Valdeor Chronicles

Sandralena Hanley

The Valdeor Chronicles

Book One
Champion of Valdeor

Book Two
Waykeepers of Valdeor

Book Three
Pilgrims of Valdeor (2022)

Table of Contents

VALDEOR

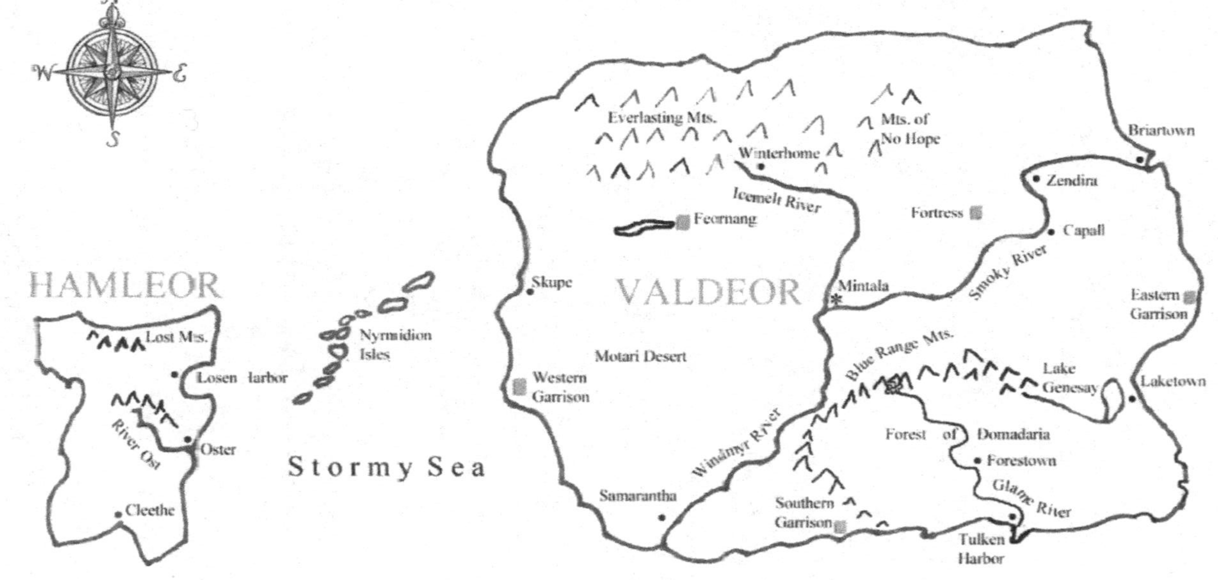

VALDEOR
Everlasting Mts.
Mts. of No Hope
Briartown
Winterhome
Zendira
Icemelt River
Fortress
Feornang
Capall
Smoky River
Skupe
VALDEOR
Mintala
Eastern Garrison
HAMLEOR
Motari Desert
Blue Range Mts.
Lost Mts.
Lake Genesay
Laketown
Losen Harbor
Nyrmidion Isles
Western Garrison
River Ost
Windmyr River
Forest of Domadaria
Oster
Forestown
Stormy Sea
Samarantha
Glaive River
Cleethe
Southern Garrison
Tulken Harbor

Alloryn parried his enemy's sword and thrust under his guard as the ruined fortress brooded above them in the darkening sky. The sheep, who played the dreaded warlord's part, bleated and ran away, then settled back to munching the grass, used to the shepherd boy's play. Alloryn swung his wooden staff and dreamed of heroic deeds.

He would turn fourteen tomorrow—almost a man. From the heights, he looked across the valley below to a streak of white mountains on the horizon. His chest ached with something close to physical pain. Longing swept through him. What he would not give to leave this valley, and these sheep, and join the soldiers of Winterhome, in the far north, who dared defy Valdeor's greatest enemy, Warlord Feornson.

Sunlight faded, bringing him back to the present. He whistled. "Shep, girl, bring the flock home. Good dog." He bent to pat the wolfhound's head.

He watched the dog round up the sheep and wondered what form the test of his manhood would take. His father had only hinted that the proving ground was half a day's walk and that he wasn't allowed to take anything with him. A shiver of fear, mixed with anticipation, ran down his spine.

As he approached the cottage he shared with Father, he saw the back of a man disappearing down the track. Curiosity ate at him while he penned the flock for the night.

Alloryn burst into the room. "Father, who was your visitor?"

Father did not turn around but kept ladling stew into their bowls. "No one to worry about. Eat. I have no time for your endless questions."

Heat flared inside him. He clenched his teeth to hold back a retort. *Why did Father keep treating me like a child? I will be a man tomorrow. A man!*

Father was quieter than usual that night. He was a man of few words at the best of times. He performed the evening chores distracted and kept glancing out the window.

Why did Father say not to worry? I was only curious. Of course, I have endless questions. He never tells me anything.

The next morning, Father woke him well before dawn and told him to dress. They did not sit at the table for breakfast, instead, Father took a loaf of bread and a skin of water, and they set out toward the hills. Father, tall and lean, took long strides. Alloryn had a hard time keeping up. Father did not stop at the sheep pen but headed for a desolate place beyond the grassy valley where they grazed the sheep. Alloryn knew better than to question him, for if Father wanted him to know exactly where they headed, he would say so. But Alloryn was impatient with excitement. He wanted to prove he was a man.

They marched for several hours through the barren wastelands, until mid-morn. Weird, twisted rock formations grew like plants in the stony ground. They went deeper into the rock forest, and a damp mist enclosed them. A stream blocked the path ahead, and Alloryn saw a hill with a gaping cave mouth on the other side. The fog emanated from the river, for it was thickest here, such that one moment he could not see farther than the water, and the next, a veil opened before him and he could see the cave again. He knew in his bones that this place was the rock forest's heart and that a presence of ancient evil resided in the cave.

Father rested a heavy hand on Alloryn's shoulder. "In that cave lies the Crestin Sword—a powerful weapon forged hundreds of years ago that once belonged to your warrior ancestor."

"I am descended from a warrior?" A thrill coursed through him.

"Aye. You must face a test of courage to become a man, son, and retrieve it. Oh, aye, I have seen you pretending to wield a sword. This is your chance to become a fighter for right and good. But beware the Kratigula. You must slay the great beast with the sword it guards. Avoid its claws, for they are poison."

Alloryn stared at the swirling mists around the cave and felt the waiting presence in its depths. His heart pounded and sweat coated his hands. He often wondered what it would take to become a champion. This was beyond his worst nightmare. He could not move his limbs.

Father turned him to face him with gentle hands on his shoulders. "When I was a lad your age, I faced the same test and failed. You can be the man I could not. Trust me. Trust yourself."

He knew fear, but his desire to perform a feat that would make him a warrior, as his forbearers had been of old, was greater. His father counted on him.

"I will bring back the sword!" He shoved his terror deep inside himself, took the lantern his father offered, and crossed the river alone.

The river proved not as swift and deep as he feared, and he soon crossed it. He stood at the cave entrance, water dripping from his trousers. He glanced back toward where he left his father, but the mist hung between them. Chilled air seeped from the cave. With shaking hands, he stopped to light his lantern, tamped his uneasiness, and entered.

Before him gaped a tunnel. He made himself walk forward. It twisted and turned for a long time before it straightened and started to descend. The feeling of brooding evil increased with every step he took. He gritted his teeth and went on. Surely his father would never allow him to go on such an errand if it were impossible.

Was it hours or minutes since I entered the cold, damp cave? And still, the path wound down, and the darkness beyond his lantern pressed around him like a living thing trying to wrap him in its arms and smother him. The tunnel seemed to have no end, and then it twisted again. He found himself in a natural chamber filled with bizarre rock formations similar to the ones outside. He held his light aloft and peered into the darkness. He could not see the immense chamber's end.

Cautiously, he made his way forward, fear twisting his gut,

wary of the weird shapes, and the shadows they threw around him. The chill air made him shiver. He stopped and listened for any sound in the stillness, but his heart thumped so nervously it overpowered any other sound. He waited until he was one with the quietness. The hairs along his arms rose. Something lurked in the silence, still and ominous. Trembling, he advanced despite his terror.

An object glinted ahead. He forgot caution and strode toward it. A metallic gleam from a niche in the wall reflected the light from his lantern. He moved faster, all else forgotten in the certainty that he had found the great sword.

He was near enough to see the oblong shape and the gleaming hilt when a movement in the shadows caught his eye. He swung around.

Four baleful eyes glared at him twenty feet away.

The Kratigula!

He did not pause to think, throwing the lantern at the monster, and leaping toward the sword.

The beast cried with pain or anger. The lantern hit the floor and extinguished. Alloryn could no longer see in the darkness which enveloped the cave.

His hands groped in the niche and touched old leather. He grasped the scabbard with his left hand and felt for the hilt with his right.

The beast's snarls filled the cavern as it dashed toward him.

His right hand clutched the sword hilt, and he yanked the blade free. He braced his back against the wall for the onslaught.

A sudden faint light emanating from the sword allowed him to see the monster. He almost dropped the sword in surprise.

The Kratigula nearly impaled itself on the blade but stopped short.

The sword's light gave them both an advantage.

The beast gave a deep growl, and the two looked eye to eye for an instant.

Two heads, like those of a turtle, sat upon long slender necks on top of a massive body. Sharp claws curled from the end of its splayed feet. Alloryn froze, a wave of terror washing over him.

The monster reared its heads and roared a cry of challenge. It slashed the air with a raised claw.

With a rush of panicked strength, Alloryn swiped with the sword at it and felt it cut through flesh.

The beast lowered one head and tried to bite back.

Alloryn turned and struck at the new menace, but only managed a light gash as the head swung away. Its foot knocked Alloryn off balance. He rolled and sliced the foot off before the beast could react. With another roar, the Kratigula backed away, screaming in pain.

Alloryn panted as he climbed to his feet.

From the Crestin Sword's soft golden glow, he could see the monster gather strength for another attack. As another claw and head reached for him, he threw himself on the ground and flung himself behind a nearby rock column.

He paused to catch his breath. He raced behind another column and crouched.

He remembered Father's training when out hunting. *Breathe softly and step gently so you do not alert the prey to your presence.* He followed those rules as he zigged and zagged around the rock columns.

Clammy sweat rolled down his back in the chill air. He pushed away the fear that threatened to paralyze him. He vaguely remembered the position of a certain rock formation he had seen beside the beast when he first encountered its glare. One rock balanced on top of a slender column. He had to find that column!

He stopped at the base to wipe the sweat dripping into his eyes. When he glanced up from his crouching posture, he found the large rock precariously perched above him. He climbed. His feet found toeholds, and the fingers of his left hand searched for a place to pull him up, while his right hand gripped the sword so tightly he bruised his fingers.

He climbed the column, sure that each loosened pebble would bring the monster.

When he was in a position to nudge the boulder over the other side, he braced his shoulder against the stone and levered the sword's hilt in a crack. He strained to rock the hilt until the stone loosened. Soon small pebbles dislodged and clattered to the ground below him.

The Kratigula came with measured tread toward the noise. Alloryn pushed with strength borne of fear and loosened the stone farther. He heard the tapping claws as the beast warily approached the column. He strained every muscle until he tipped the boulder over the edge. It crashed onto the beast's back and knocked it over.

Relief washed over Alloryn. His plan had worked.

For the first time since entering the cavern, Alloryn felt hope rise in his chest. *I can conquer this monster!*

Alloryn slithered down the column, the sword gripped

tightly in his hands.

He stood above the bellowing animal with its broken back. Both heads lashed at him, and he managed to chop off the left one, but the right one grabbed his leg and toppled him. He hacked at the remaining head with its turtle-like grip that held him like a vise. The undamaged claw raked his leg as he beheaded the monster.

A bolt of pain shot through his leg.

The jaws grew slack, and Alloryn released himself from them. His head spun when he tried to stand. He sat back down and breathed in gulps of air. His vision grew bleary.

The poison! It was at work in his system. He must return to Father. Surely he would know what to do to combat it.

Dragging the sword in one hand, he stumbled to the tunnel that led outside. He won the weapon, but he feared he was dying from the burning scratches on his leg. Still, he kept on, up and up the passage to the outside world.

Escape was all he knew.

He seemed to be coming and going in a strange reality. He found himself crawling at one point, then the mist came upon him, and he was in a dream again. He feared something behind him, as he imagined it pursued him, and he could almost feel its foul breath on his neck.

All that mattered was getting the sword to safety.

Then fresh air hit his face, he heard Father call his name, and he remembered no more.

2 *The Quest*

lloryn thrashed in the darkness, the monster gripping his leg and biting down. Alloryn cried out. He fought his way up through layers of darkness. Gasping, he felt pain throbbing in his leg. He opened his eyes, not to a cave, but he woke in his bed disoriented. *What a strange dream.* Then he moved and felt the bandages covering his leg. Father sat beside him. His face seemed more lined and his brown hair more streaked with gray than the day before.

"Here, lad, drink this." Father lifted a cup to his parched lips.

Alloryn obediently swallowed the nasty draught.

"What happened, Father? How did I get here? Was it real, then?" he asked in quick succession.

"Yes, son, the Kratigula was real. It is dead and the sword is safe, back in its scabbard, which I retrieved." He motioned to it propped in the corner. He gently stroked the hair from Alloryn's forehead. "You did the deed, after so many generations of waiting."

Father gave him a rare smile.

Alloryn could hardly believe yesterday happened. Except for the very real pain in his leg, the whole thing seemed like a dream. A scary dream.

But he had proved himself. He was not just fourteen, he was a man.

"Now you'll take the soup I bring you, and rest till you have your strength back. There's time to talk later."

Over the next few days, he lost count of the times his father fed and bathed him when he awoke before he fell back into oblivion.

He was restless after the fever passed, so he crept from his bed and took the scabbard from the corner. He sat back on the straw-filled mattress and studied it. Finely traced scrollwork decorated the leather scabbard. He ran his fingers alongside it and was amazed when a faint red glow followed the path of his fingertips. Here was magic indeed. He yanked his fingers away, fearing a burn. He waited, but nothing else happened. *Am I still feverish?*

He cautiously touched the pommel and the fine ruby embedded in the hilt. He drew the long blade forth, which was half as tall as he was. A stray sunbeam lit the blade and highlighted the fine edge. He could hardly believe he had won it and it belonged to him now. This blade was too fine for a shepherd. It was a warrior's weapon.

He awoke the next morning with the scabbard tucked under his arm, his chin touching the pommel.

Father allowed him to sit downstairs for a time. Alloryn was amazed to learn that three weeks had passed. He was impatient to know the future. However, questions got him nowhere. He waited with resignation and watched signs of spring through his window.

A morning came when Father allowed him outside. He sat on the hill and watched the newborn lambs frolic with his father's favorite sheepdog, a giant wolfhound, at his side. Shep rarely left her master's side, but today she seemed to sense Alloryn's need for company.

Late afternoon, Alloryn whistled as he walked down the hill, filled with gladness at his new freedom, Shep barking at his heels. He stopped short at the sight of the staff at the door.

Visitors were rare, so Alloryn looked through the window before going in. Father and an old man in a brown cloak shared a drink of ale. Alloryn slipped into the room.

The door creaked behind him, and they looked up.

"Here is the boy now. Come forward, son."

Alloryn stepped farther into the room. He glanced at the stranger's travel-stained clothes, shaggy hair, and leathery skin. But the man's eyes were what held him. The newcomer assessed him in turn. His gaze seemed to penetrate Alloryn's soul and weigh him.

Alloryn straightened his shoulders, lifted his chin, and stared back, not with defiance, but with pride. He came from a long line of upright men. They were poor now, but his people had not always been so. In past ages, his ancestors had been warriors who served the King, before the dark times.

As if reading his thoughts, the stranger spoke. "He has a look about him of his proud fore-bearers. Have you ever held a sword, lad?"

Alloryn glanced at Father, unsure whether to share their

secret about the Kratigula. Although a shepherd might carry a dagger in these uneasy times, swordplay forbidden to all but the warlords and those in their service.

The old man must have seen the look that passed between father and son. "Your father Yarrek has trained you well. The secret is safe with me, young Alloryn, seeing I was the one who challenged your father to win the Crestin Sword when he was your age. It is time you learned about your family history. Come, sit, and listen to the tale."

Alloryn was eager to hear about his ancestors. How many times had he asked Father about them, and received no answer? This man could answer so many of his questions.

Father secured the door, dropped a piece of burlap over the window, and added wood to the fire.

Filling his elders' mugs with more ale, Alloryn ladled himself a bowl of stew. He sat on a bench near them. The old man unfolded his story.

Many years ago (one hundred, to be exact) there lived in Mintala, the capital city of Valdeor, a good king. Arness was the last of a noble line of kings who had ruled the land with justice for many generations. He gathered the wisest men in the land. Scholars who collected all the learning of the ages to advise the king made up the Council of Mintala. The King himself was a learned man, but he, unfortunately, trusted too easily.

At the beginning of time, the monarchs of Valdeor wore a medallion that separated them from other men and helped them rule wisely. Legend had it that a spirit of light, one of the

Guardians of Valdeor, visited Gildran, the first king when his sacrifice pleased the One Who Fashioned All Things. The spirit gave Gildran six gems of great weight, glowing with their power. The stones of virtue, also known as heartstones, were different colors. Red, blue, purple, orange, yellow, and green—one for each virtue a ruler needs: courage, wisdom, justice, moderation, faith, and hope. From these heartstones, the Guardian of Valdeor took a chip of each of the six and set them in a circle in a silver medallion. The center stone was a diamond, for the greatest virtue of all, charity. This medallion passed from ruler to ruler through all the ages, until King Arness.

There were no eastern-ocean enemy sea raids in memory, and there were no uprisings among the lords for two generations. Thus, the Council of Mintala grew too powerful and power breeds evil in weak men. Myrkr, their leader, coveted the heartstones' power, and he corrupted the others.

The central throne room in the palace of Mintala was in the shape of a circle. The Guardian of Valdeor dictated the design to Gildran. And the guardian spirit set the hundred-pound heartstones in a ring, suspended in niches between the walls and ceiling around the throne in the middle of the room. In front of the throne he set the center stone, a diamond gem raised on a pedestal three feet above the floor. When the sun shone directly overhead at the noon hour twice a year, the rays from the heartstones focused on the center stone, and it glowed with a brilliant light, beautiful to behold. On those days the king would make the most important decisions of state, and judge those who appealed to him, guided by the stones' virtues.

Myrkr made his plans and called the Council of Mintala

together, all but one who was loyal to the king. This man, Justinian, was away. They locked the chamber when the king went in to sit in judgment. As he approached the throne, Myrkr stabbed him in the back. Myrkr must have thought he could take the medallion and become ruler by force, but the time was high noon on the autumnal equinox, and the heartstones were brilliant with energy. Myrkr mortally wounded King Arness and his blood fell upon the center stone. As he collapsed on it, a blinding flash of light and a resounding explosion knocked all the council members unconscious. The blast ripped the heartstones from their alcoves and no one has seen them to this day. The center stone changed from a clear gem to one of the blackest ebonies. A mighty earthquake shook the city, and tremors spread through all of Valdeor. People were terrified. They thought the end of the world had come.

At last, the rumbling stopped, and a profound silence followed. The warrior Justinian, returning from his sojourn, entered the city. He found the streets deserted, and rubble from collapsed buildings blocking his way to the palace. He hurried to the throne room, where the blast had flung open the locked doors. There he found the murdered king and the treacherous council still stunned. A moment he knelt by his sire in sorrow, but there was no time for grief. Justinian had to act. He removed the medallion and sought the young princess, who was now the uncrowned Reina of Valdeor.

Lauressa was but fourteen years old, slim and straight and tall, with russet hair and deep sea-green eyes. Justinian knew she was not safe in Mintala. With her father dead, and the Council of Mintala traitors, the warlords in the north and the south would come and vie to rule in her stead until she came of age. The most powerful of them, Lord Feorn, had coveted the throne for years. He ingratiated himself with King Arness to become betrothed to the princess, but Lauressa did not like, nor trust, him. Feorn did not stop pressing his suit with the king or his daughter until Arness publicly announced the princess's engagement to Prince Jarell of the Eastern Province.

Justinian knew that Feorn and the lesser lords, as well as Myrkr, would seek Princess Lauressa as the means to get the throne. Therefore, he immediately set forth with her for the castle of Prince Jarell.

They never reached him.

When Myrkr and the others recovered from the shockwave, the medallion was no longer on the king, and the princess had vanished. The traitors then fled the city themselves, for many people converged on the palace hoping for aid from their king in the crisis, and when they found him stabbed, they turned into an angry mob seeking the lives of those responsible. Such was the Myrkr Revolt.

Warlord Feorn, and other lords approaching the city, found it in chaos, and whole sections lay in ruin. They destroyed the city as they and their retinues fought for control of the realm. After many years of bloody sieges around and in the city, Feorn was the victor. He declared the princess dead, though her body was never found in the palace wreckage.

When Jarell heard what happened in the capital city, he set forth to find his fiancée, but he was unsuccessful in his quest. A legend spread forth at this time, that someday the Champion of Valdeor would find the Lost Reina. He would be mighty and strong and wise, and none could withstand him.

He would restore the princess to her people, and peace would come again to Valdeor, for naught but war and famine have filled the realm since she vanished.

The night was far advanced, and the fire burned low before the wanderer finished his tale. The old man pulled a pipe from his pocket and searched his other pockets for tobacco.

"Take mine, Estrell." Father took the tobacco tin from the mantle and passed it to him. Estrell filled it with tobacco and lit it.

Alloryn became aware of the lateness of the hour and his tiredness. He arched his back and stretched.

"I have never heard this wondrous tale."

Father gathered the ale mugs and empty bowl on the bench beside Alloryn and brought them to the washbasin.

"I was hoping my ancestors played a part in it. What has this to do with me, sir?"

The man puffed a couple of times on his pipe. "You think, young man, that this happened one hundred years ago, and concerns you not."

He removed the pipe from his mouth and pointed it at Alloryn. "But I tell you, the princess still lives."

He sat back, put the pipe in his mouth, and ruminated for a while. "The heartstone medallion has a power of its own, and it preserves her life."

Alloryn wriggled in his seat, wanting to repeat his question, but not daring.

"Did I not also say that you have a warrior's heritage? It is from your family line that the Champion of Valdeor shall come."

At first, Alloryn could not take in the meaning of this. He looked from the stranger to his father, who nodded.

"Aye, lad. From generation to generation this story has been handed down in our family."

"For this reason, your father sent you to retrieve the sword."

All was silent in the room as Alloryn digested this.

"Go to bed now, son, and rest. You learned enough for one night." His father put a callused hand on his shoulder.

He did as Father bid, but he did not sleep for a long time. He heard the muted sound of voices below his attic room far into the wee hours of the morning as he pondered the stranger's words. Especially the surprising truth that he, a shepherd boy, could become not only a warrior but a champion.

Alloryn climbed the hills to think in his favorite place, the ruined fortress. He found the gray-cloaked wanderer there before him with his pipe in his hand. The old man motioned for him to sit beside him on the broken wall.

"I see you are none the worse for your encounter with the Kratigula. I am sure that you are anxious about the next step in your training." Estrell's eyes glinted with amusement.

"Yes, sir!" Alloryn could barely sit still in his eagerness.

"Do not expect it to be easy, or soon done. You are the only one to wrest the Crestin Sword from the Kratigula in five generations."

He tamped tobacco in his pipe. "The first warrior placed it in the cavern when he realized he could not find and restore the Reina to her rightful throne, although he spent his lifetime trying."

The old man struck light from a flint tinder and puffed to start his pipe. "On the warrior's deathbed, a vision of the winged Guardian of Valdeor promised that one of his direct descendants would fulfill the Quest that he began, because of his faithfulness."

"Were all my ancestors sent into the beast's lair when they turned fourteen?"

"Yes, but none succeeded until now."

He could not sit still any longer. He brandished his shepherd's crook and swished it through the air. "I want to learn to fight like a real soldier. When can we start?"

"Do not think winning the sword was the greatest test you will face. Others will be harder if you are to be the Champion of Valdeor."

"I can pass all the tests if you are my teacher, sir."

"Yes, I have come to teach you. But it will take many years, for only a full-grown warrior can overcome all the difficulties ahead."

Alloryn drooped at the word 'years.' *I want it now. Why is it always later with adults?*

"Are you committed to seeing this through to the end, whatever the cost to yourself, whatever the outcome may be, though you cannot imagine it?" He punctuated each phrase with his pipe stem in Alloryn's direction. He raised his hand toward him, forestalling a quick answer. "Think before you answer, my boy."

A new sense of responsibility enveloped him. This man, who offered to be his mentor, talked to him as though he were already a grownup. He felt like an adult ever since he held the

Crestin Sword in his grip and had slain the beast. He knew fear and faced death, and now Estrell asked him to face it again for a lifetime, like the first warrior who set out on the Quest.

He squared his shoulders. "I regained the sword. I accept the challenge."

They found Father, and before both witnesses, Alloryn repeated an ancient oath as he knelt on the ground in front of the Crestin Sword. "I swear to serve the Reina of Valdeor, and succor all those in need, on my Quest to restore order to the realm."

"Now the first thing you must do is bid your father good-bye, for we go to train in distant lands." He must have seen the sorrow on Alloryn's face, because he added, "Your wants and needs come second to the mission you have taken on."

In a short time, Alloryn gathered his few belongings. He looked around his loft, and said good-bye in his heart, wondering where he would lay his head tonight and every night after that.

Father gathered supplies. Alloryn ran his fingers alongside the rough table, and let his gaze linger on the room where he spent his childhood—his mother's chair, his father's tobacco jar on the mantle, his wooden practice sword in the corner.

Father provided dried food, tea leaves, and blankets for them to take on the journey without a word, but his sad gaze seemed to take in every detail of his son. Father seemed to have aged before his eyes. His shoulders stooped, his face waxed pale, with wrinkles that had not been there before, or at least Alloryn had not noticed them.

Shep followed the three outside, tail down as if she sensed sorrow in the air.

The afternoon light dimmed, and the dark of a storm appeared over the hills and blocked the sun. The wind picked up, ruffling Father's white-streaked hair. "Take good care of my son, Estrell. He is all I have."

Alloryn swallowed the lump in his throat as he said his good-byes to Father and faithful Shep, and all that was familiar in his young life. The feeling of being a man faded, and he fought back the tears, wanting to cling to Father as if he were a small child again. The first big drops of rain fell, and his heart was as heavy as the dark cloud above as he and his new teacher trudged up the hill leading to the big world beyond.

He looked back once to the hut and Father, and raised his hand in farewell, not fully grasping the years that would go by before he saw it all again, yet fearing in his heart that it would be a very long time.

*T*hat summer Alloryn lived in primitive conditions. They roamed through uninhabited places. He learned to hunt for and find water in barren wastelands, with a bed of stones in the wilderness. He thought they would practice swordplay daily. Instead, he carried heavy pails of water from streams to their camps and cut trails through thick brush. He learned patience and endurance, but not his greatest desire—how to use a sword.

During their wanderings, they met an old woman trying to plow a field. She told how soldiers rode through the area, looted her belongings, took her crops, and burned her croft. She was planting turnips to survive with her grandson during the coming winter.

"If you let us bed in your stable, we will rebuild your cottage and plant your field."

The old woman gratefully agreed to Estrell's offer.

Alloryn did not understand how this would constitute training for a warrior. "Master, when will I learn swordplay?" he asked, as they put their gear in a dilapidated building used as a barn.

"All in due time." Estrell often answered his questions as Father had—with no answer.

He was unused to horses, whose temperaments were quite different from the sheep he was familiar with, but he found he liked the old mare. Although stubborn, she was much smarter than any sheep.

"Master, will I learn to ride?" he asked hopefully.

"All in good time," was the answer, as usual. Alloryn sighed. *I am so anxious to learn to be a warrior. Cannot the old man see that?*

His mentor showed him how to pull the plow behind the horse using a harness. "As you walk, I want you to breathe through your nose, and feel it deep in your belly, then let it out through your mouth.

"Hold the plow, line it up just below your belt. Keep it steady. Every time you hit a rock, reposition it."

Estrell, the old woman, and her grandson Rodrek followed along, planting the turnips in the summer heat.

Alloryn found it hard work, harder than watching sheep. His arms, shoulders, and lower body ached after a few hours.

This is not the life of a warrior that I imagined. After a hard day in the field, surely Estrell will give me training now.

But no, in the evenings, the old man fashioned what looked like wooden swords, while telling Alloryn a true warrior was honorable, stalwart, valiant, and self-sacrificing. But still no sword training.

Alloryn and Rodrek, who was his age, snuck away after a hard day's work.

"Do you know what 'stalwart' means, Rodrek?" Alloryn asked as they climbed a tree.

"Call me Roddy. Only Gran uses my full name." Roddy swung his legs from a branch. "You are a scholar. I am just a farm boy."

"Estrell is always using big words to describe a warrior." Alloryn sighed. "How can I be what he wants when I do not know the meanings of the virtues I am supposed to practice?"

Alloryn convinced Roddy that they should fashion their swords from sticks and play warriors. Every chance they had between chores, they spent on the banks of a nearby creek, where they slashed, thrust, and parried each other's wooden swords. When they were tired of it, they lay on the bank and watched the insects above the water and fish below.

When the crop was in, Estrell and Alloryn built a snug little cottage. They cut trees and made them into long logs using a two-man saw. The trees Estrell chose were in a deep dell. "I want you to carry the logs up the hill to the road. Balance each log on your right shoulder. But do not let it tip downward over your back. Use your left hand on the log to keep it tipped slightly up, and your right hand to bear the weight. There you go."

Alloryn grumbled, "There must be one hundred logs!"

"Be grateful you only have to carry them to the road above, and not to the site." Fortunately for him, they used the old horse to drag the logs to the house site.

Alloryn hoisted logs in place, while Estrell and Rodrek used ropes and pulleys to position them. But his shoulders and arms did not protest as much as they did before he carried the timbers and plowed.

They finished the walls, and they cemented them with mud. Next, they laid the roof and thatched it.

After they completed that task, his mentor made him cut the hayfield near the cottage with a scythe. "Swing from right to left in steady motions. Move from your hips, not just your shoulders. Remember to breathe from your belly." The old man and Rodrek gathered the hay behind him and bundled them into haystacks.

The work was hot in the late summer days. How Alloryn wished he was back with the sheep on the rolling hillsides away from the blazing sun.

At day's end, he and Roddy found shade in a wooded area and sat on logs to relax. Alloryn idly picked up a stick and swished it back and forth it in his hand.

"Why do you want to play so much at swords? Let us go swimming!" Roddy suggested. He led Alloryn to the stream at the field's end.

"I do not know how to swim, Roddy."

"I will teach you," and with those words, Rodrek pushed him in. Alloryn swallowed water and thrashed around, but in the end, he learned quickly. Rodrek showed him a deep spot and a rope swing hanging above it, and they took turns diving into the natural pool to cool off.

One cool morning, before anyone else was awake, Alloryn quietly entered the horse corral. He offered the old plod horse a carrot and rubbed his nose as he had seen Estrell do. The horse nuzzled Alloryn's pockets for more. Alloryn chuckled and gave it the second carrot. While the horse munched, Alloryn slipped the bridle over his head.

"Good boy. That's all I have for you." Alloryn gently led him to the fence, stepped on the lower post, and heaved himself up. After swinging his leg over, he found himself facing the horse's rump.

The horse, perhaps sensing the wrongness or simply not liking a rider on his back, stepped sideways, shaking his head. Then he trotted around the corral, forcing Alloryn to clamp on tight with his thighs since the bridle was behind him.

"Whoa, boy, whoa!" Alloryn tried his calm voice, and when that did not work, he started yelling, "Stop, you stupid beast! Whoa!"

The horse lifted his front feet in a semi-jump, and Alloryn found himself looking up at the sky. Only then did he hear the laughter.

Roddy bent over double with mirth, while Estrell and the old woman looked like they were trying to hide smiles.

"Maybe it is time I teach you to ride since you seem so determined." Estrell entered the corral. After calming the horse, he led him by the bridle back to where Alloryn was brushing himself off.

"An old and gentle horse is the best way to start learning."

Alloryn held his tongue, though he did not agree with his mentor's assessment of the horse. But, in time, he did learn to ride him.

They prepared to go on their way when they finished all the jobs to Estrell's satisfaction.

"I can never repay you for what you have done for my grandson and me." The old woman thanked them, pressing their hands with both of hers, tears staining her lined cheeks.

"The boy needed training. Thank the One Who Fashioned All Things for sending us, and ask Him to keep us safe on our travels. That will be thanks enough."

As his teacher went ahead, Alloryn lagged to say good-bye to Roddy, his first friend. Awkwardly, he shook his hand, now calloused like the other's. "Thank you for teaching me to swim."

"I hope the old man teaches you to fight. Though if he does not, you can always build a snug cottage for yourself and plant a crop."

As he sat with his mentor at their campfire that evening, he could hold his tongue no longer. "Master, when will I hold a sword?"

"You need to learn patience, my boy." He sighed and put down his newly lit pipe. "You needed strength before you lifted a sword. These many months you have gained in size and muscle. So today we will start with practice swords."

"Not the Crestin Sword?"

"No, else you would take harm." He removed the heavy wooden swords that he worked on in the evenings. "But tell me first, what did you learn while we stayed with the old woman?"

"That is easy. How to build a dwelling and plant a crop."

"Yes, that is so, but more importantly, you learned compassion. A man uses all his skills for the good of others. A warrior should be a man first, a fighter second.

"Now, stand with the right foot slightly ahead of the left. Not too wide. Take the wooden sword I fashioned. Swing it easily side to side. Less movement of your shoulders, and more of your hips. Move like you are using a scythe. That is better. Now feel your center. Breathe as I taught you from your belly. That is your center. All your moves must start from your center."

The old warrior showed him the first position with the other fake sword. "Hold the sword hilt at your navel, point up, toward my face. You can put your weight on either foot. This is the Plow Guard, or first position. Now I will move in closer and you extend the sword to block me."

Estrell stepped nearer. "That is position two. I must either move away and disengage, which leaves me open, or I must move your sword." And so saying, he pushed Alloryn's sword to the side with a powerful swing.

"Let us start again. Do not hold your sword like a hammer, but open the thumb away from the rest of the fingers, then curl the fingers around the hilt, and put the thumb along the hilt toward the blade." He demonstrated with his sword. "Remember to breathe. Move your front foot toward me and then reposition the other. Lift them, do not slide. Swing at me from the side."

His master blocked with the first position he had taught, overcoming the attack.

"Now the third position, the Roof Guard, is above your right shoulder. Remember how you carried the logs? Move your right foot in the rear position. Tip up the blade as I taught you. Good. Swing it down. See how much energy it takes? The whole point is maximum effect with as little effort as possible, to conserve strength."

They practiced footwork next. Besides the basic stance, he learned two others that allowed the back and front feet to switch positions and a one hundred and eighty-degree turn that he practiced, rotating around his center. Over time, he learned the other guard positions, which he also practiced.

Alloryn's heart sang. This was his dream.

For the next five years, Alloryn sweated through scorching deserts, toiled up steep mountains, and trudged through treacherous swamps. He learned to track wild animals and men noiselessly through all of these places.

As he grew in strength, so he grew in the finer points of thrust and parry, offensive and defensive stances, and attacks. His sword became an extension of his arm and his will.

His mentor did not neglect his mind either. He learned the history and geography of Valdeor in great depth. They brought books with them, and after a hard day, Estrell expected Alloryn to study. Estrell quizzed him as they made their way from place to place. Sometimes they walked on the main road, sometimes they walked barely discernible forest tracks, but they always avoided settlements when possible. Through all of this, he came to have great admiration and respect for the old warrior's stamina in the face of hardships, and his wisdom in teaching Alloryn to become a man and a champion.

One evening they came upon a small group of ruffians around a campfire. From the shadows, Alloryn listened with disgust to their tales of thievery and terrorizing the land. He would have challenged the men, but Estrell laid a hand on his arm.

"The time has not yet come, my boy, to face such as those men," he said when they were beyond hearing range.

"But you heard them! Someone must stop them. How many villages and farms have we seen in our wanderings, destroyed by the wanton cruelty of mercenaries under the warlords' patronage? I know I can defeat them." He moved to block the old warrior. "Why do you not let me try?"

"The land has known unrest for a century. If you strike too soon, all my careful planning will be for nothing. The Warlord Feornson is powerful in these lands, and he would surely hunt us if we were to kill his henchmen. Did you not see their insignia?" He stepped around Alloryn and continued down the road, away from the campfire. "A champion you will be, but not before your quest has begun in earnest. Patience for a short while, then your adventures will truly begin," Estrell promised.

Alloryn brooded all the next day. He wished to test his skill against other swordsmen. He was nineteen, and restless for his chance to make a mark on the world. Wrapped in his thoughts, he did not note the direction they were traveling, until they came upon green pastures and the bleating of sheep. He saw the land of his birth. Across the valley rose the hills where Father's hut nestled. He sought the face of his companion as they stood before the valley entrance.

"I thought it time you made a visit home. Even wanderers need a cozy fire and comfortable beds sometimes."

Alloryn strode confidently across the fields, but a crofter's burnt hut hidden from view until now stopped him short. Into his mind came the brigands' conversation heard the day before, "a lonely place, hardly worth looting." They found no inhabitants alive. After searching through the rubble, and feeling nausea, anger rose in his heart and caused him to shake with fury at the destruction of innocent farmers. He turned his gaze toward the familiar hills of home. Then a sudden fear arose in him.

"Master! My father!" He raced along the road to where his home lay concealed in the hills. As he approached it, fear squeezed his heart at what he would find. In shock, he saw the familiar cottage not burnt, but plundered, its contents strewn about the ground. Sheep and wolfhound carcasses littered the area.

"Father! Father!" he cried. Panic and desperation flooded through him as he looked around his ruined house. Maybe Father was on the hills. He clung to the slender chance with all his might as he raced for the best grazing area. Within moments, he heard a faint bark, and an old wolfhound bounded down the track. Shep growled until she got a whiff of his scent, then she nosed and danced all around him. Then she ran up the track and came back for him.

"Shep, old girl! I'm coming. Lead me to Father. Where is he?" A spark of hope flickered in his heart, the first since he'd seen the burnt cottage. Shep led him through the familiar hills, then went off the path into a gully. She lay beside her master, and all hope left his heart.

Father was on his back, his leg twisted under him at an odd angle. He had a big bruise on his temple, and his skin was gray.

His broken staff near him told the story. Alloryn knelt beside him and tears threatened to spill.

"Father," he sobbed, and with seemingly great effort Father opened his eyes. His mouth moved, but Alloryn could hear nothing. He leaned closer, and Father licked his lips and spoke with a low voice. "I hoped I would see you again. Been thinking of you and your mother Jorelyn." His brow scrunched with pain and the effort of talking, so Alloryn scrambled to the nearby spring, wet the handkerchief he wore around his neck and dripped the water into Father's mouth.

"Who did this to you, Father?" He wiped the familiar face with the damp handkerchief. "I will search, find them and make them regret this day!"

"No!" he cried. "You must not!" He gathered his strength to speak again. Alloryn leaned closer to catch the faint words. "One death, one act of revenge will solve nothing. Peace! You must bring peace everywhere. Remember."

Father struggled to speak. "You slew the two-headed monster, but beware the monsters that stalk all men: pride, lust, envy."

Although Estrell and Alloryn moved Father back to the cottage, tried to keep him warm, and helped him drink a little water, he did not last the night.

In the early hours before dawn, Alloryn lay his head on his father's chest and gave into his grief.

After a while, a hand on his shoulder roused him. "Come, my boy, we must bury your father Yarrek properly."

And in silence, they dug a grave and laid him in his final resting place.

"Surely the time has come when I can no longer watch as the wicked and greedy ravish the land and people!" Alloryn paced away from Father's newly made cairn. "I will seek Feornson and his men and destroy them and rid the realm of their kind." He swept his arm as if he could sweep away evil. He stood tall and stern in the early dawn, and his mentor seemed to shrink beside his wrath.

"You are naturally angry, but you must not let your feelings interfere with your mission." The elder man pounded his staff for emphasis. "This is not what your father wanted. I have trained you to be a warrior, not an instrument of revenge." He placed his hand on Alloryn's arm. "Think with your head and not your heart, Alloryn. Valdeor needs you."

But he was tired of listening to reason. The fight was too personal now. "Valdeor needs her wrongs to be righted, starting with those who committed these and other heinous crimes. Do not stand in my way." He roughly shrugged off the consoling hand. "It's time I fulfilled my true mission as a sword of vengeance." And with those words, he strode alone into the valley, back the way they had come.

He tracked the ruffians. After searching the campfire where he first encountered them, he found and followed their trail south toward the Smoky River.

He walked all day and most of the night until weariness overtook him. He sat to rest with his back to a boulder on the crest of a rocky hill. The wind blew in cold gusts, and he wrapped his cloak tighter around himself.

As he stared into the night sky, he remembered his childhood, looking after the sheep. He recalled his mother humming him to sleep when he was very small. He thought of how big and strong his father always seemed. Nothing had touched his world until the drought when he was six. Food was scarce, and bands of men from the warlord's garrison raided nearby farms and carried away the food, so the valley went hungry. At this time his mother, Jorelyn, died, and he knew anger. But his father taught him that a time would come when peace and prosperity would flourish again.

"Revenge gets us nowhere. The killing of a few wicked men does not change the world. More will take their place. A good ruler must unite the land. Honest men must pass fair laws and enforce them. People should not be ruled by fear, but by justice." Father's words rang in his ears. He pushed them aside.

"I will have justice for your death, Father," he promised aloud.

A campfire twinkled in the distance.

Still, he sat on his high perch in the wilderness, looking out over the land to the distant horizon that he could barely see in the moonlight. The night drew on while visions filled his mind's eye with victory over Lord Feornson and then battles with the many great warlords north and south until he had defeated them all. Then the people would hail him, the Champion of Valdeor, as their defender. He would bring justice to all the corners of the land. The people would follow his lead and he would be the ruler.

At some point in these musings, he must have drifted to sleep. The next thing he knew, something wet and insistent pushed in his face. He heard a whine. He opened his eyes and stared into a pair of big, brown eyes on an over-sized puppy's wriggling body. He recognized a smaller version of Shep, but with a bedraggled coat, as if it had traveled far.

"Where did you come from, fellow?" It held up its bleeding paw and wagged its tail a little.

He understood several things as he contemplated it. This dog had escaped the fate of its brothers back at the hut and followed his trail to these forsaken parts. His eyes were full of trust that his master would make things better, symbolic of the realm's inhabitants who waited for Alloryn to make their life better if he fulfilled his oath. Understanding stripped his glorious dreams away, and he saw them for what they were— another warlord rising to power and crushing the lesser ones beneath his feet. A great leader could bring peace from chaos, and he was but a servant of that cause. The heavy weight constricting his heart lifted.

With his newfound companion limping behind him, he hunted and fed both of them. Two days later saw them back at his old home. Finding no sign of his mentor, his shoulders drooped.

He feared Estrell had left for good.

I am unworthy. I cannot see a champion within myself, either. So it is no surprise Estrell went looking for another to train.

All through the spring, he worked to make the hut habitable again. He gathered the scattered flock and relearned the shepherd's simple life. Trekker, as he called the dog, was his only companion. Trekker was as quick and intelligent and loyal as his mother had been. He soon learned to obey every command and signal and was invaluable at keeping order among the small flock of sheep. He also showed himself to be a hunter, alert and unafraid when Alloryn roamed beyond the hills for food.

Alloryn tended Father's grave and dug one beside it for the faithful dog Shep who soon followed her master in death. Time eased the sharp edge from his grief.

The first frost descended on the valley before there came a knock on his door one chill evening. Alloryn was surprised and humbled to see his teacher in the tattered cloak with his ancient staff.

"I do not deserve that you should train me. I am unworthy to be a champion." Alloryn hung his head in shame. "I sought revenge, not justice."

"You have not disappointed me or your father." The old man still possessed the power to gaze right into his soul. "Every man makes mistakes. Only the wise learn from them."

"Come, it is time to complete your training. I am now the owner of a little boat. We will go on a journey around Valdeor's southern coast to the western seas at day's break on the morrow."

A new life on the sea awaited them. And a new, humble Alloryn listened patiently.

He learned to handle a sloop in fair weather and foul. He honed his swimming skills, and learned to spearfish, and forecast weather. This time they did not avoid the coastal towns but entered them. He learned his way around port cities and their inhabitants. His life was so different than he had ever known, and he grew to like the occasional contact with his fellow men. But he most enjoyed the stiff breeze on his face and the feel of a ship under his feet, with Trekker at the prow, looking like the bow carving.

Nearly six months they sailed the ocean before their idyllic life came to an end and fate caught up with them.

They had sailed from Briartown on the northeast coast and took on supplies at Laketown and other small fishing villages along Valdeor's southern coast. Eventually, they landed in Skupe on the western seaboard.

Estrell gathered his belongings and stood on the dock looking at the sloop, bobbing in the waves, that had been their home for so many months. "I will miss this little sloop. She handled very well, as did you."

"Thank you. I think it was easier to learn to steer a ship than ride a horse." Alloryn smiled at the memory. He turned his back to the sea and looked over the town. "Is the princess here? In Skupe?" Eagerness rose in his heart.

"No, but I know a man who will buy the sloop." Seeing Alloryn's look of disappointment, he added, "Your training is over. The next journey we take will lead us to her."

Alloryn felt hope flood his body. *Finally, I am truly a warrior!* He hardly paid attention where Estrell led him, as he mused over the future. He was in a daydream, imagining meeting Princess Lauressa, instead of focusing his senses on the here and now, when they turned a narrow corner.

The alley was dark, the cobbles slippery with recent rain. From behind a stack of crates, a scar-faced man stepped in front of them. His short blade glinted in the light as the moon fleetingly peeked from behind a cloud.

Several things happened at once. Alloryn started to draw his blade when a heavy item fell on top of him from the crate beside him and knocked him over. A net tightened around him.

He struggled, but he could not draw his sword from the scabbard.

Two more men dressed in warrior garb surrounded Estrell. A deep gravelly voice came from behind them. Alloryn twisted to see a giant of a man with a chest like a barrel and a braided, red beard stride toward them. Alloryn redoubled his struggle against the heavy ropes, but the newcomer ignored him.

"At last, we meet, old man. You have no idea how I have longed for this day for decades." He drew his sword, a long black blade. His men stepped back, while the original ruffian held his blade over Alloryn as he struggled in vain to free himself.

"Where is the princess?"

"I, betray her? Never!" The old man threw back his shoulders and took a warrior's stance.

Alloryn continued to struggle even as he watched the two men circle. He wished they had brought Trekker along, but the wolfhound was aboard the boat, guarding it in the harbor.

Blades flashed and engaged. With a graceful move, his teacher spun and disengaged. Alloryn subconsciously noted all the patterns he learned. Grunting, the attacker blocked all attempts to break through his guard. Alloryn did not see why the big man did not go for the kill, eventually realizing the aggressor's strategy was to tire Estrell.

Alloryn saw the subtle signs as his mentor slowed, and the giant warrior also noticed and went on the offensive. The old warrior now was the one blocking all the moves.

The air was full of grunts and heavy breathing, the clattering of steel on steel, all of this nearly drowned out by the sound of Alloryn's heart pounding in his ears.

The men around him were watching the fight, cheering on

their leader, so Alloryn used this opportunity to inch his sword from the scabbard as far as the net allowed. He concentrated on sawing the rope with the little bit of exposed blade.

But he was too late.

The giant man wore away at Estrell. Panting, Estrell lost his footing momentarily on the slippery alley paving stones. The giant used the opportunity to slip under Estrell's guard and strike a fatal blow. He showed his teeth in a grim smile when he pierced through his enemy. He pulled his blade back, bloody, and contemplated his victim.

"Tell me her whereabouts, or the boy dies along with you." He moved over the net, his sword pointed at Alloryn's head. Alloryn froze. He feared for himself, but he also feared Estrell would put his life above the mission.

Estrell put his hand on his chest and looked at the blood that covered it when he pulled it away. He moaned with pain as he tried to rise and reach his sword where it lay on the ground between them. He fell back, his gaze flickered to Alloryn.

The pause stretched out and Alloryn's body tensed for a blow.

"No need to harm the lad." Estrell let his hand unclench and go slack with resignation. "She is in the city of Zendira, working as a seamstress."

The assailant called his men and they left, not before one of them kicked Alloryn bowed with grief.

He soon freed himself and crouched beside his teacher. The old man was feeble and his cough produced blood. Alloryn tore part of his tunic to staunch the flow of blood but feared the enemy had pierced a vital organ.

Estrell refused to let Alloryn go for the doctor, saying it was too late.

He motioned for Alloryn to come close. For the first time since they met, Estrell looked frail and elderly, his purple veins standing out from his transparent skin. In the depth of his eyes was the same look Yarrek had when Alloryn found him on the hill after the brigands' attack.

"Is there nothing I can do to ease you, Master?" The old title slipped out as Alloryn tried to make him more comfortable, tucking his cloak around the dying man.

"Listen. The time has come to restore the Reina to her throne. You must find her and bring her safely to Mintala." He grasped Alloryn's forearm. "Remember the oath you swore five years ago and let nothing stand in the way of your quest."

"But I cannot leave you. You must come with me. We will find her together."

"My traveling is done. I leave you soon." A fit of coughing overcame him. Alloryn gave him water from the skin he carried. "My death was foreordained to be the time in which Princess Lauressa would be reinstated as ruler. My time is over, but you are just beginning."

He must have seen the doubt in Alloryn's eyes. He made another great effort and spoke reassuringly, "When you stormed away after your father died, I sought Lauressa out. She still lies safe, undiscovered by men. You will know her by the heartstone medallion she wears." He paused for breath.

Alloryn described it, giving Estrell time to recover. "A silver medallion, with a circle of colored stones—ruby, sapphire, amethyst, flame, emerald, and topaz."

The dying man gave a small nod. "I have guarded her and kept her safe for a century since we escaped the capital together." His breathing grew more strained. "But now you are her champion."

Shock rippled through Alloryn. *Did he just claim to be Justinian? The one who had hidden the princess a century ago. How could this be?*

Alloryn gazed with wonder on the man who lay before him. He never questioned the old man's identity, but called him Master, and loved him as a father. He never asked where he came from, nor inquired about his past. He respected his teacher's silence on his former life, as Yarrek taught him. He assumed Estrell was once a warlord's swordmaster, defeated by a younger man who took his place. Now more than ever Alloryn wished for his continued guidance.

"What if I fail?" he asked with trepidation and humility.

"Then you must pass on what you have learned to your son one day. But I am certain you are the destined one, for you have shown great promise since the day you faced and overcame the Kratigula. Remember all I have taught you." The tired voice grew soft. "Use your strength only for the good of others, never for base gain or revenge. Seek wisdom, not glory." The voice faded away.

"But I do not know where to find the princess. I know you did not give that warlord her true whereabouts."

"Beware Feornson. He has seen your face and will not forget you." Alloryn's heart raced at the words as panic threatened to overwhelm him. *That was Feornson? The most powerful warlord in the land is my enemy now?*

Words came with difficulty, and Alloryn had to lean close

to hear. "Lauressa is on the island nation of Hamleor in the seas west of here."

Sorrow threatened to choke Alloryn as the dying man spoke his final words. "She is in the shadow of the mountain. Find her." Soon after, Justinian, the loyal councilor and warrior of the Royal House of Gildran, entered peacefully into his final rest.

Alloryn crouched beside his mentor, lost in grief. He was now alone in the world.

How can I complete the quest alone? He did not feel he had the srength for such an undertaking.

Shadows fell across the alleyway, and still, he stayed, overcome by sorrow.

Cramps throughout his body eventually brought him back to the present. He could not leave Justinian here in the alleyway. He deserved a state funeral. The least he could do was bury Justinian's body with as much reverence as he could.

Unfurling himself, he stretched and headed to the main stables in town, where he had seen a hand cart earlier in the day. He borrowed a shovel too. He lifted the body into the hand cart and grasped the handles. The single wheel rumbling along the cobblestones broke the silence in the wee dark hours of the night. Fog drifted in places, as grim as his heart.

Up through the port town's streets, past the last house, he went into the hills above the town. He reached the cliffs overlooking the sea and he dug a shallow grave. The early morning sun touched the clouds as he put the cairn's last rock over his mentor and friend.

He offered a prayer for the old hero's soul as the sun broke over the sea.

A drizzle fell in the hour before dawn. Ships creaked in their moorings. Dockworkers unloaded and reloaded vessels on the busy dock. The man and his dog received few glances, since those at work had none to spare, and everyone else on the dock sought refuge from the rain. Alloryn pulled his cloak more securely around him and waited with other passengers to board the frigate.

After placing Justinian in a cairn on a cliff overlooking the sea, he sold the little sloop. He used the money to purchase his passage to the largest port city on the island of Hamleor, once a part of the realm of Valdeor. An elected official now governed the land. Upon arriving at the port of Oster, on the River Ost, Alloryn planned to travel north along the coast until he came to the Lost Mountains, possibly named for the Lost Princess. He could not think beyond that. Justinian had given him no further instruction. He would have to rely on local legends.

The first mate, who indicated that Alloryn could board, brought him out of his reverie. Trekker got a few stares as he followed his master on deck, most likely because of his great size. He was no ordinary sheepdog, but a mighty wolfhound, full-grown, his head higher than a man's waist. Other passengers and crew steered clear of the fierce-looking dog and the stern-faced young man wearing a sword half-hidden under his cloak.

The crossing took three weeks.

Alloryn landed in Oster and was glad of his familiarity with port cities. He wasted no time but set about to find a horse and supplies to take him north to Losen Harbor, at the foot of the Lost Mountains.

The Red Swan was a tavern at the bustling port's wharf. He went inside and ordered a meal and a mug of ale. He thought it likely to be the last meal he ate among people for quite a while. His purpose was to learn local legends concerning the Reina.

"I have heard stories at my mother's knee about the doings over the eastern sea," said the barkeep to his questions. The barkeep's look was one of wariness. His gaze traveled over the other's weather-stained clothes and bulky sword. The man's voice indicated he believed they were fairy tales. A few nearby patrons stopped to look at Alloryn as well.

Alloryn retreated to his table with his ale, but he kept one eye on the sailors in the tavern. He saw men look his way and whisper, but many strangers came and went in a busy place like this. He waited a little while longer, but no one approached. He had so little to go on. Justinian told him to come to Hamleor, to look under the shadow of the Lost Mountains. It could take months to comb the whole range for a cave or a hut.

Trying a new tactic, he showed himself ready to buy drinks for all who would entertain him with a good story. This allayed the bar patrons' suspicions. Stories were stock in trade to sailors who spent months at sea, spinning yarns to entertain themselves. After listening to several sailors' unlikely tales, fabricated to gain themselves as much ale as he was willing to pay for, he perceived one old sailor was a true storyteller. The others hailed the man as one who could relate every story since the dawn of time. After letting the man warm up with several fantastic tales—which the patrons had heard before, good-naturedly ribbing him not to leave out the best parts—Alloryn invited him to his table in the back and led him onto the subject of the lost princess.

"Aye, there be several tales I can be telling you about her. 'Tis said she fled here when she was sought by the evil Myrkr."

Alloryn saw he must not push the storyteller, or he would go into another embroidered tale. He motioned for a jug to be set at their table and filled the sailor's mug.

"The young are not so thoughtful of an old man these days." He squinted a knowing eye at Alloryn. "And what is it you're after? You rightly look like one should be living his tale, not listening to one."

"I seek where the princess may be found."

"Oh ho, a young man with a quest." He surreptitiously glanced at the half-concealed sword.

"The legends say that the Lost Mountains in the north are named for her. A crescent-shaped canyon is on the eastern coast. Some say it's called Moon Canyon because of its shape, but others say the entrance leading inside the mountain can be found only at a full moon."

The storyteller's voice dropped as he looked around to see if anyone else was listening in. Alloryn leaned forward in his seat, eager to catch every word.

"The heart of the mountain is a crystal cavern, with gems so beautiful it blinds you to all else but the desire to possess its wealth. 'Tis said that the ancients mined the very heartstones from there. They were reputed to be the most brilliant objects, short of the sun itself."

The storyteller finished his mug and poured more from the wine jug. The interruption only made Alloryn desirous for him to continue.

"If you can avoid the allure of vast wealth there, look for a mirror-like pond in the cavern's center. Anyone who gazes into it will see the object their hearts search for. Mind you, most men seek riches, and so would only see the reflection of the wealth around them."

The sailor took a swig of ale and wiped his mouth with the back of his hand. "The princess is supposed to be asleep, hidden in another chamber nearby."

The man leaned back, obviously done. Alloryn pushed the jug toward him and thanked him. The storyteller drained the last of the jug and sauntered back to the bar where he rejoined his companions.

Alloryn pondered the old man's tale while he finished his drink.

Another patron at the bar piped up, "Tell us about the time you married a mermaid." Others shouted with laughter, and many urged him on.

Alloryn paid his bill and left, as the patrons clamored for the tale.

He knew from Justinian's geography lessons the Lost Mountains Range start in the northeast, extending to the west. At the eastern tip lay the town of Losen Harbor. He would start his search in earnest there.

The next day, Alloryn bought a horse and headed north. For days he and Trekker traveled through sea towns and into the low hills. The track wound through flat coastal plains beside gentle waters for a day and a half. Towns grew scarcer and farther apart. The sea's smell and sound were never far away. The mountains loomed as a distant blur on the horizon, but with each day that passed, they grew until their craggy tops filled the whole sky. Even in the high summer, snow and ice coated the forbidding peaks.

On the ninth day, he entered a forest path that would lead him to the town of Losen. He camped in the woods and hunted for food, saving his supplies, since he did not know how long they must last. He had money from the sloop's sale, but he would use it for the passage back to Valdeor with the princess, supposing he found her.

He avoided the fork in the road that led to the east and Losen Harbor, the town at the foot of the mountains. Instead, he turned the horse's head west, upon a narrow winding track that eventually led into the mountains. Soon he found himself in the foothills cloaked with forests of pine.

The path wound back and forth, the air became cooler, and after another day the vegetation ceased to grow. As night fell, a chill wind rose, and he pulled a fur-lined cloak from his saddlebag and wrapped it around himself. Trekker, ever tireless, trotted in the lead.

The sky above the looming mountains had the look of an approaching storm. He quickly gathered kindling and filled his canteen in readiness.

He scoured the landscape for any trails leading off the main path to the cave he sought.

The clouds grew leaden, and a pinkish haze settled over everything. The wind picked up, so Alloryn hastened the pace. Snowflakes drifted down, soon becoming faster and thicker.

A squall overtook them, and within moments visibility was a few feet. He called to Trekker, "Shelter, boy!" and trusted the animal's instincts to find it, bred as he was to seek protection for the sheep on a winter night such as this. He dismounted and led the horse where the wolfhound indicated. They found themselves in a winding canyon sheltered from the worst of the wind. It narrowed so much that the horse could hardly pass. They soon left the falling snow behind. He found himself in a natural fissure in the mountainside.

He fed the animals and built a fire, thankful for the kindling he had gathered. He noticed in the flickering flames the fissure did not end in this little cave but went further into the dark heart of the mountain. He remembered the sailor's tale of the moon-shaped canyon and realized he had stumbled on it. But as anxious as he was, he did not explore it until he ate a meal of dried meat and hard bread, and his clothes were sufficiently dried. He lit the torches he had the foresight to bring with him and entered the narrow crack.

The walls and floor were smooth, polished obsidian. The place had a strange, unnatural feeling. As he ventured deeper, the floor and walls changed into hard granite. He entered under the mountain itself through a large chamber with natural columns and felt as if he was in the halls of some long-forgotten king. At the far end, the path continued, winding down and down in a gradual sweep. Eventually, he came upon steps cut in the stone. Maybe the stories were true. The heartstones could have been mined in this mountain.

His first torch nearly burnt out before he reached the bottom. He lit another before the flame died. He calculated he had traveled about two hours. He figured that if he did not reach the bottom of this stair in another two hours, he would try to sleep on a landing. He wondered at the labor it had taken to chop stairs into this deep place.

Roughly an hour later, the passage flattened. For a moment, he thought that he had reached the end, but then realized that it went around the corner. The way became like a sinuous river. He was unprepared for the stunning sight around one bend—a room of stalagmites and stalactites twinkling in his flame. As he entered an enormous cavern, he thought this must be the mountain's heart. The many flickering colors were actual jewels. The light dazzled him, and he moved the torch this way and that to see all the colors of the rainbow reflected on the walls and floor and ceiling.

The legend was true!

He realized he was holding his breath, so he made himself breathe again as he went farther in the room. He became aware the flickering light was an indication that his torch was dying. Only then did he tear his gaze away from the beguiling wealth around him, and search for the mirror pond. He forced himself to concentrate on the path, not the beautiful gems scattered at his feet. He accidentally found the pond as he stepped around a cluster of gleaming emeralds and saw their image waver.

Kneeling, he reached for one of the green stones but felt water instead. Ripples spread out, and the surrounding wealth, mirrored there, blurred and became unreal. It was as if a spell broke. The smell of damp dirt tickled his nostrils, and the steady drip of water was magnified in the silence, which had been at the edge of his senses, but unacknowledged until now. A day's travel on horseback, combined with the hours of descending through the granite stairs, pressed him with weariness. An overwhelming urge to sleep seized him as he gazed at the mirror pool's changing image. His last conscious thought was to wonder if the water was enchanted and if it was more deadly than the lure of wealth after all.

In his enchanted sleep—or was it merely a dream—he saw the Lost Mountains in the moon's wavering light. Under it, he saw a sign with a mountain's image. The longer he stared at it, the more detailed it became. He could see the rough board as it swayed slightly in the wind. He could even hear the chains creaking. He became certain the sign was that of an inn.

He woke to find himself in total darkness. He remembered he was at the mountain's core, where no sunlight ever penetrated. Fighting a sudden sensation of panic at the thought of being buried under the mountain's weight, he felt in his pouch and sighed with relief when he found flint and tinder. After a couple of tries with shaking fingers, he lit the remaining torch, and with the light, his fear of confinement receded. The cavern looked the same, but he felt disoriented. He remembered growing heavy with drowsiness. How long had he lain on the smooth black floor? He looked at the water indirectly, in case it were to enchant him again, but he saw nothing but the room's reflection. The spell was no longer on him. His first emotion was a disappointment. He sought to see Princess Lauressa, to gain her location, but he had failed.

His next idea was to search to see if any rooms led from this one. Had not the old storyteller said Princess Lauressa might inhabit the cave? His heart beat faster at the thought of finding her. But it did not take him long to make a circuit around the room. It was not as large as it first appeared.

The dream sign's image intruded on his thoughts even as he struggled with its meaning. How was the image of an inn his heart's desire? He recalled Justinian's last words to him: "She is in the shadow of the mountain. You will find her there." Losen Harbor was the only town in the Lost Mountains' shadow.

Maybe she resided at the inn.

Maybe she was in plain sight—not in an enchanted state, but living a secret life among ordinary people.

He turned to head back but stopped before he left the room. He held his torch high and looked at all the wealth at his feet. *I do not wish to be greedy, but if I do find her we will need funds for a passage over the sea, food, horses, and places to stay on the mainland. Mintala is a long way from here.* He knelt and gathered small gems into his pouch. The large ones twinkled at him, but he knew they were the hardest to dispose of and would raise too many questions. But he could barter the little ones for goods and services. He gathered enough jewels to help in his journey and left a vast fortune behind.

Three days passed before the storm cleared and he could blaze a trail through the drifted snowbanks back down the mountain. He traveled three more days to reach Losen Harbor, which was a merchant town, the port farthest north on the east coast of Hamleor.

He rode into the center of town. Everywhere he looked, a variety of goods filled the stalls. The precious metals and gems from the mountain found their way here, as did pearls from Cleethe. Merchants sold exotic fruits from Samarantha, and even sheep from his valley here. Avoiding the vendors eager for him to buy their wares, he asked a man in the street where he might find an inn called the Lost Mountains.

"The Lost Mountains is a respectable enough inn, though they are probably full since this is market day." The man looked him over. Although his clothes were travel-stained, Alloryn looked respectable. The man also noticed the sword he was carrying. Alloryn figured the man probably thought him a soldier of fortune. No one else wore a sword these days. He gave Alloryn further directions and added, "Mention my name—Kelvan—and you might get a room yet."

"I'm Alloryn, and I thank you greatly." He shook the outstretched hand.

The streets were too crowded to ride through, so he led his horse and wove through a maze of streets. He found himself in more quiet avenues. But somewhere he made a wrong turn—and there had been many—because he found himself in the byways. He passed doors that looked more like gaping holes spewing forth evil odors than entrances to homes. He was on the point of turning back and trying to find his way to the marketplace when he saw an elegant carriage pass the alleyway's end. He went that way and stepped onto a broad avenue and saw an inn a block away with the Lost Mountains drawn on the sign. In front of the inn's steps, he saw a beautifully dressed lady get into the carriage. He thought of the mirror pool. *Here might be my heart's desire after all.* He hastened his pace.

As he passed a dark alley, he heard a cry.

His gaze tried to pierce the darkness as thoughts raced through his mind. It could be a falling out of thieves or some such thing, and he did not relish the idea of barging in and getting a knife in his back for his trouble. And yet, he was supposed to be the legendary Champion of Valdeor. He could not hold that title if he did not try to champion all good causes and people.

He dropped the horse's reins. Squaring his shoulders, he removed his dagger with his left hand and unsheathed his sword with his right and walked stealthily into the alley. As his eyes adjusted, he saw two men who had a third backed into a corner. The lad brandished a small piece of metal pipe at his opponents, but they threatened him with wicked-looking knives.

"Have done!" the nearest man to Alloryn cried. "We have you cornered."

"If I'm not mistaken," the other interrupted with a sneering laugh, "this is no lad behind the boxes, but a girl. A regular she-wolf at that."

"A wench? Well, well," the first voice said. "We do not wish to hurt you. Just scratch our backs and we'll scratch yours." He guffawed.

Alloryn had heard enough. "How do you like this scratch?" He came up silently behind them and slashed the wrist that held the knife. The man howled and spun around, dropping the weapon. The second thief circled the newcomer warily.

"Behind you!" the girl cried.

Alloryn swung around and saw a glint of a blade as the second ruffian launched it in the air straight at him. He deflected it with a swift movement of his blade without losing his forward momentum. He continued on a course toward the attacker and followed with a thrust when he was in range. The next knife flew from the attacker's hand before he could throw it. As metal hit stone, the defeated thieves ran away.

He turned back and stepped toward the girl crouching against the wall. Her age was hard to tell. She was thin and wore a rough homespun dress, and a strand of her hair fell across her face, but there was no hiding the fire in her eyes and determined look as she watched the ruffians disappear around the corner.

She turned her attention to Alloryn and examined his tall and straight form. He gave her his most winning smile and stood with a non-threatening posture. She seemed to decide to trust him, and her fearfulness fell from her like a discarded garment.

She straightened to her full height and took a step toward him. "Thank you for rescuing me."

"Are you alright?"

She nodded.

"I was on my way home from my work in the bakery. If you care to step in my kitchen, I brought a few buns," and she held up a bundle she carried under her arm.

He thought of the carriage he saw earlier and was ready to refuse. She must have seen it in his face, because she added, "It is the least I can do to repay you."

At those words, he nodded his agreement. The finely dressed lady must have driven away in the carriage by now, anyhow.

After putting his horse in the stable at the inn and paying for its feed, he left his faithful hound with the horse. The girl led him another block to a poor but respectable neighborhood around the corner from the Lost Mountain Inn. He surreptitiously watched the graceful girl as she laid worn but clean crock-ware on a simple wooden table. The lodgings were clean and neat, but sparsely decorated. As for the girl herself, she was tall and carried herself well. Her hair was chestnut, pulled into a knot on her nape. Her oval face was smooth and creamy, as were her arms as she cut the chunk of cheese. Her features were fine, with sea-green eyes, as he had noted before, a long noble nose, arched eyebrows, high well-defined cheekbones, and a wide mouth made for smiling, although she was serious as she worked.

She seemed not to notice his regard. When she did look up, with a slight smile she indicated a rough bench which he pulled to the table. He removed his sword and propped it beside him.

As they shared the simple meal of bread, cheese, and a hot drink, they made small talk.

"I arrived today in Losen Harbor. I was heading for the Lost Mountain Inn."

He asked about the town, and she spoke of the many travelers who came from the inland, as well as the ships and their crews who traded in this city, the second-largest port of the island continent of Hamleor. In turn, she inquired of his travels, and he told her about his trip across the sea but did not expand on his reasons for coming to the island continent.

She deftly cleared the table when they were both finished eating. From a cupboard, she produced a bottle of homemade cordial and offered it to him.

Standing beside him, she reached out and touched his sword. She rubbed a finger lightly over the scabbard's scrollwork. He opened his mouth to tell her not to touch it but sat amazed and frozen in place as light suddenly ran alongside it where she traced the design. The only other time he had seen the same thing was after he had won it from the Kratigula and caressed the intricate designs himself. He believed he had imagined it the first time, but now this girl had the same effect on it.

The Crestin Sword had its own legends. It belonged to noble warriors and reacted to their touch.

She became aware of his open-mouthed gaze. "Where did you come by this sword?"

The question was unexpected. He thought she should apologize for her forwardness, not demand an explanation for what was not her business. He nearly said so, but her stance and tone were one of command, not subservience.

He found himself answering, "I gained it through a test of courage. It belongs to my family." He unconsciously puffed out his chest. "I come from a long line of warriors."

"And you seek someone." She made it a statement, not a question.

He scrutinized her face but saw no cunning, only a sort of hunger. He stood and faced her. "Yes. I seek the Princess Lauressa, the rightful Reina of Valdeor."

"Then you are the Champion of Valdeor."

He was surprised again. What kind of baker's apprentice was she?

Reading the look on his face, she lifted her chin and smiled. "Seek no farther. You have found her."

He stared at her in disbelief, watching as she drew forth a chain from around her neck, and handed it to him. He stared at the medallion in the palm of his hand. He recognized it as the one Estrell had described to him many times—round and silver with a clear stone in the center, surrounded by six stones of different colors: red, blue, purple, orange, yellow, and green. As he held it, diffuse light came from the stones, similar to his sword a moment ago. Power emanated from it, and he could feel it pulsing within his hands.

He had found the princess and in the most unexpected way.

He dropped on one knee before her and bent his head. "My Reina! I serve you with my life."

"Arise," she said in a soft, but commanding tone. "I accept your service gratefully."

As he regained his feet and met her gaze it seemed that she had changed. Or maybe he was now aware of her regal bearing, her graceful hands, and her direct gaze because he knew her for what she was. He realized that he still held her medallion and hurriedly gave it back to her, embarrassed by his lack of manners, unable to say anything. Her smile dazzled him, and his heart beat faster at her nearness.

All her earlier weariness seemed to drop away.

As she slipped on the heartstone medallion, in the window behind her the sun hung above the horizon. Her chestnut hair gleamed in the setting light, causing a halo to shine around her head. The rough homespun dress and poor surroundings were back-lit and dimmed into insignificance. She stood ramrod straight before him, the medallion shining with its light, giving her face a soft glow. She could have been a queen. In fact, she was.

The quest for the lost princess of Valdeor ended.

Returning her to her rightful throne began.

Lauressa sat before the campfire, braiding her newly-washed hair. She was aware of Alloryn trying not to stare at her. He was a handsome young man, serious and confident. Judging by his size—the wide shoulders and height over six feet—she did not doubt that he was powerful. Justinian would have trained him well in the use of arms. Their gazes met, and she blushed and turned away. She found him equally attractive.

Until now she had kept a strict watch on her heart. She still had a mission before her—the greatest of her life—but maybe when it was over... *Though I fear even then that I will have to marry for political reasons, such as an alliance between families.* She looked surreptitiously at Alloryn casting a spear into the stream. *Too bad. For Alloryn is appealing.*

They fried the fish that he caught in the River Ost. The fire gave a crackling, warm flame on the late summer night.

They had traveled south after he bought a cart from Kelvan, which was cheaper than buying a good horse for Lauressa. It also drew less attention to them. Since the island continent of Hamleor broke away after the kingdom's dissolution, they had no nobles, but elected officials. They and their wives traveled in comfort in luxurious carriages, while the peasants walked or rode in carts. The inhabitants of Hamleor were mostly fishermen, farmers, and merchants.

Lauressa came back to the present and broke the silence. "Justinian and I escaped the capital and were on the road for weeks, camping under the stars like tonight. We headed for Prince Jarell's castle, my fiancé's home on the east coast, but war erupted before we got there. I assume the turf wars between the warlords have worsened over a century. Raiding parties began as the hierarchy of law disappeared across all Valdeor."

Lauressa took up a stick and aimlessly poked it in the burning embers as she relived her past.

"In the end, my father's friend and swordsman, Justinian, and I shared the same dream that showed us the path to take. We both dreamed that a Guardian of Valdeor descended as we slept. He spoke secret words over the medallion and made it glow. The colors spun, orange mixing with green, purple, and yellow shimmering in the air, then coalescing with the red and violet, till all turned fiery white. At that point, I had to turn my face away from the pulsing light. The Guardian bid me rise and kneel, at which point he replaced the medallion around my neck. In a thundering voice that echoed around the glen where we slept, he said, 'As long as you wear this medallion you will not age until the chosen champion shall find you. At that time, when the Crestin Sword draws near, it will break the bonds I put you under tonight.' The Guardian then ascended into the sky and grew distant till he appeared as a star in the firmament."

She ceased speaking and stared into the fire, which had dwindled to embers. The night sky and the many stars seemed to press closer as if the Guardians themselves listened to her lovely voice tell her story.

"I could not stay in one place for more than ten years at a time," she unconsciously touched the medallion around her neck, "or people would become suspicious. So Justinian and I moved from town to town. He acted as my father, but he also left for long periods, gathering information, waiting to see who would gain the Crestin Sword. I worked as a baker's assistant, a weaver, an innkeeper's maid, and a milliner's assistant in different locations. We would move on to a distant town after a while and start over again. When I came back to any area, fifty years had passed, and no one remembered me.

"Justinian was right to hide me here till the proper time. Meanwhile, he waited for a sign of the Champion to be born." She stopped fiddling with the medallion and leaned forward. "Now that I have told you of myself, tell me how you won the Crestin Sword." And Alloryn obliged.

Ten days later they reached Oster, the biggest port.

Alloryn had been unsure how the princess would do on the journey, but he need not have worried. She did not complain, not about the long hours on the road, nor sleeping on the straw in the cart, nor the meager food.

The wharf was cold and damp. Lauressa huddled into her cloak. Alloryn spoke to the first mate of a schooner, the *Silver Spray*, a tidy looking vessel that occasionally took passengers if the pay was right. The short, burly man left to obtain the captain's approval.

The voyage's start did not look favorable. Gray mist swirled, dimming the early morning light, and gave disconcerting glimpses of the schooner and the quiet preparation around it. Fog muffled the sounds of clanking chains and the ship's creak as she pulled against her mooring.

A freak gust of mist blew around them and when it passed Lauressa saw the captain and the first mate standing in front of them, as if they had sprung from the planks beneath their feet. She almost gasped and stepped back, but held herself still.

The captain was tall, on a height with Alloryn, but gaunt. His gaze was direct and appraising.

"I will give you a passage for half again as my first mate bargained for," he said, and inclined his head toward Lauressa, "because women on board are bad luck, and we are already short of luck due to this here fog. You must pay beforehand." Lauressa saw Alloryn carefully show a small purse. She knew he hid a purse with the bulk of their coins in his clothing. He used the money from the sale of the horse and cart to purchase their passage. He had told her he planned to buy horses when they reached the mainland of Valdeor.

She hoped the ship and the captain were reliable.

"We sail in forty minutes," the first mate said pointedly to Alloryn, never glancing at Lauressa before he followed the captain into the rolling fog. His disembodied voice drifted back to them. "Do not be late. We do not wait for any man, and certainly not for a woman."

Lauressa followed Alloryn to the place where they had left Trekker near a stack of crates. They divided the food they had procured earlier between them. She had sewn some coins in her gown back in Losen Harbor in case they were separated. The rest of her small savings were in his hidden pouch.

Alloryn glanced at Lauressa as she closed her satchel and hefted it over her shoulder. "The captain seems honest, but as the only woman aboard you must be careful. Pirates are on the seas between here and the Nyrmidion Isles. I think you should have a weapon to brandish if the need arises." He removed a small scabbard from his belt and handed it to her.

She drew the deadly-looking dagger from it and held it confidently. She turned it in her hand, examining the blade edge. "Thank you." She re-sheathed it and stowed it in the sash around her waist.

They boarded as the sailors untied the last mooring and threw it aboard. The captain glanced at them once and then ceased to regard them. Lauressa's stomach lurched as they moved from the sheltered harbor into the open sea, but it quickly passed.

Like a hand letting go, the mist unclenched them, and the sun dazzled their eyes. It seemed like a morning for clear sailing. A feeling of freedom engulfed her with the crisp sea air. Too long had she waited for this day to arrive. Too long had she wondered when she would see her homeland again.

She caught Alloryn's admiring gaze, ignoring his heated embarrassment as he realized he was staring and smiled at him. "I was fourteen when my father was murdered. I have not been on a ship in almost a century."

What she left unsaid was, she had sailed from the mainland to Hamleor, the distant reaches, long before he was born.

Her cheeks glowed with excitement, and her eyes sparkled when she spoke. "It feels so fresh and free." Wisps of hair escaped her braid and blew around her face as red-gold curls in the morning light.

She thought the *Silver Spray* was an apt name for the schooner, as water mist sprayed her uplifted face.

6 *Nyrmidion Pirates*

*T*he pirate ship bore down on them. The storm raged furiously. Waves threatened to swamp the schooner, and amidst the water washing over the deck, Alloryn watched the sailors trying desperately to outrun the enemy ship.

As the schooner crested another wave, the rough seas exposed rocks in the trough. The captain valiantly tried to change course and avoid the collision, but it was too late. As the *Silver Spray* reached the trough's bottom, the impact threw the crew off their feet. Many washed overboard as another wave crashed on top of them.

Alloryn grabbed on to anything he could and pulled himself across the slippery deck toward the door leading to the cabins below. It flew open when he was twenty feet away, just as another wave lifted the ship. He saw Lauressa framed in the door, but before he could reach her, the schooner slammed back onto the rocks and flung her toward the railing. As the next wave pummeled the deck, she lost her precarious hold on the rail as the wave swept her overboard. Trekker skidded after her, and Alloryn managed to make a running leap and flew into the raging sea.

His body absorbed the shock of the dunking, and he pushed his head above water. He located her bobbing head near the wolfhound paddling toward her. He swam with strong strokes, never more thankful for Rodrek's swimming lessons. He battled the sea and the flotsam from the fast-breaking wreck behind them.

At last, he reached her side and locked his arm around her neck. He held her, both of them gasping in the storm's fury, as he sought his bearings. He sighted the wreck behind them, then headed for the shore of the Nyrmidion Isles, where the *Silver Spray's* crew spied it before the pirates made their appearance.

Trekker disappeared in the waves, but Alloryn could spare no more than a thought for his faithful companion. Trekker was a strong swimmer, and he would have to trust the animal to smell land and head for it.

The storm surge pushed them toward shore. As they rode the next big wave, he made for a gap in the rocky coast ahead, which became visible, else the surf would smash them on the sharp boulders that rose along the shore. The last wave carried them safely to the beach, and he used the last of his strength to fight the wickedly strong undercurrent that dragged at their legs and nearly pulled them back to sea. He let the girl go and collapsed, taking deep breaths and coughing up seawater. He then turned her on her stomach and pumped the water out of her lungs. Once he was sure she was breathing and no longer retching water, he tried to look around but collapsed with exhaustion.

When he next opened his eyes, he saw lights bobbing and thought he was still unconscious. Men with torches climbed down from the cliffs above to the shore. Rescuers?

He started to push himself up to call them when he saw their odd clothing and headdress as they scavenged along the shoreline. These were the dreaded Nyrmidions. The realization that the pirate ship had purposely wrecked the *Silver Spray* off the island coast for their people to pick over what remained of it made his stomach turn.

He pushed himself on his feet and reached for his sword, but realized with great dismay that it and its scabbard were lost at sea in the struggle to gain land. His hand clasped his knife hilt as he measured the distance to the nearest Nyrmidion compared to the distance to the tropical forest, and the likelihood of Lauressa gaining its shelter while he fought for the time needed for her escape.

Too late. The nearest Nyrmidion brandished his scimitar and called to his brethren as he stood.

The enemy reached the two survivors, so he had no choice but to pick up the now exhausted princess and follow them back to their camp.

Their destination was a cluster of rough-hewn dwellings a league inland from the still-pounding surf, where they met the stares of old men, women, and children with barbaric tattoos and an assortment of armor covering their bodies. Some had on breastplates, and others wore vambraces that covered their forearms, while others had the greaves to protect their shins, though the most popular piece was a modified helmet with horns attached. Pieces of ships and their cargo were in evidence everywhere as well—boat hatches used as makeshift doors, crate lids used as shutters, and pieces of masts used as support poles. The inhabitants of this island depended on the shipwrecks that happened naturally—or, Alloryn thought more likely, given their predicament—that they contrived.

The people stared at them with frowning faces, showing an avid desire for their belongings, reaching out to touch them as they passed. He feared they gave no quarter and had no compassion for the poor souls who survived the shipwrecks.

The crowd grew as the men who captured them led Alloryn, still carrying the princess, now awake, to the largest building in the enclave. When they reached it, he set her down. One man entered. In a few minutes, another exited the tent with the first, and the crowd hushed. The new man was almost a head taller than anyone present, with a commanding mien, long hair past his shoulders, bulging muscles in his arms and legs, and a fierce scowl. He wore a complete set of armor, though none of it matched. Large, red-painted horns decorated his helmet. No doubt this was the Nyrmidion leader.

"We found these survivors on the west beach, Mighty Lord. Shall we put them with the others?"

"Yes. Strip their goods and weapons and throw them in the cage," he commanded. With rough hands, the Nyrmidions pulled off Alloryn's and Lauressa's cloaks, took their daggers, and any possessions they still retained on their belts.

A warrior as tall as Alloryn pushed through the fierce crowd, who gave way as if even they were frightened of him. He wore a breastplate with an image of a bull's head. His helmet had a rectangular plate between his eyes to protect his nose. His biceps were as stout as a thick limb. He stopped in front of Lauressa and looked her over with a cruel grin. He reached to grab her arm but found himself held in a grip like a vise. His surprised gaze followed the offending hand up the arm to Alloryn's equally fierce scowl, as he held him off. In a few heart-stopping seconds, they took each other's measure.

"If it is a fight you want, I will be glad to oblige," Alloryn challenged. The warrior shook off his grip, and Alloryn stepped back. The newcomer looked at the leader who gave him a nod. A circle of Nyrmidions quickly widened around them, and the people cried for their hero to overcome the shipwrecked stranger.

The two men circled for a moment, judging each other, then swiftly came to combat. The newcomer went for Alloryn's head with his right fist. Alloryn spun out of his way, and clutched his opponent from the back, around his neck. Like an enraged bull, the warrior spun around, clawed at Alloryn's arm, and finally flipped him over his head. Alloryn quickly rolled aside and got to his feet before the man could stomp on him.

They made quick jabs with their hands, followed with kicks and dodges. Then the Nyrmidion combatant enveloped him in a crushing bear hug. Alloryn found himself unable to break free of the arms like tree trunks that encircled him, crushing him, so he made himself a dead weight while kneeing him and dragged the warrior to the ground. They rolled, each trying to get the upper position. Alloryn got one arm free and used his fingers to stab the eyes of his opponent, who roared with pain and slackened his hold.

Alloryn found himself loosened, broke free, then rose to his feet and kicked the man in the chest.

The warrior jumped up, pulled one of the spectator's swords, and attacked. Alloryn weaved in and out, ducking the deadly blade, but with no weapon nor armor, he knew he did not stand a chance.

The silence was absolute, as the spectators crowded in a ring around the combatants, expecting the kill. Lauressa, with her hands steepled over her mouth, looked as if she prayed earnestly for a favorable outcome. A loud, menacing growl broke the silence. Even the enemy stopped while the crowd jostled one another as something broke through their ranks. To the astonishment of all, Trekker appeared, dragging a scabbard, and jumped on his master. Alloryn used the momentary shock and unexpectedness of it to pull forth the Crestin Sword, and they resumed their fight.

Although the warrior was strong, he depended too much on his strength alone, which Alloryn used against him. Alloryn, the more agile of the two, sidestepped a particularly vicious thrust, brought his sword down on the other's hilt, and kicked the warrior in the knee as he moved past, causing him to drop his sword.

The fight was over, with the Crestin Sword at the warrior's neck. Panting from the exertion, Alloryn spared a glance at Lauressa. She lowered her hands from her face, gripping them tightly in front of her. She gave an imperceptible shake of her head. Her champion stepped back a pace, still in an offensive position. "By the right of the victor, I choose to spare your life."

The headman made a sound of disgust and a combined grunt of dissatisfaction sighed through the crowd. To the victor belonged the spoils. The man rose to his feet, a look of burning hate in his eyes, a promise of a dagger between the ribs if they ever met again. But the rules of combat would not allow him to re-challenge the obvious winner. The once-proud warrior slunk away through the crowd, with boos and hisses following him.

Their original captors stepped in and cleared the crowd now that the struggle was over. Several men subdued Trekker and dragged him away on a chain. With a dagger held at her throat, Lauressa had no choice but to be recaptured, and she saw Alloryn allow his sword to be stripped from his grasp when the man holding her threatened to cut her throat if Alloryn did not surrender. The islanders yanked them behind the center building where a crudely-made cage hung suspended in the air. Guards lowered it, opened the door, and shoved the two in.

Appalled, she realized what had looked like scarecrows inside it were prisoners crying for mercy to their captors, who hauled the cage once again into the air. The guards tied the giant hawser, once used on a ship, to what appeared to be an enormous mast stuck in the ground.

Lauressa, though at first horrified by the creatures in the prison cage with them, realized with compassion that these were prisoners who had been here a while, survivors from another wrecked ship like theirs.

She soon learned her surmises were correct as she spoke to the man next to her. His age was hard to tell as he was gaunt from lack of food and care. He told her he was a missionary priest who had come to preach the All-Seeing God of creation to the superstitious Nyrmidion tribes. The pirates captured him and his companions several weeks earlier and gave them bread and water once a day. They had not long to live. The islanders only waited for their most important festival, Winter Solstice, when they would light the bonfire under the cage and burn the captives as a sacrifice to their goddess of death.

Lauressa shuddered in her light clothing, partly from fear, and partly from the chilled, damp, dress. But she managed not to otherwise show her fear. She could not believe she had lived such a prolonged life to die on an obscure island. She told herself she had to have faith that her life was not meant to end here and now. She had a destiny to fulfill. They would escape, and she would see to it that these poor souls escaped with them.

Alloryn wished for his sword. If events had not happened so fast, or he had not been so exhausted after the swim, things might be different. He despaired as he thought he only saved the princess from death by drowning to face a more horrendous death by burning alive.

He saw her shiver more and more uncontrollably as the storm's wind blew, and shared what little warmth he had with her, putting his arm around her and warming her as best as he could in the wooden cage's corner.

Her nearness started his blood pumping, but he pushed his feelings away and studied their prison for a way out.

He studied the cage, looking for a weakness he could use. Tree limbs wove in a tight grid, bound together by rough hemp cords. An iron chain locked the door by which they entered. The top and sides had only space enough to push a hand through. He could easily use his sharp dagger to cut through the rope, but the Nyrmidions had taken that, along with everything that he could use as a weapon.

The evening lengthened, and the breeze diminished. The storm blew itself out, but it left behind an unusual chill for the tropics. The prisoners mostly bunched together for warmth in the cage's center, where the natives' sticks and stones could not reach them. Alloryn and Lauressa drowsed as the hours passed. Even their cold, cramped, and miserable state could not ward off sleepiness after the hard-won fight with the sea and warrior earlier.

The morning light brought a small measure of relief, as the pirates lowered their prison so that they could pass bread and a pail of water through the door. No escape was possible with two pike-wielding warriors guarding the man bearing their food.

As they ate hungrily, a keening sound reached them, which grew in volume. A procession of wailing women grew nearer. They tore their garments, and they pulled at their wild hair in a loud display of grief. At the procession's head, a woman in bright flapping robes, covered with occult symbols, held a cup in the air and chanted in the Nyrmidion language.

"What is happening?" Alloryn asked the man nearest him, a sailor with long straggly hair and a scar on his cheek.

Before the man could reply, Lauressa translated, "The priestess calls upon their goddess of death to spare someone close to death. It sounds like a child is dying—" she cocked her head and listened "—the headman's son."

Lauressa stood with difficulty, her cramped legs protesting, and stepped toward the open door while the guards' attention focused on the wailing women. When they noticed her, they swung their pikes and pointed them at her midsection. Ignoring her danger, she called in their language, "I am a healer. Take me to the boy before it is too late." They did not respond, so she repeated it, with greater emphasis. "Do you wish the Headman to learn that you did not heed a healer who offered her services, only to let his son die when you could have prevented it?" Her words finally affected one warrior, who removed his weapon and spoke in a low tone to the other two Nyrmidions. He gave her another glance and disappeared toward the largest structure in the village.

Alloryn grabbed her arm, "What did you say?"

She assumed the alarm on his face was for her.

She repeated her plea. At the stern look on his face, she soothed, "This is our chance. We must take it. If I can heal that boy, we can win the Nyrmidion leader's respect, and secure our freedom."

She could tell by the expression on his face Alloryn did not like it. Neither of them trusted these people to make a bargain and keep it, but if she did not risk it, they had no other option that she could see. The more time they spent pent in this cage, the less able they would be to run or outwit their captors as they lost strength, mobility, and hope.

The man came back, and with him was the leader with the red horns, striding quickly. They stopped before the cage. Red Horns gave her a searching look and spoke harshly in the common language. "You claim to be a healer. I fear this is a trick, but you have no place to go on this island that my men cannot find you. If you are lying, you will suffer great tortures, and the fire ceremony to the goddess of death will seem a blessed relief."

Lauressa raised her chin and stood her ground, though her knees trembled beneath her dress. Courage in the face of adversity was what Justinian had taught her.

"I need to see him, now, before it is too late."

The Nyrmidion headman locked eyes with her. She could feel his commanding presence, the strength of purpose, and vitality that radiated from him. He was a man who bowed before no man, trusting in his strength of arms to fell all before him. But nothing in his arsenal could conquer illness and disease.

He paused a few moments, then without a word, motioned the guards to let her pass. Alloryn stiffened beside her. She reached for his hand and squeezed it once before leaving their prison and following the headman.

The boy lay in the main structure's inner room.

His eyes were unfocused when she lifted the lids. The women around her muttered under their breath as she stared down his throat and laid the back of her hand on his forehead. She asked the nearest woman who hovered protectively around the boy a few questions.

After her inspection, she said, "He has all the symptoms of the Hedonian Fever." She told the woman she would need to speak with the headman who waited outside the sickroom. "No. Speak me. I boy's mother, Irda."

"Are you an herbalist? Can you make a brew if I tell you what you need?" Irda shook her head no and called over the woman leader of the earlier procession, standing at the bed's foot.

"This woman herbalist. She help you." The priestess looked at Lauressa with contempt. Her face was pale, her hair was long, jet black and wild looking. She was wearing necklaces of what looked like human teeth mixed in with feathers and small animal bones. She hissed at the princess in the Nyrmidion dialect. "My prayers cannot save this boy. What does one like you know of potions and powers? Pah. This is a waste of time." And she stormed from the room.

The mother looked from the retreating witch's back to the girl standing before her. "I speak to my lord husband. You save son." She rose from kneeling beside her son's bed, lifted a curtain, and went through the door.

Within moments the headman appeared with his wife. Irda led him to Lauressa. Standing before her with a stern face he asked, "What can you do that the witch Malfressa cannot for my son? Nothing my priestess can conjure will save him, she says."

"I know of herbs and healing potions. If one of your women can bring me herbs, I can cure his fever and his illness." She named the herbs needed, and the boy's mother nodded at most of them, except for a few key ingredients. "I not know of what you speak," she said.

Lauressa then pleaded with Red Horns to gather the herbs from the hills deeper in the island, but he denied her request. "You seek to trick me. No. I will hear no more."

"Wait!"

He paused in his retreat and looked back at her.

"Send my companion and he will gather the necessary plants. I will stay as your hostage. If he does not return, you can kill me."

Red Horns considered her. She was in earnest, and she hoped he saw her words were a true indicator of her character. She tried to impress him—fearless, with determination in her demeanor.

"You show no weakness or hysterics as past female captives have. I will give you a chance, for the sake of my woman, who looks at me with pleading eyes, and for the sake of my favorite son."

Hearing the conditions, Lauressa could see Alloryn was not pleased. "What if I cannot find these herbs on this island?" He reached for his sword at his side, frustration apparent when he realized it was not there. "Do you trust him to let us go even if I do find them?"

"I know you are worried about my safety, but we will both die if we do not try." Lauressa put both of her hands on his arms and tried to project her confidence with her eyes. "We must have faith."

As their eyes locked, she felt a connection with him that she had never felt with another. She realized she was only inches away from him, and still gripping his arms. She quickly let him go and stepped back, lowering her eyes, to cover the feelings she was experiencing,

She described the plants she desired and their quantity.

"I know the plants. I learned the same plant lore from Justinian, using them to heal wounds gained in training, and fevers caught in the swamps and jungles."

Besides Red Horns, the women, and the guards, many villagers gathered outside the boy's sickroom. They watched the situation avidly. A few wore looks of hope on their face, while others wore looks of skepticism. Alloryn did not doubt that they would exult in Lauressa's torture and death if he failed to return.

Warriors led him from the village, with a huge following—

seemingly every Nyrmidion on the isles wanted to see him depart on his mission. He followed a path that led to the inland mountain where he hoped he could find the herbs Lauressa needed. He prayed that they were on this island, far from the Valdeor mainland, and that the Nyrmidion boy would live long enough for this to work.

The vegetation closed in on him soon after he left the village. After forty-five minutes, the path veered steeply upward, hardly more than a goat track at this point. After another fifteen minutes, trees and ferns stopped at a rough cliff wall. If the herbs were to be found at all, they would be in the foothills of the mountain now towering above him. So he left the path and climbed the cliff. Foot by foot he reached with his hands, or his fingertips, for purchase on the vertical rock. He reached a ledge one hundred feet above the path without too much exertion, although it was a while since he had done any serious climbing.

In a sheltered area, he found the first necessary herb, called Mountain Balm, clinging precariously to the rocky slopes. He carefully removed the whole plant. He put it in a pouch he brought specially to preserve the herbs. For the next half an hour, he scoured the ledge, which was as wide as thirty feet in places and one hundred feet long. He managed to harvest a dozen plants.

He stood on the mountain scar overlooking the canopy below and saw the far-off sea stretching to the horizon. A constant breeze from the heights made it cool. He brought his mind back to the task and searched below for a likely area for a stream, where the next medicinal plant, Alisma, would grow. He headed back to the cliff face when he discerned a faint spray of water.

An hour and a half of walking passed before he heard the rushing waterfall from the mountain heights above. The heavy vegetation, mostly ferns at this point, parted on the scene of a mountain stream full of rocks below him. He clambered down the canyon, careful of his pouch with its precious contents. The gurgling river beckoned to him. He knelt and tasted its icy cold, sweet water, drinking as much of it as he parched throat demanded. As he stood, he saw a native island deer watching him, before it bounded from sight. He kept the watercourse on his left, and he headed downstream. He followed its course, pushing branches out of his way. He detoured around impassable areas of thick brush and fallen trees, always keeping the water's sound and smell within reach, until it glided into a meadow. Here where the stream meandered, he found the marshland needed to grow Alisma. He hunted through the mud and grass until he found a patch. He gathered as much as his pouch would hold, then he straightened and stretched his back.

The sun was getting low. He did not have much time left in the day. He longed for his dog Trekker, who the villagers captured and tied up after his dramatic entrance during the fight. The dog would have no problem finding the way back to the settlement. Using the mountain behind him to take a bearing, and the sea smell that tickled his nose beyond the marshy smells, he headed in that direction. Once he found the shore, he would follow it back to the village and hope he was not too late.

Lauressa prepared the herbs that the boy's mother had given

her in a room near the sick room. She boiled some of them, and others she pounded into a fine powder. The woman watched her on occasion, leaving her son to the care of others. At one point she had asked in her simple way why the princess did not chant over the herbs as she prepared them.

"I am not a witch. Not a priestess. I pray silently to the One Who Fashioned All Things in my heart, not with my tongue."

"The witch, Malfressa, she speak much, mutter, roll her head and eyes. I not like her. She jealous of my power with my man. You be good. I hope your man come back soon with good medicine. I not want see you die."

Lauressa hoped that one day these people would put away their superstitions. Maybe this one act would plant a seed. At least she could dilute the witch's power and reputation among these people.

As the day wore on into the night, she stepped outside to watch for Alloryn's return. She did not try to go beyond the guards around the building. As the dusk fell, she stood in the doorway as long as she could and stared at the path where he disappeared. She imagined his tall, strong body as she had seen him during the fight. She had feared for him as he fought the warrior who wanted to claim her as his own. Twice now Alloryn saved her from a horrible fate.

Now she was worried, but not in the same way. Time was running out. She needed him, but she also wanted his companionship. She knew she was more attached to him with every passing day.

She went back inside and lay a hand gently on the lad's forehead. The fever was higher, and delirium set in. His mother tried to keep him from casting off the covers. She gazed at

Lauressa with hopelessness. "Say many prayers to your god," she begged.

A sound of voices and footsteps drawing closer announced the arrival of Red Horns and his retinue. His grim look in the torchlight spoke more than words. Alloryn had not returned. The women muttered and cast dark looks her way. Lauressa trembled inwardly, but would not show her fear before these people.

A shout in the distance, wild barking, and many voices raised drew everyone's attention. Within a moment, guards brought Alloryn in. Wearily he detached the pouch from his belt and passed it to her with unspoken hope in his face.

She hurriedly took the precious plants into the adjoining room and finished the herbal preparations. She brought back a poultice that she placed on the lad's chest. She motioned Irda to prop his head on her lap since he was not able to hold the drink in his hands. She carefully spooned a concoction into his mouth, and with his mother's encouragement, they got it all down his throat.

Lauressa eased back and wearily stood. Red Horns and all present watched her face.

"Now we must wait for it to take effect."

She sank on the floor beside Alloryn at the bed's foot, and he put his arm around her shoulders. Everyone in the room waited in silence to see if the boy lived or died this night.

She prayed fervently that he would live because her fate and her companion's would be the same as the headman's son.

As the dawn broke the boy stirred, opened his eyes, and reached for his mother. "His fever is gone!" Irda's face lit with joy, and she sought out Lauressa's eyes. They exchanged a look before she ministered to her son. The unbearable tenseness in the room eased. In no time he was able to sit and drink a little broth.

Lauressa claimed he was out of danger after she examined him.

Seeing for himself that Lauressa had healed the child, the headman glanced her way. He spoke a word in the guard's ear and strode out of the room.

Women served Lauressa and Alloryn food and drink, then provided rooms to freshen themselves and get a little sleep.

That afternoon they met again, and the islanders led them to a different meeting room. They walked into a large hall with high ceilings. Banners and weapons of every kind hung on the walls—spoils of battle from all known peoples. The whole tribe gathered before a wooden dais with a massive carved chair. The crowd moved aside as Alloryn and Lauressa entered and left the two standing in front of the empty dais.

A hush settled over the room as a curtain parted and the Nyrmidion leader strode to the dais and took his place on the throne. In a loud voice, he spoke. "Listen, my people, and hear my words. I, Marjek Red Horns, release these two from bondage. No harm shall come to them within or without our realm by any of the Nyrmidion tribe here or elsewhere." He motioned with his hand and two warriors came forward with salvers. From the first one, he removed a brooch of finely wrought silver in a fantastical design. His wife Irda stepped from behind his throne and with a shy smile pinned it on Lauressa's dress. Then the second warrior proffered a salver to Red Horns. He removed a dagger with a jeweled hilt and

Nyrmidion designs scrolled on the blade, which he presented to Alloryn.

Looking from one to the other, Marjek Red Horns formally intoned, "As long as you live, you shall be honorary members of our tribe, welcome in our village, given all respect, and all your ancestors shall receive the same for what you have done today."

He opened his arms with surprising humility, and added, "Ask what you will, and we will provide it if it is in our means."

Lauressa stepped forward and her voice penetrated the hall for all to hear. "We thank you, Marjek Red Horns, the great leader of the brave Nyrmidion warriors for the honor you have shown us this day. I, too, am a leader of a nation, and I am honored to be a part of your tribe. I will not forget you or your people when I come into my power and sit on my throne."

A surprised thrill went through the room at her words.

She resumed. "We will open trade agreements with you at that time if you wish. Today I ask that you release the other prisoners."

When Red Horns motioned assent to his chief warrior, she continued, "I suggest that we give thanks to the One Who Fashioned All Things for your son, because He has cured him. I was His humble instrument. He has great plans for your firstborn."

As she began her speech, her medallion glowed with a faint red light. When she finished, its pulsing light was discernible to all present. Nyrmidions fell back from them, and even Red Horns brought his hand up before his eyes as a strong reddish light bathed the room.

Lauressa's countenance went from calm and regal to intense and excited. "Alloryn! The heartstone is near! The gem of courage is here on the Nyrmidion Isles."

She rushed outside, with him at her heels, followed by Marjek Red Horns and all the warriors and Nyrmidion populace. She froze in amazement at the bright red light, mimicking the setting sun's splendor as it shone from the mountaintop where Alloryn found the herbs. Gasps echoed all around, and everyone pointed to the phenomenon. They glanced from it to her and the medallion that now hummed, as well as shining like a small sun. The circle of people around them moved back several paces and many fell on their faces to the ground.

As suddenly as the orb began to glow it disappeared. A noise like a thunderclap rang overhead and those gathered no longer saw the ruby heartstone in the mountain peak. The light from the medallion also dimmed, then faded away.

"Who are you, O Lady of the Light?" The headman cringed before her show of power. "If you are an enchantress, why did you not strike us down instead of allowing us to capture you?"

"Fear not, Marjek Red Horns. I am a human the same as you. My name is Princess Lauressa, true Reina of Valdeor, Ruler of the House of Gildran." And she told those gathered a shortened version of the tale of the lost heiress to the throne of Valdeor.

The Nyrmidions held a great feast, celebrating the headman's son's return to life, and the stone of courage's miraculous return. After feasting a few days, the whole village again turned out to watch Lauressa, Alloryn, and the now-freed captives board a pirate ship to set sail for the mainland.

Irda shyly hugged Lauressa. "Thank you, Great Lady, for my son's life." She stepped back and put her arm around her son's shoulders.

The islanders also returned their possessions and gave them provisions for the journey as well.

The missionary priest stayed behind, at Red Horns' request and the princess's negotiation. They wished to learn of the One Who Fashioned All Things after He had defeated their greatest god, the goddess of death and destruction.

Unseen by anyone, a figure in black watched the ship go over the horizon. From her vantage point on the cliffs facing the east, she cursed the two who discredited her and made her an exile among her people. "You have not seen the last of me," the witch Malfressa cried as the last glimpse of sails slipped over the horizon.

7 Mintala, The Capital City

*I*n Mintala, the citizens went about their business, including one man named Odem. He was a man of many talents—a wayfarer, an intelligence gatherer, and a fierce soldier. Some would call him a spy. He considered himself a watcher.

Odem was the second son of an innkeeper. He was approaching thirty years of age. His older brother would inherit the family business, which suited Odem just fine. He loved to travel and had seen much of Valdeor. But right now, he was in the capital on business. He found his father's inn, with its popular tavern, a wonderful place for collecting information.

He had learned many years ago that there is always a market for good information. What made him good at his job was his ability to notice subtle details, read other's expressions, observe their nervous habits, and make judgment calls on what was important and what was not.

Odem's assessment of the current state of the citizens was that over the years the wars and feuds to control the biggest city on the continent of Valdeor had wearied them and made them a silent, suspicious lot. No one wanted to be noticed, no one wanted to draw attention to themselves, for if one did, the guards of Feornson, the city's current warlord, would be sure to take one in for questioning. They would claim a trumped-up charge, such as disturbing the peace, and the offender would disappear into the dungeons. So the inhabitants kept to themselves, and their charity grew cold. Helping their neighbor might get them in trouble, and trouble is what all wished to avoid.

The city was once the most prosperous of all the realm. Odem found in his many travels to and from the plains surrounding the hill where the city stood, it still looked grand until one entered the gate, then the disrepair was noticeable. Gazing around as he walked from his father's place, the Crown Imperial Inn and Tavern, to the marketplace, he could see the houses needed paint, the roofs needed repair, the streets were unclean, and warehouses that were once full were now shuttered. And everyone complained the jails were full.

This particular day was the weekly market day. Farmers from outlying areas brought in their wares—pigs, cattle, and produce. Their wives brought in their crafts—woven items, cheeses, and freshly churned butter. The marketplace also had wares brought from far-flung ports—wines, bolts of cloth, rugs, pottery, and all the things one would expect to find in a large city's market. Missing were the work of goldsmiths, silversmiths, as well as jewelry and fine linens. The poor could not afford those luxuries, and a century of war and unrest had reduced even the once-proud nobles to poverty.

Odem entered the market, which was full of vendors and buyers at mid-morning. Carts and wagons of all shapes and sizes negotiated the streets leading from the gates to the central plaza. As he reached the outer stalls, smells of horses and humans, and, strangely enough, onions assaulted his nose. The deeper he penetrated, though, freshly baked meat pies and fried bread filled the air and made his mouth water.

As he bought a meat pie to eat, Odem's thoughts turned to his job. His main buyer of information these days was Preedim, ruler of Winterhome. Preedim closely watched Feornson's troop movements.

Odem did his best to blend into the crowd. The presence of Feornson's guards watchful for trouble kept the noise of a city muted and the air somber. Odem covertly edged closer to the soldiers, seemingly intent on eating his pie but listening to their chatter.

Hearing nothing of importance, his mind wandered. His eye fell on the palace walls above.

In the palace on the highest hill in the capital city, Odem knew the throne room sat empty. Although Feornson claimed the palace as his main residence, he only used the western portion. Everyone from the lowest scullery maid to Feornson himself considered the throne room, and the king's chambers leading from it, haunted since that fateful day of King Arness's death.

Months before, he had received a note from his old friend Estrell, telling him the time was near for the stones of virtue to reappear. Odem had secretly visited the throne room to see the place of legend. The only occupants were spiders busy spinning their webs, and rodents scuttling across the room as they traveled from one end of the castle to the other in search of food. The throne itself sat in the judgment room's center, covered in cobwebs. The center stone, the last gem of power left, was still opaque, dull black. Occasional drafts of air caused dust to swirl in spirals. The air came from the six encircling window embrasures, which had once supported the six heartstones.

Odem, although having a soldier's courage, could understand why others considered this place haunted as he looked around that day.

Odem's thoughts returned to the present when a tremendous boom shook the marketplace. Some citizens screamed while others cowered in place.

Seeing the sky above the palace turn red, Odem remembered the words Estrell had written: *Watch for the stones of virtue to appear in the sky. These signs will precede the Champion bringing Princess Lauressa to Mintala. Prepare the city.*

People in the marketplace ran for cover, thinking a storm had suddenly blown in. The fiery red glow, which lasted several minutes, drew Odem toward the palace. Many citizens crying, "fire!" ran with him. A deep red glow engulfed the palace and surrounding buildings and slowly faded, leaving a ruby in the west embrasure. Soon a large crowd gathered on the street under the palace's western end to gape at the heartstone as it dimmed.

Describing the events in a letter to Preedim, Odem wrote, "Over the next hours, many city inhabitants came to see for themselves the red gem which magically appeared in the palace wall."

Fortunately for Odem, many then quenched their thirst for drink and companionship at his father's taproom. Odem heard their accounts firsthand.

A young man bragged to his companions, "I saw many of Feornson's other servants fall on their faces in fear as the thunderclap reverberated overhead." He took a slurp of his ale. "Of course, I stayed calm. My mother raised me to be fearless."

"That's funny," the lad at his elbow piped up. "I thought for sure I saw you hiding under a table." The group around the table sniggered.

A soldier at another table was telling his companions, "I was in the room with Feornson, giving my report. I thought that judgment day was surely upon us. Why even the red-bearded warlord himself blanched at the sound and brilliant light that followed."

"I heard a terrible thunderclap from as far away as a day's walk from the city," a merchant told Odem when he brought his meal.

Odem went on with his written summary, "News of it spread far and wide over the next few weeks as those who came a long distance to the market told all they met about the stone's miraculous return. None were old enough to remember when all six stones sat in their place at the king's judgment seat, but old tales were circulated of the glorious age lasting five hundred years, which ended a century before.

"It is as if the red ruby's presence, heartstone of courage, gently prod the inhabitants to face their lot in life with strength and perseverance. I have observed they square their shoulders and hold their heads a little higher, and their eyes reflect a determination to overcome difficulty. No longer do they hunch over and look at the ground as the soldiers stride about the city, but they face Feornson's mercenaries as men."

The red gem of courage returned to its rightful place, and

Odem saw how a down-trodden people hoped for a brighter future.

Alloryn and Lauressa spent the long weeks aboard the Nyrmidion ship *Relentless* discussing how to gain the next stone of virtue. They chose to go south first, which meant crossing the Motari Desert, the largest in Valdeor.

Alloryn was standing at the bow when the ship's crew sighted the port of Skupe. The pirate captain knew his ship would be unwelcome and did not want a fight with the many vessels at anchor in the trading port. So he turned south and sailed a half-day, till he reached a little cove where crew members took the passengers in a skiff to shore.

The group parted ways on the beach as the shipwrecked sailors and other ex-prisoners chose to walk to Skupe in search of a passage to their respective homes, while Alloryn led Lauressa toward the main north-south road along the coast. Short of it, away from prying eyes, they partook of breakfast consisting of salted fish and hardtack soaked in tea.

Heading straight across the plains to Mintala, in the center of Valdeor, was not the goal at this point. Lauressa needed to gain the other stones of power before they faced the warlords in the middle lands. The northern provinces had snow now in the eighth month of the year. So this was when caravans headed south. They carried goods such as iron weapons from the forges in the great northern city of Winterhome, and gems dug in the Mountains of No Hope in the cold north, where they traveled during the warm summer, and brought them to the south's gentler winter climate. There the merchants would trade the weaponry and gems for fine woven cloth and rugs from the south's fair city, Samarantha.

"We will head for an inn, or caravansary, where the caravans stop when they have left Skupe behind, but before they cross the desert." Alloryn passed Lauressa chunks of fish. "It is the last oasis before the true desert starts. Many times the caravans wait until their numbers swell before crossing. The desert is dangerous, yes, but also the bandits hiding in the desert places who watch for the richly-laden wagons. The Nyrmidions might be the fiercest of tribes, but they have a certain sense of honor. The bandits are more barbarous, leaving their victims to die in the merciless sun."

She shuddered. "How terrible."

They walked until they came to the Four Winds Caravansary. Here Alloryn negotiated with a horse trader for two desert horses which could withstand the desert's heat and harsh climate. A week later a caravan arrived. Along with Alloryn and Lauressa, the Four Winds Inn's inhabitants left their chores to see it. At first, all they saw was a dusty track in the distance. It resolved into a colorful procession the closer it came. Sixteen covered wagons were on the train, with all different colors of canvas on the wagons. Noise filled the air with much stomping of feet, the jangling of horse tack, and merchants shouting merry greetings.

From the lead wagon a tall, rotund man alighted. He verged on fat, yet his arms looked muscular when the sleeve of his robe fell away as he reached for the reins to lead his horses to the stable. He wore a bright red vest over his garments, and several rings on his fingers flashed in the light.

Alloryn remembered how nearly a year ago, he and Justinian traveled the route from this caravansary to Samarantha. They signed on as swords for hire, since the route led into the badlands frequented by outlaws who preyed on unwary travelers. He still remembered the lay of the land, the possible nooks and crannies most likely for ambushes, and the places where water could be found in times of need. Instead of traveling as clients paying for the caravan's protection, he hoped by offering his services as a mercenary, he could save precious coins.

He spoke with the innkeeper regarding the caravan leader.

Wiping down the spotless bar, the innkeeper replied, "Yes, he comes through here every year. You could do no better than to join him as you travel across the desert. He has a well-earned reputation as a canny one. Bandits do not tangle with him in general. His outriders are fierce, but they are nothing compared to him when brigands threaten his wagons. I heard he killed five bandits himself in a raid a few years back. He is an honest man, but no fool."

After the caravan merchants settled in the taproom, with food and ale before them, Alloryn approached the caravan's leader.

"What can I do for you, young sir?" The big man shrewdly assessed Alloryn's honest face, plain garb, and his soldierly stance. His gaze slid to the intricately tooled scabbard where it peeked from under his cloak. "If you are offering your service to join my outriders and protect my goods till we reach Samarantha, I will take a chance on you. I will pay handsomely upon the journey's completion, but beware, I, Eleedur the Hawk, came by my name, as I can discern an honest man from a con man. Any man who causes trouble on my march will have to deal with me." With that said, he laid the dagger he used as a knife on the table where Alloryn could see over a dozen notches on the hilt. "Aye, no one gets the upper hand with the Hawk."

"I am a good scout too. I have ridden this way before. I would be pleased to pledge my sword to your service while we travel the Motari Desert. My traveling companion and I seek to journey in safety with your caravan."

"Then we have a common goal. Come, sit with me." He called the server over and ordered more ale. "We might as well get to know each other. We will pass the time with ale and song until my cousin and his caravan join with us in a week. The more mighty the company in number, the less likely bandits will target us, although in this business there is no guarantee we will be entirely left alone."

As Eleedur promised, a week passed before a smaller caravan joined them, with only eight wagons, not so colorful, and not in as good condition. But the wagoners were hearty, as they told tales of peril on the road and toasted companions not seen in months. Whereas Eleedur and company had come south from the stronghold of Winterhome, his cousin Rappallo came southwest from the capital city of Mintala.

A few hours after the second company arrived, Lauressa found Alloryn in the taproom and joined him as the two newly merged caravans sat around, while the news and ale flowed.

Rappallo spoke to the gathered travelers. "I heard of strange goings-on in the capital a few weeks back. Seems that during the weekly market last month a miraculous event occurred."

"'Oho, miracles. Are you sure they were not induced by your ale?' 'Here comes a miraculous stretch of my belief.' 'What tall tale shall he tell next?'" and such jests met the statement.

Pressed by the Hawk's group for details, he took a long swig of ale, wiped his mouth and replied, "This is not a traveler's yarn, and I embroider not the truth. I saw with my own eyes the first heartstone return in the windows of the old palace.

"I jest not," Rappallo repeated to the sounds of disbelief. "Hundreds witnessed the bright red glow of light and the great thunder and quake that preceded it." Conversation buzzed at the announcement.

Lauressa sat rapt by Alloryn's side. She knew when the stone winked from their sight in the Nyrmidion Isles it would appear in Mintala in the embrasure where it had originally been set millennia ago, but she was still glad to hear of its safe arrival and the effect it had on those present. Since she planned to claim the throne, she wanted the people to know and be prepared for her arrival. She needed the populace behind her to finally abolish the oppression her people were under and return to the old ways.

She was as thrilled to hear Rappallo's tale as she had been when the stone appeared that day on the island. She would need the courage the stone represented to continue facing the new obstacles that were sure to appear.

"I, for one, would like to meet this princess," Eleedur motioned for the innkeeper to fill his mug and wiped his mouth. Others nodded around them. "A girl alone could not take down Feornson."

"'Tis said a champion will defeat all who oppose her." Rappallo poured some ale from the pitcher brought by the innkeeper.

"Champion? Magic stones?" Eleedur guffawed. "I think whoever told you these tales must have smoked jimson weed."

Lauressa felt Alloryn tense beside her. She placed a hand over his hand when she was fearful he would speak out.

Now was not the time to defend herself or reveal her identity.

Two days were spent dickering over the price of goods and loading on all the many provisions they needed for the three-week march through the desert.

"It is a balancing act," Eleedur told Alloryn as they watched his men load the food and barrels of water. "If you take too much, you needlessly burden the horses, which you cannot afford to lose. But if you take too little, you may die of starvation or dehydration in the wastes."

Soon all was ready. The merged caravan pulled out, dust swirling behind them. The entire Four Winds Caravansary household watched them go, calling farewells and wishing them safe travels till they returned.

The merchants began the journey light-hearted and jolly. They chose the life of the open road, seeking new wares, new treasures, new business, and adventure on the way. Even the steeds seemed glad to be back on the roadway.

For the next seven days, they made good time. The scenery became flatter, browner, with less vegetation the further they traveled from the coast, and the sun became harsher and glaring, causing all to squint at the distance. Grass gave way to weeds. The few trees gave way to scrub brush, which became scarce. The sea's smell gave way to the smell of dry dust. The light mood slowly turned into a plodding steadiness.

Alloryn rode with the outriders who kept a constant circle of surveillance around the slower-moving wagons. The outriders took turns standing watch during the chill desert nights, while they guarded the wagons clustered together.

Lauressa rode on her horse, and other times in the women's wagon, Trekker running alongside it.

During the seventh day, all was quiet in the drowsy afternoon. The horses' hooves sent up puffs of dust, which the light breeze caught and caused to swirl around the wagons as they passed.

Alloryn was absorbed in his thoughts when a spare horse tied to the last wagon reared with a loud whinny and broke its lead. It bolted into the hills. The caravan slowed their horses, and the outriders rode to the back of the wagon train. A coiled snake on a rock had spooked the horse. One of the outriders killed it.

Alloryn volunteered to leave the group and bring the horse back. Eleedur agreed. Alloryn rode to the top of a nearby hill. Before him lay a vast, trackless wasteland dotted with brush and cut with zigzagging gullies among the hills. He saw dust hanging in the air and wheeled his mount in that direction. He followed the hoof prints until the ground became too stony to see them. He could no longer follow the prints on the baked earth. He got off his horse and searched the ground for signs.

He recalled his training days with Justinian. He looked for turned over pebbles and stones, disturbed earth, broken scrub brush, and hoof marks. He saw minute signs of life in this barren place: mice, snakes, birds, and other tiny creatures' marks. Eventually, he found the direction the horse headed, mounted his steed, and followed the tracks. He found the lathered horse standing on its lead, unable to run. He gently coaxed the beast with water from his waterskin poured in a pan. He gathered the rope, and slowly retraced his steps.

A couple of hours later he rejoined the caravan, leading the stray horse. Rappallo and Eleedur were impressed with his tracking skills in the harsh land.

On the tenth night, as he was relieved of his watch, he came to the fire for a cup of tea to warm himself before turning in for the night. He sat companionably with the others around the campfire.

"This is bandit territory," the lead outrider said. "Before us are hills with deep canyons and many hiding spots over the next rise. Best be on the lookout and keep your eyes and ears alert. They ambushed us here one year, even though we managed to kill more of them than they killed of us."

The next morning before the sun rose a degree from the horizon, the caravan was on the move. The flat land dropped before them over the next hill. A huge canyon stretched from a few miles northeast to the horizon on the southwest. A well-used, wide trail led to the bottom. Eleedur sent six scouts ahead of the caravan, including Alloryn.

The trail reached the bottom of a ravine and followed a dry stream bed for the first few leagues. Then it narrowed to allow one wagon enough margin to barely pass. Alloryn realized this was an ideal spot for an ambush. He removed his sword from its scabbard and held it across his lap. He re-strapped his dagger from his belt to his thigh where he could reach it easily. He tied his reins to the pommel of his saddle to free both hands. "Scout," he commanded Trekker, who lopped off with his tongue hanging out in a doggy grin.

An hour into the narrows, a pebble suddenly came trickling down the cliff wall. Alloryn shouted a danger signal to the other riders and gripped his sword.

Soundlessly, a bandit slid down a rope with a sword in his hand, almost on top of him. With quick reflexes, Alloryn parried the sword's down-stroke and whipped his dagger into the other's exposed belly. More ropes and bandits appeared around the scouts, who fought back in the confined space. Alloryn swung his horse about and attacked the nearest bandit who fought a comrade. With one stroke he cut off the thief's sword arm. Then he charged his horse at another bandit who pulled a scout from his horse. A hoof in his back and a swipe with the sword finished the third one, but he was too late to save the rider.

The air was rent with injured men's cries as the five outriders and one wolfhound fought the remaining eight raiders. They gave a good account of themselves, but Alloryn was like a whirlwind released, everywhere at once. He smote with his sword, kicked a man trying to grab at his horse, and came to another's rescue. Soon they overcame the bandits.

"Go back to the caravan. Make sure this was not a diversion. My dog and I will ride ahead and look for more attackers."

The men left.

For the next hour, he expected more men to ambush him from around every bend and intersecting canyon, but none did. He found their camp and the loot they stole from others passing this way, including bolts of many colors of silk in the first group of bags. He moved beyond them to another heap, but gagged at the "bags," which he saw were sightless bodies strewn by the marauders. Alloryn forgot any lingering regret at having killed the bandits earlier in the horror before him.

He buried the unfortunate travelers' bodies heaped beside the treasure.

Eleedur praised him, "You led my outriders to a victory today. You earned the spoils you found." At first, he declined the ill-gotten goods, but Eleedur shook his head. "The owners do not need these silks where they are now. You can buy more beautiful goods at Samarantha for your lady. What woman does not wish for pretty baubles and lace and lovely gowns? They have this and more at the fair city."

Alloryn finally agreed to keep the stolen goods, not for those reasons, but to buy more provisions.

A week after the ambush, the landscape changed to a rocky wasteland. Little vegetation grew in this part of the Motari Desert. The trail wound through weird stone shapes that fierce winds sculpted as they blew through the land.

The first sign of a disturbance was a brown cloud to the north. It grew larger in the passing hours. As it loomed closer, Alloryn realized it was a gigantic dust storm. Others realized it at the same time, and Eleedur frantically motioned for the wagons to circle. The last horse hardly found his place when it overtook them. Those who drove and rode in the wagons deserted their places on the seats squinted in the wild wind and made their way into the wagons with the goods. They closed flaps with quick fingers against the dust, which poured into every crack. Those on horseback were less lucky. The wind blasted them forcefully before they were able to gain entry inside the circle as the dust storm hit. Most managed to gain entrance inside the wagons, and a few managed to crouch below the wagons.

Lauressa, who drove a wagon today instead of riding in one, scrambled inside quickly with the other women. Alloryn, who rode beside her, covered as much of his face as he could with his cloak till he gained entrance inside her wagon with Trekker at his heels.

The howling wind deafened them. The sandstorm was like a great predator roaring and shaking the wagons like prey.

The hours passed and the sand blew. Inside the wagons, they tried to block the sand from entering, but the blowing dust kept finding its way in. The air was stifling. They choked over the tiny particles. Lauressa tore strips of cloth from a bolt of fabric, and they tied the pieces over their lower faces to keep from breathing it in. Their meal consisted of dried fruit and nuts. They drank sparingly from their canteens, having no idea how long it would be before they could refill them from the barrels attached to the chuck wagon.

It lasted for twenty-four hours, making the day as dark as night.

Alloryn awoke from sleeping hunched in the corner and became aware of a lack of noise. He stretched his stiff limbs and opened the flap a crack. The once colorful wagons were unrecognizable. Dust covered them all, making them blend into the dull brown landscape. He brushed the dirt blocking the entrance and turned to help Lauressa descend. Sand had drifted over the wagon wheels in places. Others clambered from their hiding places within the caravan and assessed the damage. Two horses were dead, as well as an outrider who had not made it into a shelter in time. They found him buried in the sand under a wagon where he had taken refuge from the monster storm.

The company spent the day digging out from the storm. No goods were lost or damaged in the sturdily-built wagons. The worst misfortune was finding two water barrels full of sand.

"I fear a thief among us dipped into our water supply for his benefit and did not secure the lids properly. When I find that person, I will personally remove his boots and leave him to the desert sun and animals. We no longer have enough water to reach Samarantha." Eleedur's sharp gaze looked at each person in turn. They all stared somberly back, but none looked away or refused to meet his gaze.

At this point, Alloryn stepped forward. "I know an oasis that is further south, slightly out of our way, but we can fill our water barrels and have a better chance of survival."

Eleedur and Rappallo conferred. The Hawk asked, "How sure are you of this source?"

"Very sure. A spring flows there, which does not rely on the seasonal rains. Although off our original path, it will give us enough water to reach Samarantha."

More wagoners nodded their heads and murmured in agreement with the new plan. Eleedur spoke for them all. "Very well. Our chances of reaching the city without water are not good. Lead on."

And so after half a day's travel, the caravan came to a little-used side track that was easy to miss between two hills. If not for an ancient stone marker, which was easy to miss if he had not known to look for it, Alloryn might have bypassed the track altogether. Since he was on the watch for it, he recognized the way. He led them through the shallow hills, which slowly became foothills of buttes that stretched through leagues of red sand. Red dust covered their clothes and bodies, so much that they tasted it, leaving a gritty feeling on their teeth.

Even the desert-bred horses plodded along slowly conserving water.

They traveled until they stopped before a trackless waste of dunes. The travelers held another council. Several were wary of crossing because they had little water left. One-third of the wagons wanted to turn back and trust the well-known trail they had used in the past.

"No!" The Hawk climbed onto a wagon seat and loomed above the others with a threatening scowl, daring anyone to oppose him. "We have wasted too much time already having come half a day out of our way." He addressed Alloryn, "How far does this wasteland go? How long before we sight water?"

"Another day and a half should see us at the oasis. From there we should be able to reach the city of Samarantha within three days, which would be three days past our original schedule."

"Get ready to move. We will cross the sand." No one questioned Eleedur further. He shepherded the group back into their wagons and lead the caravan forward.

The grim wastes stretched to the horizon before them. They all silently prayed they would find water at the oasis.

The sand cruelly reflected light from the sun's rays, so the travelers covered everything but their eyes. The pace was slower than before, the horses plodding with their heads hung low. Water was almost gone. The group made more stops to rest themselves and the beasts in fear that the heat would overcome them.

At mid-morning the caravan crested a steep dune and they gazed over the land, looking for a place to rest until the cooler, dark hours. They saw before them what at first looked like discarded bundles laying at the dune's foot. Riding closer, the scouts realized they were a nomadic tribe lying in the scorching sun. Alloryn jumped off his desert horse and brought his canteen to the nearest person, giving him little sips. Using the cloth strip he kept around his neck, he dipped it in the precious water and wiped the man's parched lips.

"Sandstorm," the man croaked. Of the twenty-five nomads, six were dead, and the rest badly dehydrated.

"We must take them with us, or they will die, even if we had any water to leave them, which we do not," Alloryn said to the merchants who gathered around.

"Our horses are nearly spent. Nineteen more travelers aboard the wagons might tip the scale and kill them, stranding us in this forsaken land," Rappallo complained.

Lauressa knelt nearby, dripping water into a child's mouth. "I will walk so the children may live," she volunteered. The men could not do less than her, so as they began their march again in the early evening coolness, the wagons went driverless, the men walking beside the horses.

The foothills of a lone, barren mountain grew larger on the horizon. The more they picked up their pace to get there, the more it seemed beyond their reach. The caravan spent that night reaching the foothills.

Blistered feet joined the misery of their parched throats.

As the group shared rationed food and little water, Lauressa and Alloryn sat apart from the rest. She stroked the forehead of a child. She gave him a little broth made from boiled jerky.

The mood around camp was somber. No one knew how long the food and water must last, so Eleedur ordered very little given out.

"In the first years of my exile, most of the crops were casualties of war. Horses trampling the fields as warlords and soldiers fought over the land meant a time of want. The fields around Mintala are the best for growing wheat. Much of Valdeor depends on it." Lauressa seemed to contemplate those days as she slowly ate her ration, having taken care of the child's needs before her own.

"It must have been difficult."

"Starvation was a constant companion for most of the following decade. Just when things would seem to settle down, another skirmish would break out, and the little wheat planted would suffer." Lauressa gave the now sleeping child back to its mother.

In the cool of the next afternoon, Alloryn collected the empty canteens, mounted his horse, and pushed ahead, leaving the others to rest. He wandered through the dry and desolate places following an imperceptible trail made by the few animals that could survive in this harsh environment. If he had not ridden here before, he doubted even he could find a track. The horse suddenly picked up his ears and he knew it smelled water. He gave the horse its head and in a short time they turned a corner and looked upon a hidden canyon with cottonwood trees, grass aplenty, and a bubbling spring-fed pond. Steep walls overhung the area surrounding the canyon, shading it from the bright sun.

The horse burst with energy to reach the cool water. Alloryn let it drink its fill. He dismounted and slaked his thirst. He let the crystal drops dribble off his chin, and sheer joy surged through him at the cool water's feel. Then he dipped the canteens one after another into the clear spring.

The ride back seemed much quicker, made easier by his newly marked trail, and his exuberance to share the good fortune with the others.

The caravan had progressed little. But with water for all, including the horses, the group rode with hope to the hidden oasis. The men unhitched the horses for the first time since they left the Four Winds Caravansary, and they were let loose to drink and graze. After refilling the canteens and water barrels, the travelers washed in the cool, clear pond. Much splashing and levity followed.

Lauressa and the few women on the trip wrung the water from cloths into the nomads' parched lips and bathed their faces. After a time even they revived.

All the merchants decided unanimously to stay an extra day or three in the shady, secret spot until they and the nomads were rested enough to go on. They sat or slept in the grass and under the trees instead of within the wagons, and even Alloryn decided not to keep guard, leaving his dog and wary desert horses to warn them of any danger. He kept the Crestin Sword unsheathed under his hand. The whole band slept deeply under the desert moon.

After the third day in the oasis, the nomad elder was well enough to sit and speak with the merchants, while the scouts kept a watch around the canyon from above. "My people and I are very grateful for your care. Without you, we would be carrion for the desert creatures and birds. The terrible sandstorm came upon us without warning. Drought has lasted for three years in this area. Our usual watering holes dried up, so we risked heading for this one, but we were too weak to outrun the storm. I lost my wife and my youngest grandson, as well as other kin, but we will refresh ourselves here till the rains come again."

"You have Alloryn to thank for finding this oasis and saving all our skins. And Lauressa, his traveling companion, to thank for the room made in the wagons for you and your people. Without their knowledge and compassion, I am afraid we would have left you behind," Rappallo said shamefacedly. "They reminded us of our duty of hospitality to our neighbor, even with the likelihood of death if we helped you."

"Receive these goods to replace what you lost in the storm. Their value will help you to trade with others for the necessities your people need." And with these words, Alloryn passed the bundle of ill-gotten goods that he found at the bandit lair to the elder nomad.

"I, elder Nathum, of the tribe of Josper, thank you, great lady and lord, for saving us. We have little of worth, but if you call on us, we will gather the might of the desert tribes to ever come to your aid."

As he finished speaking, the medallion around the princess's neck began to glow from beneath her dress. She drew it out, and the emerald of moderation brilliantly pulsed with life.

The gathering gave a collective gasp, then grew silent as an answering light shone from a crevice in the canyon's walls above the spring. It bathed the area in its soft green light, rivaling the sun in its brilliance, yet it's cool color refreshing. A sigh seemed to echo around the canyon, with peace and calmness at its heart. Then a loud snap followed, reverberating in endless echoes as the medallion and crevice ceased to shine. Lauressa and Alloryn won the second stone of virtue.

Early in the evening in the capital city of Mintala, Odem walked the streets from the docks to the center of town. The inhabitants were closing shop for the day, most likely looking forward to the family meal, as he was when a thunderclap and quake shook the city. Odem froze. Knowing the source was likely to be a return of a new heartstone, he joined the many people rushing into the streets before the sound stopped rolling through the air.

Up the hill he ran in the lead, until out of breath, he stopped with the others before the throne room walls. A blinding, emerald green gem shone in the southern window embrasure

The stone of moderation and temperance's presence seemed to touch their cold hearts, with a little spark of softness for their neighbors in the days that followed.

Odem was amazed to see citizens all over the city share their coins with beggars they had passed by before, until the poor supplicants' cups overflowed.

The next day he witnessed a family with a long-standing feud calling to their neighbors to share their evening meal.

The Crown Imperial Tavern was abuzz with the story of how a carriage stopped and a well-known miser dropped off food baskets for less fortunate families and widows.

In his next letter to Preedim, Odem wrote, "A smile or a kind word slowly is more common, traceable to the stone's arrival in their lives.

"Rumors fly daily which say the princess is arriving, or someone saw her in the next town over."

"The heartstone's appearance has had other consequences. Over the last weeks, inns around the city are full as more people travel to Mintala to see the miraculous stones, hoping to be present when the next one materializes. This has led to more jobs, more goods sold, more eating places opened, and more business in general.

"In fact," Odem summarized, "the capital thrives."

But from the remarks he heard, the stone did not touch Feornson and his followers. "Even the heartstone's appearance could not overcome the stone that was their hearts," Odem concluded in the report.

Once leaving the oasis glen, the well-rested travelers made good time on the short leg to Samarantha, with many good wishes from the nomads for a safe journey and a happy return to their homes. The wagons stretched in a colorful line as they used a shortcut Nathum led them to, which met with the main road.

The caravan followed this road leading to Samarantha, the jewel of the southern provinces. Scrub brush soon gave way to prairie grass. Gently flowing hills and grassy plains surrounded the city. Known as a land of plenty, the region was still prosperous amid the war for the throne. The fair weather and fertile lands meant none went in hunger and abject poverty. Farms dotted the landscape as far as the eye could see as they neared the city. Orchards hung heavy with fruit, succulent and juicy even in this advanced time of year.

They joined a long line of farmers with wagon loads of produce for the market. A few simple coins bought them a bag of ripe fruit to eat as they rode on the hard-packed dirt avenue leading to the city gates. Samarantha was set on a slight rise above the fruitful plain. The clay baked walls reflected a rosy, pink glow. The houses were painted in many different colors, all with terracotta red roofs, making the city look like a child's toy land, more cheerful and less dilapidated than Mintala.

Alloryn and the princess parted company with the caravan at the main city entrance. Eleedur and Rappallo headed for the main market square, while Alloryn searched for an inn where Lauressa could bathe and rest.

"May the wind ever be at your back, and the road ahead wreathed in joy." She gave the traditional parting to their friends.

"May we meet again and share the journey," Eleedur said in time-honored response. "Go in peace."

When they passed through the gates, the sights and smells and sounds assailed them. Wherever their glance fell they saw a riot of color. The houses sported every color of the rainbow, and window boxes competed from house to house for the gaudiest blooms and most unique arrangement. Food stalls lined the main street past the entrance and offered fried and roasted meats, sizzling vegetables, rustic breads, and delicate pastries. The vendors hawked their wares, their voices mixing with the sounds of horses clopping on the cobblestones, wagons rolling along, and conversations of those buying goods.

The people dressed more colorfully, they smiled more frequently, and they were known for their hospitality, compared to Mintala.

Alloryn left Lauressa at the Red Swan Inn while he sold their spent horses and purchased new ones. As their trail would now go east mainly through farmland, they did not need the desert-bred horses, which fetched a good price.

He kept his ears open for the next few days in the taproom and at the marketplace for news. The return of two heartstones must have had an impact on the population. Especially of interest to him were the warlords' movement, who knew the princess's return meant their expulsion from power.

Meanwhile, Lauressa sought an audience with the ruling family. She entered the rose-colored stucco palace and looked around her as she walked the cool halls. The throne room swarmed with people, most who ignored her in her simple traveling gown of homespun cotton. On the throne sat a middle-aged man decked in gold fabrics, from his golden turban decorated with white feathers and pearls, to his gold trousers which ballooned out with padding. Prince Xander glared suspiciously when the Master of Ceremonies announced her. Perceiving her as she stepped forward and bowed her head, he changed his mien to a welcoming smile.

It was soon apparent what changed his heart when he introduced his son, Prince Gensard. He sent the rest of the courtiers away and granted her a private audience.

The prince arrived as the servants finished laying out a variety of refreshments. He looked about nineteen, dressed in the height of fashion, with a wickedly curved sword belted on his hip.

"My father tells me you have come to seek our aid. You are right to do so. We are a powerful house. We could raise an army on your behalf." He strutted around her like a rooster.

"I do not need an army at this point. My quest is to prove I am worthy to sit on the high throne of the realm by practicing virtue."

Prince Gensard stopped his pacing and stared at her. His father's face became blank. In the silence, Prince Xander tapped his ringed hand on his armrest as he studied her.

"Virtue is all well and good in its place, but a king rules with might. Only a strong ruler can hold his land against all takers with a mighty army at his back." Xander twitched his fingers as if shooing her words away like a pesky bug. "Kindness does not hold a realm together. It allows others to find and exploit your weaknesses."

His smile did not reach his eyes as he leaned forward and patted her hand with his fat, beringed one. He tried for a fatherly look. He lowered his voice, though there was no one else to hear. "What you need is a powerful husband at your side. One that the people fear and respect, and then they will respect you. Consider a marriage with my son, and the might of my hand and army will be yours."

He looked fondly at his son and gestured her to consider him. "He is not only handsome but a fierce swordsman. You will find no better. I have raised him to be a leader, and you will need wise counsel."

Gensard smirked at her and held out his hand. "Come, let us walk in the garden and get to know one another."

"I fear you mistake me. I have not come seeking a husband, nor a champion. I already have a fine swordsman at my side, and for many years I had the wisest council guiding my education." She looked from the gaudily dressed father to the proud son. "I simply came to ask if I could count on your allegiance when the inevitable war with Feornson comes."

Prince Xander frowned at her and played with his rings. "My people depend on me to protect them. I cannot commit an army to your cause if there is nothing for my people to gain. We will see what the future brings. Until then you are free to stay in my city. But think well on your refusal of my son. There are few men as brave and handsome as he fit to be your consort."

He motioned for Gensard to escort her from the audience hall.

"I would cross swords with your champion if I could. Then you would see who is the best swordsman in all of Valdeor. None in Samarantha can best me." Even in all his finery, Gensard had a sharp edge to him. She did not doubt he was a formidable foe.

Alloryn was not only strong, and a superb swordsman, but he was kind and gentle. She was thankful that Alloryn was her champion.

Lauressa reported the meeting to Alloryn. "I have to be satisfied that although Xander is not a staunch ally, he is not a sworn enemy."

Far away in a castle, a minor warlord named Bastil contemplated the news of a second gem appearing in the capital. The first had made him doubt the messenger's veracity, seeming no more than a fairy tale. But proof soon followed in Feornson's declaration, warning the lesser warlords of the event and demanding their loyalty to him as supreme overlord and master of Valdeor. Feornson offered a reward to the man who captured the princess.

This missive made Bastil pause. Being a jealous man, and a vain one, he believed he should rule all of Valdeor. He needed a lever to gain control. Therefore, he spent much time pondering how he could use this information to his advantage.

The messenger from the southern province brought a tale of a second stone. The good news was the information came not from Mintala, which was at a greater distance from his stronghold, but fresh from Samarantha, which bordered his lands.

Bastil prided himself on his intelligence and cunning. Pacing and pondering this new development, he decided this news meant one thing—a witness to the stone's finding must have told his tale in Samarantha. That boded well for his plans. The finders—the princess and her champion—would likely travel in his direction. He reasoned that the first stone, the red one, appeared in the west window, and the second appeared in the southwest window. The original explosion, which flung the heartstones from the palace, sent them in directions away from their positions on the compass.

Bastil sent for his learned men, the archivists. "Find what stone faced this direction from the palace in Mintala. And confirm for me the colors facing west and southwest." They scurried to the little-used book and scroll repository under the main castle keep. They reported back to him after hours of research.

"It is the stone of justice, my lord, an orange-colored citrine gemstone that faced your land, in the kingdom's southeast corner." They also confirmed the ruby and emerald gemstones came from the west and southwest, respectively.

He was sure now that he could use this to his advantage. He would locate the stone before the princess did, and then use it to bait a trap.

"Find me the citrine heartstone." His archivists looked amongst themselves with fear and bafflement. The eldest man spoke for them all, "Lord, the stone has been lost for over a century. How do you expect us to find it when others have tried and failed?"

"Read your useless tomes! The old chronicles must hold a clue. If these gems appear with claps of thunder and quakes, perhaps the same happened when one found a place of rest in my kingdom." He towered over the cowering men. "Must I think of everything? And you call yourselves learned men. Begone! Do not come back until you find me where it is!" The archivists hurried away in great fear. They could buy themselves time while searching in the files for the information, though none of them believed they could find what he wanted.

Bastil was a hard master. He was fond of justice, but a cruel justice, not necessarily in line with the crime committed. And he had a long list of crimes such as begging, being behind on taxes, or being too sick to work.

The chief industry of Bastil's kingdom was the cutting of trees from the extensive Forest of Domadaria, which engulfed his realm from the Blue Range mountains between him and the land of Samarantha, to the shores of the eastern sea. From the main seaport, barges carried the timber to the northern cities where workers fashioned the lumber into all sorts of things from furniture to great ships. This was the lifeblood of Bastil's realm.

A century before, the Domadarians, as they were called, were great craftsmen and carpenters, known far and wide, carving intricate designs on all their goods, from delicate jewel boxes to the throne of Mintala itself. But good quality took time, and the masters spent long years learning the art, starting as apprentices. The master craftsmen, in turn, expected to be paid well for their fine work. But their northern neighbors living in poor lands with no vast tracks of trees and no fertile soil for farms offered themselves as cheap laborers to work with timber. Bastil's forefathers had been as greedy as he, and banned the crafts in the realm, requiring all able-bodied men and women to fell the trees for a quick profit. Carpenters put down their tools and picked up weapons to defend their way of life. But mercenaries were cheap to hire, and the warlords eventually forced the Domadarians to log swaths of their beloved forest.

Although the people did as much as they could to delay clear-cutting the woods, the forest suffered much damage.

Leaving behind the caravan, Alloryn and Lauressa, with Trekker, journeyed from Samarantha with supplies to cross the Blue Range mountains. After traveling for two weeks through the southwest plains and farmland, the hills became more rolling, and they began to climb imperceptibly. Soon the gentle hills turned into foothills, and the farms became ranches with herds of cattle ranging the grasslands. A long low range of distant mountains frosted with snow appeared on the horizon.

Although the winter was well advanced, the weather remained autumn-like in the southern climate. But as they climbed to higher and higher elevations, the temperature dropped, and they wrapped themselves in thick cloaks, which they had the forethought to purchase in Samarantha. The evergreen trees began to thin, and the wind was fiercer. Quick snow squalls blew up, changed to little hail, called graupel, then ceased for a time before starting the cycle again.

Alloryn remembered the trails he rode with Justinian. The mountains here were not as tall or as treacherous as those in the far north, but one still had to be careful. The greater danger in the southern ranges were avalanches, but the spring thaw was still months away.

Eventually, they reached a crossroads. "The trail to the left is steeper but faster; the trail to the right travels alongside the range for another day and crosses a less steep pass." Alloryn turned in his saddle to face Lauressa. "Which one do you want to take?"

"Which one do you recommend?"

"If you want to avoid the worst snow and wind, the route that is farther south is our best bet, but outlaws and bandits are known to frequent the lower pass, although they are in greater force in the warmer months," he warned.

Lauressa pulled the hood of her cloak back over her head. "Then we shall ride on the left trail and take our chances with the mountains." They tugged on the reins and sent the horses up the winding path through the sparse trees.

Within a few hours, the snow fell more heavily and stuck to their cloaks, and the horses plodded slower and slower.

The trees thinned entirely, and they were on the range's bare slopes. They rode in a single file. Alloryn rode first, with Trekker balancing on the horse with him. The snows swirled around, and soon visibility became too difficult and the snow too deep, so he tied Lauressa's reins to his pommel. The track was barely discernible, but he knew of a snow cave where they could shelter until the storm passed. Squinting in the snow, he kept a sharp lookout for a waypost he knew would be near the cave's entrance.

When they reached it, they took the saddles off their horses. Lauressa tied feed bags on them. Alloryn used firewood he gathered earlier at lower elevations to make a warming fire. The cave was not overly big, but large enough to hold them and their horses. The wind and snow did not penetrate it. Others knew of it, for they found dry wood stacked in the back.

"How did you find this cave in the storm? I could barely see the tail of your horse in front of me." She put tea leaves in a pot over the fire.

"Estrell—you knew him as Justinian—taught me to look for stone markers, called wayposts. An ancient people scattered them throughout Valdeor. The legends say way keepers watched over them, and that is why you find a shelter nearby, and often even a well, though some of them have gone dry over the centuries." He put bigger branches on the fire. Soon they had hot drinks to go with their dried food.

"No one remembers why the markers were erected, or where the people who used them were traveling. Were they pilgrims? Merchants? No one knows. Sometimes the waypost is in an out of the way spot where even the road it once sat on has long disappeared.

"How mysterious." She poured the dregs of her tea on the ground. "I never heard of them, but now I will have to watch for them on our travels."

The storm howled for the next three days, but the cave was warm with a fire. They melted snow in pots and Lauressa added a few leaves for a hot reviving drink. She also used a bit of dried jerky and herbs to make a soup. The cave was big enough for them to walk around to keep warm and stretch stiff muscles.

She passed the time by telling him tales of her many jobs in different cities. She learned many skills and met many people while in exile. Alloryn was surprised to learn that she had not spent all those decades in Hamleor.

"Justinian traveled with me to Hamleor when we did not receive word of Prince Jarell. He deemed that with all the Valdeoran warlords looking for me, I should leave the continent."

"Your life was in peril."

"Not only that. Any warlord who married me could take my throne. They would have used my presence to win allegiance from the citizens, while others might have disposed of me after the marriage. Either way, their rule would be legitimized."

Lauressa put down her bowl of jerky broth. "I was once a spoiled, pampered princess. I loved jewels, dresses, and parties. I think my father must have felt sorry that I lost my mother and so he gave me everything I wanted."

She paused, dipping her hard biscuit in her bowl. She twirled it around, soaking up the last bit of broth at the bottom.

"I took all my privileges for granted. I had no thought for my servants or tutors. That is until I was forced into hiding with Justinian. I did not know how to peel a potato, or sweep a floor, or even fix my hair." She put a chunk of bread in her mouth.

Lauressa wiped the crumbs off her fingers. "I learned what it was like to work and sweat to provide for myself. I hope I shall never take my position in society for granted again."

Lauressa brushed the hair out of her face and gazed into the fire, as if into her distant past. The firelight played on her lovely features and made her chestnut hair flicker with red lights.

Alloryn grew ever fonder of her. *Well, fond was not the right word. I love her, not as my queen, but as a woman. She is warm and kind and thoughtful, as well as the loveliest woman I have ever met.* He realized he had no desire for the storm to abate and their journey to continue. *I am not looking forward to the end of our quest. It will mean that I will lose her—to the inhabitants of Valdeor, but also to a warlord or prince*. In other words, to marriage with someone else other than himself.

His attention snapped back to what she was saying. "I visited the Forest of Domadaria several times with my father. He went for the hunting, and I spent time with my mother's family. I wonder if I still have cousins there. I would like to rally their support for my cause. I never went back since that dire day. The family resemblance is too marked. I take after my mother's side of the family."

"You never speak of your mother."

"Her name was Lorelle, daughter of the royal house of King Stellin. She was not only beautiful but known for her charity toward the poor. She was full of joy and peace. Many suitors sought her, but my father won her heart. He was a very gentle man. My mother died when I was very small—maybe four. Her cousin, who I called Aunt Bethia, raised me. She died in a great battle for the palace. No one I knew is alive. That is the hardest part of living for so long."

Alloryn could find no words to comfort her.

"We have something in common." He looked at his clasped hands. "My mother Jorelyn died when I was born. My father's female relation looked after me till I was six, then I joined my father in the hills and became a shepherd."

"When I am crowned Reina, I plan to help the orphans. We both know how it feels to lose parents at a young age. Too many of them are in the city streets, begging and stealing for food and the necessities of life. I plan to build orphanages and fund families willing to take the lost children into their homes."

A good and wise ruler looks after her subjects. He gazed at her and saw beauty both without and within. He knew he must find a way to rally support for her in the eastern province of Domadaria.

The head archivist came fearfully before Bastil. "My lord, we think we have narrowed the search for the citrine stone. The chronicles of your great-great-grandfather's time record a brilliant flash. A few miners saw an orange streak of lightning, which shook the ground near the Glame River waterfalls on the Blue Range Mountain's flanks. Other than the miners, no one went near it."

After dismissing the man, Bastil called Hakal, his third-in-command. "Take a company of men and journey quickly to the Thunder Falls on the Glame River. Take as many loggers as you need with heavy digging equipment to dig a huge, round orange gemstone from the ground. You will need a cart to carry it back to the castle. And I want this done secretly. No rumors or I will have your men killed on their return. Do you understand?"

Hakal spoke, "Yes, my lord. It shall be as you order." He knew how to discipline his men. He had not reached such a high rank in Bastil's army by being soft. If necessary, he would kill the loggers once they finished the work. No need for any loose tongues telling their mission.

The same day Bastil had another stroke of luck. His chamberlain came to him as he was sitting down to dinner. "A woman insists on an audience with you, although I told her to come back tomorrow when you hold court. She says she has news of the lost princess."

"Send her in," Bastil commanded.

His chamberlain ushered in a tall woman dressed in black.

Her face was striking in its paleness, and her dark brows gave her a brooding look. She did not fawn before him as other courtiers would, but strode in with a mien of command. He frowned at her impertinence and nearly sent her away. He liked citizens who held him in awe, but he curbed his annoyance. He burned with curiosity. If he could capture the princess, he could rule all of Valdeor, not simply the Domadarian Province.

"My man says your news cannot wait until tomorrow. It had better be important enough for me to delay my meal."

"I am Malfressa, priestess of the goddess of death. I seek two travelers, a man and a woman, headed this way. The woman claims she is the lost heiress of Valdeor. The man she travels with is a warrior, strong and handsome. He defeated our best fighter in the Nyrmidion Isles. They seek the lost gems, the heartstones of old."

"Why do you come to me?"

"I am a stranger in your land, great lord. The stone holds power, and you are a powerful man. Would you not seek even greater dominion than you have?"

"What are you offering? You do not tell me where these travelers are. You do not offer me the stone," he sneered.

"But I know how to defeat them. With my black arts, I can make the princess love and obey you. If she were in your power, no one in Valdeor could defeat you. You would sit on the throne in Mintala and rule the world." She drew near to Bastil as he sat at his table. Her voice and eyes were hypnotizing. He could feel himself falling under her spell.

"What is in it for you?" he managed to ask, fighting the desire to give in to her enchantment.

"Revenge. Because of her, the Nyrmidions banished me

from the islands. The goddess I serve is no longer honored there. I only ask for a little land of my own in your vast realm— a place where I can practice my art." She smiled, but it had no warmth in it. "I think we serve the same god—the one who destroys our enemies."

He found himself agreeing.

Lauressa had never been so cold. Snow caked her cloak, her gloves, her horse, and everything as far as she could see.

She and Alloryn had waited as long as they could for the storm to abate in the Blue Range mountains.

Alloryn was equally covered in snow, even his lashes. "We should push on before the pass is entirely blocked with snow."

Lauressa heard his unspoken words, "...or it would be impassable till the spring thaw."

The deep snow slowed their progress, but the wind had carved tunnels in areas, making it easier to tread there. The narrow path along the cliff edge was the greatest menace now. Lauressa shuddered and sent up a prayer. A single misstep meant tumbling down hundreds of feet below. The snow blinded her. She had to trust her horse to find its footing. Her muscles were stiff with tension.

Trekker bound ahead, keeping an ever-present lookout for danger. She envisioned snowcats living here, blending into the landscape. She was in such a grip of imagination that she felt her heart rate jump as she stared into the gusty snow swirls, sure that she saw the outline of a big cat.

They reached the Blue Range summit's pass without incident and started down the slope. The veil of snow lifted and she saw the white-covered forest of Domadaria stretched out to meet them. Lauressa was relieved when they reached the cover of the woods. The snow lay less thick here, as the evergreens blocked much of it, making it darker since the pale winter sun did not reach the forest floor. The woods felt like a silent, almost magical place to her. The only sounds were the hooves and horses' breath blowing. She was warmer as well since the summit's piercing winds no longer reached them.

Hakal and his soldiers and the small band of miners reached the Thunder Falls on the Glame River a week before Alloryn and Lauressa entered the Forest of Domadaria. They searched for three days to find the orange heartstone, and then they found it by accident. The men were crossing below the bitterly cold falls when a horse slipped on the rocks and his rider fell off. After they hauled him to land and dried him beside the fire, he told them what he saw under the water.

"I saw a big boulder under the falls," he described with chattering teeth. "It is smooth."

"I would expect a boulder under a waterfall to be smooth," his commanding officer interrupted.

Before the officer could walk away and rejoin the search, the other made a stopping motion. "You do not understand. I saw a strange, fiery, orange-colored boulder. Were we not told to look for a giant gem?"

The officer brought him before Hakal where he repeated his story. Hakal positioned men with towlines on both banks. He forced a logger to dive under and attach a rope to the stone. The men made many attempts, and several loggers died of hypothermia before one of them was able to secure the lines. They hitched six horses to the lines that pulled mightily. They spent all afternoon, but they could barely budge the heavy stone, especially as the ropes kept slipping off the round shape.

Hakal abandoned the plan to drag it up using ropes.

Alloryn and Lauressa spent several days crossing the forest. The snow tapered off the farther south they went. Eventually, the forest opened into meadows where the path merged with the southern trade route that Lauressa had chosen to skip to save a few days. She thought it had been the right decision at the time, but in hindsight, she would not do it again. The snowstorm had nearly stranded them until spring. She decided she would put more trust in Alloryn to make those decisions since he had more recently traveled these roads.

Lauressa was pulled out of her reverie as Alloryn slowed down and waited for her to come alongside.

"It is twilight. We should seek shelter." He looked wearier than she had seen him before. She knew he was worried because their supply of food was nearly gone.

Around the next bend, a small band of travelers came into view, sitting around a campfire.

Alloryn stopped his horse, and Lauressa did the same. The smell of roasted meat awakened her hunger.

"Hail, friends," a heavyset man called to them. "Join us. There is plenty to go around."

Alloryn dismounted and helped Lauressa down. She accepted some meat in a bowl and served Alloryn first, as he sat next to the man who invited them. Although Alloryn often attempted to serve her, as was her royal right, she acted as an equal, even a servant, as was the custom of females serving their males. She wanted nothing to draw attention to them on their journey. And the young princess she once was, who expected all around her to pander to her every whim, had matured in the struggle to survive.

As Lauressa served herself from the pot, she heard Alloryn ask, "Which direction are you going, friend?"

"We are heading to Forestown, the small city that encircles the castle of Bastil."

"So are we. May we join your band on your journey?" Alloryn dipped his bread in his bowl and ate.

As if reading Lauressa's mind, Alloryn asked the question, "Do you know anything of the ruler Bastil?"

No one had any good to say of him.

"He is a hard master, who cares for profit more than his soul. The inhabitants go in fear of him and his soldiers." The heavyset man finished eating and stretched his legs toward the fire. "We do not plan on staying in Forestown." He caught the eyes of several in his traveling band, who murmured in agreement. "We plan on passing through Forestown to get to the sea, then catching a boat north."

Lauressa wanted to stop before they reached the main city to hire someone to carry messages to her relatives if any still lived. So they parted ways with their new acquaintances and stopped at an inn, which was in the village before Forestown and the castle.

After purchasing writing materials for her and leaving her

composing her notes in a private parlor, Alloryn rode a league to the city gates. He found a taproom and listened to the news. Among the things he heard was that a small band of Bastil's handpicked soldiers recently journeyed on a secret mission. No good was likely to come from it, was a general opinion. He paid his tab and was ready to leave when he overheard a patron tell his comrades that lately, a foreign-born witch had set up residence in the area. He was alarmed to hear it was in the small village where he left Lauressa.

Alloryn hurried back to the inn, turning over the information. Almost no witches were known in King Arness's time, but after the Myrkr Revolt, more and more began practicing the ancient arts, teaching the old superstitious beliefs. People in desperation consulted them in their problems, as neither doctors nor judges were available in these lawless times, and people took matters of sickness or revenge into their own hands.

That the witch was foreign-born disturbed him the most. Witches who practiced the dark arts stayed in their region, growing in reputation. This meant the new witch either was hounded from her region, or she was on a mission that brought her here.

He found Lauressa in the private parlor, with a packet of letters ready for delivery. She had spent her time writing them and questioning the landlord on the different noble families still living in and around the city. The landlord promised his son should deliver them for her since he recognized a lady when he saw one, even if she did not dress in finery.

Alloryn filled her in with his news and his suspicions.

"I would not be surprised if it is Malfressa." She paced

around the room, her hands clenched. "She would bear a grudge. She could not heal the chief's son, and the missionary's presence would mean she no longer had a job.

"You say she is possibly in this village? I fear she might have our description. Not many travelers have a wolfhound, as we do. We must move." He had been thinking the same thing.

They quickly paid their bill, telling the landlord they had urgent news and had to leave. They were not happy to go, as he seemed an honest man, and they did not want to stay in the city, under the castle walls. But they considered it prudent.

Malfressa hired spies at all the inns with the money she convinced Bastil to part with, and the charms she sold to the locals. She did indeed learn of the princess and the champion's presence soon after they arrived. Her spy followed Alloryn to the city.

Her plan was simple. She needed to separate them. Once she had the princess alone, she could enslave her will to do Malfressa's bidding.

She recalled the informants, on loan from Bastil, and instructed them to cause a distraction on the main thoroughfare where the two would traverse the city.

Leaving the inn's safety, Alloryn unknowingly led Lauressa into her trap. They passed the main west gate into the city of Forestown and rode through the main east-west corridor. He planned to find an inn at the end of town, as far from the castle's watchful eyes as possible.

As they rode along the busy road, two horses pulling a cart careened around the corner, the driver slumped in his seat. Passersby, women, and children were in its path. Alloryn spurred his horse ahead. He caught up with the spooked team, grabbed the slack reins and pulled it to a stop. People screamed and threw themselves out of harm's way. The cart managed to knock into a few stationary objects that added to the confusion.

While the hubbub died away, he extricated himself and checked the unconscious driver. He found a knife in the man's back. The unexpectedness of it sent him into high alert. He scanned the crowd and realized he no longer saw Lauressa on her horse anywhere on the street. His horse stood alone. Not even Trekker was in sight.

A mantle of despair settled over Alloryn.

My fault! I should have been more diligent!

He feared the whole episode was staged, and Malfressa was at the bottom of it.

Energy surged through him like before battle. *I will search until I find Lauressa.*

10 *Imprisoned*

*L*auressa automatically pulled her horse to the side when Alloryn started his rescue. She had a sense of danger seconds before she felt—rather than saw—a man step too close beside her horse. He hustled her into a bag and dumped her in a passing cart.

She was trussed in a bag that smelled of onions and dust. Her assailants did not have time to tie her, but as she was unceremoniously thrust into the wagon, an abductor threw several large items on her—bags of onions from the smell and feel of round balls pressing her down. She could barely breathe through the rough material and weight on top of her. It effectively pinned her down, and that was as good as being tied. Struggling made the bags settle tighter around her, so she ceased. *It will be a different matter when they let me out!*

The wagon rolled and bumped along for at least forty-five minutes by Lauressa's reckoning.

Soon after she noticed the horses' hooves and the cart's wheels began to have a different sound. She heard a louder, echoing, and magnified sound as if they were in a tunnel. The city sounds dimmed, then disappeared altogether. The load shifted and she figured they were going uphill.

The cart stopped a short while after that. As her captors lifted the bags from her body, she prepared to fight and scream. She thrashed her body the moment the last bag freed her, but two men lifted her from the cart, and another wound a rope around her. Her cries for help echoed weirdly back at her, but she heard no other sound. Eerie silence pressed all around them.

A man carried her over his shoulder for another ten minutes, before he lowered her to a hard floor.

"Untie her. Let me see her face," a familiar female voice spoke above her.

Rough hands removed the rope and Lauressa struggled to remove the bag. She took a deep breath of dank, musty air. After a while, her eyes adjusted to the scarce light. Standing above her was Malfressa, the witch, and a tall, cruel-looking man who leered at her.

"Your plan had merit. I did not think you would be able to capture her so quickly." The man ogled Lauressa with a malicious grin while he spoke with the witch. He wet his lips and the way he looked at her made her feel unclean. "Now you must make her mine for the taking."

"Who are you? What do you want with me?" Lauressa rose to her feet. She would not cower before her abductors.

"Ah, Your Highness. Let me introduce myself. I am Bastil, your future husband."

She blanched at these unexpected words. He knew who she was, thanks to the witch, but he was not asking ransom. Her worst fears were realized. Here were two people who wished to use her to rule over Valdeor and remove all hope for freedom for her people.

"Never. I will die first." She put her chin up and gave them her most withering royal glance.

"We will see about that," Malfressa said with an evil grin. "Give me a few days, lord, and she will beg you to marry her," she promised.

"See she is not marred too much. I wish my wife to stay lovely and recognizable by the people as their Reina. If you succeed, she may live to be my consort, else I will kill her once the ceremony is over."

He stared at her with a nasty smile. "You see, you would do well to cooperate with us. Against your will or not, you will be my wife long enough to claim your throne. Living beyond that is your choice." He made a mock bow and strode from the dungeon.

"I think you better accept his generous offer. I would not be so gentle with you." Lauressa looked at the pale, beautiful face of the priestess. Her long raven black hair fell to her waist, but the heartless gaze destroyed her loveliness. Eyes are the windows of the soul, and these eyes enjoyed the pain and suffering of others.

Malfressa pointed out a nearby cell to her captors and they shoved her in. "Some time alone is what you need to ponder your fate, Your Highness."

The cell was dark and dank smelling. Moisture dripped down the walls. Lauressa could pace five steps in either direction, which she did until she was tired enough to sit on the pile of straw in the corner and rest. She pulled her cloak around her and prayed for Alloryn to find her. She trusted his resourcefulness more than her own.

After hours passed, one of the jailors unbolted a small opening at the door's bottom and thrust a cup of water and a crust of bread into her cell. Any hope of reasoning with her captor or escaping dwindled in her heart. She would have to wait till Malfressa came back.

She fell asleep trying to devise plans for her escape. Her last thought was to wonder if the water or food was drugged, as she could not keep her eyes open.

When all the attention was on the runaway horses and the danger to pedestrians in the street, no one saw what transpired except Trekker. With long untiring strides, the dog chased the cart concealing the princess. As in many big cities, stray dogs were plenty, always on the hunt for food, so no one paid any mind to the wolfhound.

He lost sight of the wagon, as it outpaced him, but it did not matter. His nose could track the strong smell of onions as it wound through the streets and into the tunnel under the keep.

He easily snuck into the tunnels, running on the far side of a wagon while the soldiers were checking it out.

But when he caught up with the onion wagon in a side tunnel, it was empty. So he curled up under it, rested his heaving lungs, and waited for his master.

Alloryn spent a fruitless afternoon asking the spectators if they had seen anything leading to Lauressa's disappearance. As he feared, no one had looked in that direction during the runaway cart incident. He knew the trail was growing colder by the minute. He finally left the intersection of streets and led the horses to a stable on the far side of town, all the while keeping an eye out for his dog. Eventually, he checked himself in for the night, taking both their saddlebags.

He could not stomach the thought of food. He paced around the room. *How can I find her in this city? She could be anywhere. Malfressa could have whisked her away to Mintala.* He felt the weight of despair wrapping itself around him.

He thought of what Justinian would tell him to do if he were here. *Distance yourself. Be objective. Do not let your fears paralyze your mind.*

He pushed his fears for Lauressa to the back of his mind. He reasoned who would want to seize her, and why.

With the heartstones appearance in the capital, word traveled wide and far that the princess was not a fable after all, and she was on the move, earning the stones of virtue, proclaiming her imminent return. The warlords must be worried by now. But few people had the resources and cunning to find her whereabouts, plan a daylight attack, and have a place to take her in the city. The likeliest person with that much manpower and informants in Forestown was Bastil.

Alloryn scouted around the castle in the twilight. It looked impenetrable with two entrances—the main gate and the service gate—both well-guarded. He whistled a few times when he saw a shadow move, hoping it might be Trekker. But they were just cats on the prowl.

He crafted a plan before he turned in for the night. Tomorrow he would try to gain entrance to the dungeons.

Deciding he would be less conspicuous on foot, he walked

to the river before dawn and hung about asking for work. Captains and merchants could always use men at the docks to unload the cargo brought from Tulken Harbor's seaport to Forestown.

The castle sat on the cliffs above the city. Leading to it were steep stairs carved in the rock face. Guards could easily defend the castle that way. Trade was conducted at the cliff's base with a heavily guarded gate that opened into a large cavern. Alloryn took a job loading carts of wool and saw that tunneled ramps went under the castle and wound through the stone cliff to the Keep on top.

He hitched a ride in the cart that drove into the passage, passing the guards' inspection. The cart wound through a wide tunnel carved into the rock face. The rumbling sound echoed back from the walls. Tunnels branched off here and there from the main tunnel. At one branch, he spotted an unlikely sight—a dog hiding behind a stack of boxes. Alloryn paid the driver with a gold coin and leaped from the slow-moving cart, ducking into the tunnel before the next wagon rolled along.

The dog wagged his tail and licked Alloryn's hand.

"Good boy, Trekker. Find Lauressa!" he commanded. Trekker went in search of her scent. Unsheathing his dagger and holding it under his cloak, Alloryn followed the wolfhound's lead.

Lauressa woke to find herself chained to the wall. She straightened her spine and took the weight from her tingling arms. A noxious smell made her choke. She fought not to retch as it swirled around her cell. Malfressa hunched over a cauldron placed in the cell. She was muttering a strange language to herself as she added something dark and oozing to the brew, then sprinkled powder from her hand, which cause a small eruption in the pot.

"Breakfast is almost ready, my pretty," she purred as she saw her prisoner wrinkling her nose at the evil brew's smell.

"I doubt anything so vile could cause me to fall in love with your co-conspirator." She put her chin up.

"You would be surprised what my brew does. He believes I will make him irresistible to you, but what he does not know is I plan to make you obedient to my commands. Once you are married to him, I will guide you in all you do, and I will be the true power behind the throne."

She scooped the thick liquid into a clay cup and brought it to the princess. She grasped the girl's throat and tilted her head back. Lauressa was powerless to resist and was forced to swallow it. She did not fight the urge to gag and coughed most of it up onto Malfressa's dress.

The witch screamed and slapped her.

Alloryn followed Trekker through the ever-narrowing tunnel under the Castle Keep, which was deserted so far. He trusted the dog to know where they were headed.

At that moment, a guard backed out of a room. Alloryn jumped him, but the guard must have felt the rush of air, or heard a tiny sound, and alerted, he began to draw his sword. It never left the scabbard as Alloryn slashed him where he stood.

The doorway opened onto an armory where six other guards stood. Hearing their companion hit the stone floor, they whipped around. Seeing the naked blade, four of them unsheathed their swords, stepping forward to fight him, while two others held back in reserve.

Alloryn did not like the odds but knew he must stand and fight. He slashed at two of his opponents before they fully drew their blades and made them stagger back. The next two came in from his right side. He spun on his forward foot and parried their attacks. He entered further into the room, then feinted and dove for one of the pikes along the wall. Holding off the four with his blade, he reached blindly behind him and snagged a pike, which he thrust into the lead assailant's midsection, taking him out of the fight. He grabbed another pike and faced his assailants. He drove forward with both weapons, cutting the knees out from under the next two guards. Trekker leaped on them as they fell on the floor and kept them occupied.

Armed with long and short swords, the two in reserve joined the one man left. They stepped warily, trying to circle him, but he kept them at bay with the pike's sharp point.

Alloryn used the distance the pike afforded him to sheath his sword. Then he put both hands on the pike, turning it into a staff of destruction. All three soldiers jumped him, but he blocked the blows with the staff. He swung it left, hitting the soldier on that side hard in his ribs while kicking the middle man with his foot. With a lightning move, he thrust the pike into the man's chest, on the right. He used his momentum to swing the man between himself and the remaining two soldiers.

Letting the pike go, he unsheathed his sword again and parried the blows they rained on him, moving to the room's center to stop them from boxing him in on either side. His superior swordsmanship soon dispatched the last two men.

Alloryn removed the weapons from their hands. He locked the room behind him. That would stop reinforcements for a while.

He held his sword in his right hand and taking a pike in his left again, he reentered the tunnel.

At the next intersection, Trekker raced to the left. Cell doors lined both directions. Alloryn followed. Trekker sniffed under each door. Soon they heard a woman screaming and swearing. They ran toward the sound, Alloryn's heart thudding with fear that he might be too late.

The guard watching the corridor was too slow to pull his sword when the hound leaped on him and ripped his throat.

Malfressa held the evil-smelling potion in another cup. Her hand grasped Lauressa's neck and she let her nails draw blood, her cruel face inches away. Before she could pour the brew down the girl's throat, Lauressa thrust her knee into the witch's stomach, expelling the woman's breath. The brew stained the princess's gown as Malfressa clutched her middle in pain.

"I am not hungry this morning."

The priestess stood painfully and glared at her.

After a few minutes, Lauressa's head spun dizzily from the little sip of the brew she had not been able to keep from swallowing. She shook her head from side to side, trying to clear her vision.

"You cannot fight it." The witch's voice filled her, blocking any thought. "You will listen to and obey my every word." She managed to pour a little more brew down the throat of her unresisting captive. Stepping out of reach, she chanted in a singsong voice, her voice rising and falling, in hypnotizing cadence, finally reaching a crescendo.

Lauressa fought to look away from the eyes that spun before her. She concentrated on the medallion's weight around her neck. She willed the stone of courage to come to her aid.

"You are mine. Say you are mine." The evil priestess's voice spellbound her. "No one is stronger than the Death Goddess. She conquers all in the end."

"No, no. Faith. Hope. Courage, courage." Lauressa's voice faded on the last word. When she thought she could no longer resist becoming the witch's slave, the red gem began to glow, shining through the gown she wore.

Malfressa stopped her chanting with a harsh cry and tried to rip the medallion from around Lauressa's neck. Waves of red and green light poured forth from the medallion. The witch pulled back her hands with a scream, clutching them as if they had been burnt. She seemed amazed that the stones' powers equaled hers. She raised her arms, the long black sleeves falling back to reveal pale white arms covered in blood mingling with the black brew dripping onto the floor.

Alloryn burst into the room. Before Malfressa could summon her false goddess, he grabbed her around the waist from behind and thrust her to the floor. He held the Crestin Sword above her head. She whirled around on all fours to face him. Her eyes widened as she saw the sword pointed at her head. Before he was able to strike, the sword crackled with power, joining the medallion's multicolored lights. Red energy entwined the witch caught between the medallion behind her and sword in front of her. She threw her arms before her face. A bolt of energy from the medallion and sword flashed together and enveloped her. With a high-pitched scream, she dropped lifeless to the floor. The light receded.

Alloryn pushed her with his boot tip. Seeing that she was truly dead, he disappeared into the hallway and came back with a keyring.

A quick, tender glance passed between Alloryn and Lauressa, uniting them in their gladness to see each other whole and unharmed.

Alloryn rapidly released Lauressa's shackles. She almost collapsed into his arms. He steadied her then he hefted her up and cradled her tenderly. She started to speak, but he hushed her.

"No time for speech now. We must escape this vile place before the dead and unconscious guards are found." Trekker bound into the hall and headed further down the passage, away from where they came in, seemingly not a moment too soon, as he heard a hue and cry in the distance. Bastil's men must have discovered the destruction in the armory.

Torches lit the way that led from the cells to the bottom of a staircase. They had no idea what lay ahead, but the way behind was blocked for certain, so up the stairs, Alloryn went. It seemed to go on winding around in a spiral forever. Breathing hard, he stopped at the top to peer around the corner. A wide hall stretched both ways. The sound of a door opening and voices made him lean back in the stairwell. They waited for silence again.

Lauressa lowered her voice. "I can manage. You need to have your sword ready." He nodded and set her on her feet.

The dizziness was wearing off, probably because she avoided swallowing much of the brew. The fuzziness was almost gone, replaced by a bad taste and a growing headache. She was thankful she had not been chained long, or else it would be impossible to walk on her own. But the numbness and the pins-and-needles feeling were passing.

Alloryn peered around the corner and seeing no one, he sidled along the hall to the left. Lauressa followed, holding his hand. He headed for the window at the hall's end. If he could get his bearings, they might still escape. The Keep's square courtyard was below them. Tradesmen unloaded wagons, guards changed shifts, messengers carried packets, and castle inhabitants went about their daily business.

"To avoid detection, we must hide in a wagon. But the soldiers examine them as they come in and as they leave."

"Malfressa's henchmen brought me in on a cart through what sounded like a tunnel."

"Trekker and I came through the tunnels as well. They are probably safer than the main stairway down the cliff face." He gripped her hand and searched for a stairwell leading back to the tunnels.

Alloryn led them back to the wagon's access route. Their trek was not quick or easy, since several times they had to make a detour or hide when roaming bands of soldiers searching for them blocked the way. But eventually, they came to a short corridor underground that branched off to a longer one. He listened while they hid behind a stack of crates in a dark side corridor.

He heard a deep, echoing rumble, and he knew by the sound that several carts were coming. As the last one rolled by, he flung Lauressa aboard and jumped on himself. He helped her into an empty barrel, put the lid on her, and chose one for himself. Trekker leaped aboard as well and sat on the backboard as if he had every right to be there.

The three carts rattled over the cobblestones and the bored guards waved them through. Soon they left the castle environs behind.

Alloryn waited until the wagons stopped rolling and he heard silence before lifting his barrel lid. They were at the docks where he had started many hours ago. Once free of their barrels, they easily lost themselves in the hustle and bustle of the wharf and headed back to the inn.

They were safely ensconced in a private room at the inn. Lauressa used her skills to bind up his cuts and scratches. She shared her story of captivity while eating a hearty repast.

"How do we bring Bastil to justice?" Alloryn put his fork on the table and rubbed his brow. "We cannot take on the whole castle ourselves. We were lucky to escape with our lives today."

"My messages—do you still have them?"

"I gave them to the Red Swan's landlord. He sent his son to find the recipients."

"Then help should be on the way." She smiled at him and tore another chunk of bread. Her smile after their ordeal and the worry that he would not find her in time warmed his heart. He remembered the feel of her in his arms, such that he did not concentrate on what she said next and had to ask her to repeat herself.

"I asked the descendants of my Stellin cousins to meet us at week's end in the forest glen where the royals used to have picnics. The stone of justice must be nearby. It would have landed in this province, seeing how far the others traveled. Our best chance to gain it is with their help."

Waiting, Alloryn found, was harder than action, as the hunt for them continued. They stayed in their rooms or private parlor, waiting for the meeting date. When not peeking through the parlor curtains, they played a game of strategy with a borrowed board and pieces from the innkeeper. He over-thought his moves, while she made decisive decisions. Yet he won as many times as she, as they were evenly matched.

CHAPTER 11 DOMADARIA

11 DOMADARIAN FOREST

On a drizzling morning the two travelers and the dog journeyed to the forest glen. Fog tendrils reached out their ghostly arms to them as they neared the Forest of Domadaria. The only sound was the jingling harnesses and the clop of the horses.

Alloryn rode with his drawn sword on his lap. No one would catch him unawares.

Trees on either side came close enough to touch as the path narrowed. Dampness dripped from above, finding its way down their necks. Lauressa shivered and drew up her hood. The silence was like a blanket thrown over them, as even the horses' hooves ceased to clatter in the pine needles. The woods smelled damp and earthy. As they went deeper into the gloom, even the sun could not penetrate through the thick canopy.

The gently sloping trail wound through the forest. Lauressa unerringly pointed the way when they came to each crossing.

They rode through a thick patch of fog, then it became lighter and lighter. It let go of its embrace and they found themselves in a green meadow in a forest clearing. The sun was high in the sky. They both blinked in the sudden light. A ring of riders sitting astride their horses on the clearing's far side drew their attention.

The eldest horsemen walked his horse to where Alloryn and Lauressa sat on theirs. He was a middle-aged man with a grizzled, gray beard. "Welcome, Your Highness. You look like the portrait of your beloved mother, whose memory is still fond to us. I am Stepan, your great-great-grandnephew." He bowed from his seat.

"Greetings, King Stepan."

Lauressa removed the medallion from under the bodice of her dress and showed him the token of her identity.

"We have waited long for this day," he said gazing on it.

"Thank you for meeting us here. This is my champion, Alloryn." Stepan motioned two young men over. "These are my sons, Talud and Tris." Two very similar young men bowed their heads. The princes were around Alloryn's age.

Then he introduced the others with him. One look at their clothing and serious mien let her know they were warriors all. "We have much to discuss," he said. He turned to his entourage. "Set up the meeting tent."

They dismounted and Stepan asked for a moment alone with the princess.

"You plan to re-establish yourself as High Ruler." He crossed his arms. "What assurances do we have you will not be another tyrant, as Feornson is?"

"I will only declare my right to the throne when I have won all the stones of virtue, which only come after I practice and perform all the virtues needed for a good ruler." She removed her medallion and pointed out to him, "I won two of them."

"And how will you govern?" He looked sternly at her.

"The High Kings are the last resource for justice. I would make you king over Domadaria, as custom dictates." She slipped the medal back. "I have seen government works best at a local level. Too far away, and a ruler is out of touch with his or her subjects."

"Then you will not reconvene the Council of Mintala?"

"No. I will allow the provinces to have their hereditary princes, as it was before my father's rule."

"Then you have my support." He extended his hand, and she took it.

Even though they agreed, Lauressa wondered if Stepan would eventually seek a marriage alliance. Stepan's backing would be stronger if she was married to one of his sons. But she hoped she could count on Stepan's help without that.

The warriors soon erected a tent, and the council met to decide how to oust Bastil and reestablish the Stellin line as rulers of Domadaria.

"The people would see our line restored if they could. Bastil has not endeared himself to the inhabitants. He is a tyrant," Prince Talud told those assembled. A grunt of agreement went around the room.

"Each of us can raise men and women to fight the soldiers of Bastil with you to rally them, Your Highness," Stepan promised.

Deliberations continued the rest of the day and into the early night. As dawn broke, Lauressa rode with Stepan to distant villages to speak to the people and gain them to her cause. Her presence was imperative to their plans.

Alloryn volunteered to go with the sturdy warrior Talud, Stepan's son, to Thunder Falls. As they rode, Talud explained their mission again. "We spied a small force of Bastil's handpicked men traveling through the woods a few weeks ago. It piqued our interest since our informants in the castle heard no rumors of it."

Alloryn gave him a look, which Talud answered. "Yes, we have men in the castle itself. Rebellion has been brewing here for many years. Until twenty-five years ago, we mostly managed to avoid the wars that ripped Valdeor. Unfortunately, Bastil promised prosperity at a time of famine. He meant prosperity for himself." He frowned.

"But as for this band of soldiers—they traveled to the falls, which is odd for this time of year. Men dive into the whirlpool at the waterfall's base. We do not know what they search for or why."

After traveling several days, they followed a road to the north. Another day brought them to a steep offshoot of the main path. If not for Talud knowing of it, Alloryn feared he would have passed it by. The narrow trail climbed a steep slope, zigzagging back on itself several times. They broke from the tree line and soon stopped short of the crest.

Talud dismounted and Alloryn followed suit. They crawled the last few yards and overlooked a small valley. The roar of Thunder Falls was loud even here. The falls fell hundreds of feet into a pool below. Alloryn counted roughly three dozen men on either side with ropes hitched to horses and several men on a raft, in the pool's center, guiding something. Talud passed him the spyglass.

Alloryn could see a camp on the east shore and what looked like graves–mounds of rocks or cairns–that testified to the operation's danger.

They slithered back to the horses, where they could speak and hear each other. "We have to get closer. I have an idea what they are doing, but unless we can see better, I cannot be sure," Alloryn said.

They ate dried meat and rested in the noon sun. He had the germ of a plan. With just the two of them, they did not have many options. "How are your climbing skills?" he asked Talud.

Lauressa spoke with Stepan as they rode to the first village, a day's ride from the meeting place. She had already told him and the others briefly of her century of hiding with the wise councilor Justinian's help. She spoke of their adventures since Alloryn proved himself her champion in the dark alley months ago. Stepan listened gravely, made few comments, and asked pertinent questions.

"These are marvelous things, indeed. And you say the heartstones, once won, disappear when their light fades?" He had not heard of the stones' miraculous appearance in the capital city.

"Yes. I first thought we would have to find a way to carry them with us on our journeys, which would be more impossible than finding them. We would need a wagon train to carry six stones of one hundred pounds each."

As they spoke, they entered a small village in a forest clearing. The little wooden houses were immaculately kept, if poor. These were people with pride in their appearance and their village. They quickly gathered around Stepan, whom they knew well. They gasped with delight when he introduced Lauressa as the uncrowned Reina. One mother held up her little child for the princess to bless, and soon a crowd pressed closer, each with a child. Touched by the gesture, she smiled at each little one, briefly laying the medallion on their heads.

The village headman bade them enter the largest house. Women brought food and stayed to listen to Lauressa's tale and Stepan's plea for men to join with them against Bastil. All swore their allegiance to the heir of the Royal House of Stellin, Lauressa's mother's family.

Alloryn spent the rest of the afternoon circling to the west side of the Thunder Falls, on the Glame River's side opposite from the enemy camp. At the appointed hour the next morning, Talud climbed down the cliff they had reconnoitered the day before. It did not take long for the men standing watch to see him, as he was purposely obvious. He was out of the bowmen's range, fortunately, as planned.

While the enemy was thus engaged in trying to reach the intruder, Alloryn was able to use the flat of his sword to knock out the two men guarding the raft on the bank and steal it so that he could drift over the spot under the falls where the men had been working. The turbulent river was impossible to cross without a raft or boat, and too slippery to climb over with the spray turning to ice along the side of the falls.

He saw their latest attempt to haul up the stone with ropes woven into the netting. He also recognized the orange gemstone of justice, almost entirely buried under a century of silt washed downstream by the roaring waterfall.

A man on the right bank spotted him and sounded the alarm. The bowmen across the valley tried to get close enough to Talud to shoot their arrows. Their occupation left Alloryn free to paddle the raft back to shore safely. He escaped back the way he came, his mission fulfilled.

Talud stopped his climb, apparently to watch the bowmen trying to get into range, but Alloryn knew it was to truly see how Alloryn fared. Once Alloryn was back onshore, Talud climbed the short distance back up the cliff and headed along the trail to their prearranged meeting place.

After they met and rode far enough to be beyond the men's reach, Alloryn told Talud what he had spied under the water.

"But we cannot leave it for them!" he cried as he reined his horse in.

"Never fear, they will not get it out of that river. It is buried too deep in the silt, and too close to the falls."

"How will the princess recover it? Should we not wait and steal it from them if they do haul it up from the riverbed?"

Alloryn gave a lopsided smile and shook his head. "She will earn it. That is how she won the other two. Once the virtue is acquired the stone disappears." Seeing Talud's look of disbelief, he continued. "I have witnessed it, or I too would think like you." And he expounded their earlier adventures as they rode back to meet Stepan, Lauressa, and the others who had joined forces with them.

"'Tis unbelievable," Talud frowned at the end of the tale. "For the size of the stone you described to just disappear... But I trust your word. This is something I look forward to seeing with my own eyes." Under his breath Alloryn heard him mutter, "She must be as virtuous as she is beautiful."

Disturbed, Alloryn realized Prince Talud was not just an ally, but a contender for Princess Lauressa's hand. He tamped down the sudden flare of jealousy of his new friend.

Both groups met again in the forest glen.

Sentries stood guard around the tents. Stepan's best generals gathered in a war council, along with a few village leaders, Stepan's sons, Alloryn, and Lauressa.

Alloryn and Talud reported that Bastil's soldiers had found the heartstone under the waterfall, and, fortunately, their inability to budge it.

The men reacted the same way Talud had, so Alloryn glanced at Lauressa, his expression making it clear she should tell them how she would recover it. Their disbelief was apparent, though they did not voice it. Being men of action, they quickly turned the meeting back to things they understood—how to overthrow Bastil.

Lauressa and Stepan reported of the Domadarians rallying to the Stellin family.

"I think the time has come to act," Stepan said.

Lauressa nodded her agreement and told him to proceed.

Stepan sent forth trusted men to alert those inside the castle to put their plans in motion. The minutest detail was gone over with those gathered. They would take the castle on many levels if all went right.

In the next few days, men and boys began arriving from the forest villages, arrayed in battle gear. Blacksmiths worked feverishly producing weapons. In two more weeks, the castle's allies reported ready. Also, the last of the warriors arrived from the forest's farthest points.

Arrayed in fine armor, Stepan led his trusty band of men toward the city's east gate. His son, Tris, guided a smaller band of men disguised as merchants into the city's heart. Loyal men inside the castle would open the lower gates, where Alloryn and Lauressa had so recently escaped, to those disguised. The other generals staged a large frontal assault at the main west gates as a diversion. Alloryn and Talud would climb the cliffs at the stronghold's back, where no one expected resistance, and strike a surprise attack from the inside.

A watchman burst into the room where Warlord Bastil was conducting business. Before Bastil could berate his lack of manners, he cried out, "Lord, a host comes at the city from the west!"

Bastil threw back his chair and raced for the window at his tidings. A large host of warriors marched from the western hills, their bright armor gleaming in the sun like a river of war approaching. His general rushed into the room.

"Lonquil, how have I not heard of this army on my doorstep? Where are the advanced post watchers? Where are my spies? What have they been doing as an enemy marches across my land?"

Lonquil blanched at his commander's tone. And so he should since his was the first head that would roll as Bastil's head general.

"Sound the command to man the gates. Close the city!"

Bastil cried with fury, veins standing out on his forehead.

Lonquil raced out of the room, bellowing orders.

The alarm bell sounded. Bastil stood at the window and watched as soldiers ran to their assigned stations. They shut heavy gates leading to the city from the west from the inside. Bowman quickly armed themselves and posted along the walls facing the army, now only a league away.

"Fools! I am surrounded by incompetent fools!" muttered Bastil under his breath, to no one in particular. If only the witch had been successful. He cursed her as well.

Tris and his men had ridden into the city at mid-morn with a large load of fine wine. They mingled with the wagons waiting to enter at the castle's base. The wagons rolled up the ramps, and when their turn came to enter the castle, a sudden diversion of one barrel seeming to escape from the last wagon stopped further traffic from entering. Chaos erupted further when Tris told the guards the wine might be damaged, so they could have it for themselves. Tris and his band were unnoticed when they left the cart and raced on foot through the tunnels, leaving one man with their wagon of wine casks. Lauressa had drawn the castle's layout for them, so they headed unimpeded for their designated spots.

The alarm bells were the signal for Tris and his men in position outside the castle armory. They whipped their swords from concealment and blocked the weapons room at the end of a narrow corridor.

Tris knew that on the eastern gate when the To Arms signal sounded, his father Stepan and his band would pull their swords from under their merchant cloaks and attack the guards before they could close those gates.

These were just diversionary tactics. The princess's rescue would come from within if Alloryn could sneak into the castle while the fighting kept the enemy force occupied.

Tris could only do his part and hope all went well.

Alloryn and Talud, who had shown himself an excellent climber at Thunder Falls, scaled the cliff face with ropes and pitons soon after dawn that morning. No one guarded this side, because no one had ever before tried attacking from the cliffside. They found it tiring, with rough handholds to grasp with toughened hands, and feet barely managing to find purchase. Talud went first when they reached the last third of the climb, as he was the more experienced climber. He drove pitons in the sheer face and tied belaying lines to it. They had no fear that anyone would hear notice above, they were so far away. Stepan delayed the overall attack so the two could reach the castle at the same time as the other bands of men.

Once over the cliff, they found themselves on a narrow sill that overlooked the main keep courtyard. The castle itself had been partly built from the cliff. Instead of joining the soldiers and the household members who were loyal to the Stellin royal line who battled in the courtyard, Alloryn and Talud climbed the castle until they entered through a window into the hallway. Using the castle map, they drew their swords and fought their way to the throne room.

They met a band of soldiers racing along the corridor and engaged them. Their skill with their blades outmatched the soldiers, who they soon dispatched. After a few more minutes, they skidded to a halt at the heavily guarded door to the throne room, where Bastil was directing his leaders. These guards were better trained, but they could not withstand the onslaught of Alloryn's blade. The Crestin Sword moved like slashing lightning in his hand.

Soon putting the guards to rout, Alloryn and Talud burst into the throne room turned war room. Leaving Talud to deal with the other soldiers, Alloryn headed straight for Lonquil and Bastil. Lonquil stepped in front of his lord and fought, thrusting with power from his superior size, but Alloryn was quicker and nimbler. He let Lonquil believe he was failing in strength, and when the bigger man slashed down as if to cut off his head, the Crestin Sword blocked the blow. Alloryn used his concealed dagger with his left hand, which he buried up to the hilt in Lonquil's left side. The man dropped, staring in shock as his blood spouted.

Alloryn glanced around for Bastil. He saw a household servant wielding a spear join Talud against the soldiers. On the edge of his vision, he saw a tapestry on the far wall move, as if a passing wind had stirred it. Bastil was nowhere in sight. He hurried to the tapestry and thrust it aside to find a secret stair. He raced down it without a pause.

Lauressa sat on a horse on a hill to the north, looking down at the city, with Trekker crouched at her feet. She used a spyglass to watch the tiny figures of Alloryn and Talud scale the cliff walls. She outwardly showed patience, though she fretted for their safety on the inside.

For the first time in a hundred years, she dressed in royal garb. Stepan's wife Talina had given her the silken dress and cloak edged with gold the day before. She hoped to ride victoriously into the city when it was safe.

Talina and some of the other village women whose men fought today sat sidesaddle beside her waiting to escort her into the city when their husbands and sons won the battle.

All knew their men's mettle. All trusted the day would be theirs.

Lauressa turned her spyglass toward the west gate, the army composed of men, young lads, and even some women at the back to swell the ranks, as they used a battering ram to knock down the gates. All was going as planned.

Next, she swung the glass to the east.

Stepan had gained entrance at the east gate. Lauressa imagined the sight of him in his polished battle armor with the griffin emblazoned on his chest plate, royal red cloak billowing behind him, and his flag bearer carrying the royal gold griffin fluttering on the breeze. He would rally the citizens, who recognized the hereditary leader. She smiled when she discerned the city inhabitants grabbing weapons from their homes, or improvising with whatever was at hand, as they followed behind Stepan. The crowd surged forward. She could hear their cheering from this distance as he rode with his warriors toward the castle at the city's heart.

Reaching a landing, Alloryn found himself in a cramped corridor. The narrowness of it made him realize that he was inside the castle walls. He followed the sound of racing feet.

Bastil must be a short way ahead of him. A light showed in tiny beams along the right-hand wall. He did not stop to look through them but assumed they were spy holes.

Alloryn saw his quarry for ahead and made himself go faster. With one glance back at him, Bastil plunged down another stairwell. Letting himself skid into the corridor's end, rather than losing any speed, Alloryn grunted as he hit the wall with his side. He raced down a spiral staircase, catching brief glimpses of Bastil not far below him. He was gaining. He almost shot past an opening in the wall beside him, but the scrape of feet alerted him that the warlord had taken a new direction. He stretched out a hand and followed the wall of a dark corridor with no torches. The swaying of a door at the end let him see his way before it slapped shut.

He stepped back into the stairwell and wrenched a lit torch from its place. He reached the short hall's end, and he found not an actual door, but another tapestry blocking it. He paused to regain his breath, gripping the Crestin Sword in one hand, and his torch in the other. He thrust the tapestry out of the way with his foot. A blade sliced through the air where his arm would have been if he had not shown caution. He used the lit torch to thrust around the tapestry.

He heard a cry as Bastil clutched at his burnt arm. Alloryn barged through the opening. He did not pause to let the man regain his balance but launched an attack. With a wolfish grin, Bastil fought like a madman, though he was panting and grunting with the effort. Alloryn kept the upper hand and pressed him farther into the room. The room rang with swords clanging, their heavy breathing, and their boots stomping.

Alloryn lunged at his opponent and locked blades with the

weaker man. They stared grimly at each other, both unwilling to give ground. He shoved the torch into his opponent's face and as Bastil jumped back, Alloryn struck away his sword with a mighty thrust.

"Mercy!" Bastil cringed. His craven attitude made Alloryn angry.

"Justice, rather." He put the blade's point at the man's throat.

He had no time to look around before, but now he became aware that they were not the only ones in the room. Two elderly men, wringing their hands, watched the scene. He saw neither was armed.

"Get me something to tie this tyrant with." They scurried to obey. After they had tied him, Alloryn doused the torch and finally took in his surroundings.

They were in an underground chamber lit by torches. All around were shelves built into the walls, full of tied scrolls. In the room's center was a table, also piled high with parchments covered in writing and maps. Banners and ancient artifacts covered the little of the wall that remained.

"What is this place? And who are you?" he asked the nearest man.

"This is the archive room. The lore and historical treasures of a realm long past are stored here. We are the custodians," answered a gray-bearded man. "My name is Libran."

The second man pointed with amazement at the sword still in Alloryn's hand. "You bear the Crestin Sword? There is none like it in the world."

The question reignited his need to learn everything he could about the sword. With Bastil safely tied up, he decided he had time to indulge his curiosity. "What can you tell me about it?"

The archivists stepped forward, eagerness on their faces. Alloryn held the sword so the two men could examine it closely.

"One legend claims that Gildran received it from the Guardian sent to him from heaven. But most believe that story is a myth. Its origins are wrapped in a mystery, but it is forged from rare metal. May I hold it?" Alloryn passed it to him. Libran ran his fingers down the scrollwork. "The fine etchings are the work of a master swordsmith. Hunston was the greatest who ever lived, two millennia ago. My guess is this is of his making." He handed the sword back, then grabbed a banner leaning against the wall. He held the metal pole horizontally. "Hit this with the sword."

Alloryn hesitated, but both men showed innocent fervor. He swung the sword at the middle. The pole broke in half. He glanced from it to his sword. Not a mark could he see on the sword's edge.

Libran then ripped a piece of cloth from his robe, holding it between both hands. "And now the fabric." The Crestin Sword passed through it as easily as if it were butter.

"It is true! No metal can break the sword. If wielded with enough power, it can break any sword in the land. But it is so sharp it can also cut through a cloth. A wonder, indeed!" They examined the slit fabric, which the sword had finely sliced, not even fraying it.

"Tell us, is it true that the heir apparent of Valdeor travels with you? The Reina yet uncrowned?" the other eagerly asked.

"Yes. I am the Champion of Valdeor and I protect the Princess Lauressa from scum such as him," he nodded at Bastil, as he sheathed the Crestin Sword. "And she shall pronounce judgment on you," he threatened the warlord.

Through her spyglass, Lauressa saw Stepan gather a multitude around him. He dismounted, surrounded by the best warriors of his clan, and stepped onto a dais in the center plaza, the castle a mighty backdrop behind him. He sent one of his followers with his banner into the now open castle gates.

As soon as Lauressa saw the griffin banner carried toward the castle, she and Talina, and the village women with them, rode into the city by the east gate. Tris and his warrior band met them and escorted them to the plaza. The crowd parted to let them pass. With a borrowed golden circlet on her head, they had no doubt who she was. Men bowed, and women curtsied, and children gazed with awe.

She dismounted and with regal grace joined Stepan on the dais, and all watched as men raised the new standard above the castle keep. The proud gold griffin replaced the boar. The whole city cheered.

The army, which had battered down the west gate, marched into the plaza amid glad shouting. Soon the troops gathered all Bastil's soldiers and retainers and threw them into the dungeon.

Stepan signaled for the crowd's silence. When they quieted, he spoke.

"You all know me, Stepan, heir of King Stellin the Just. And you have recognized Princess Lauressa, soon to be crowned Reina of Valdeor. We have retaken Forestown for the people of Domadaria!" Cheers and shouts of joy met these words.

"We come to bring justice back to the realm. Too long have tyrants bled our coffers dry. Too long have our sons and daughters labored under the cruel reign of Bastil. Too long have our forests dwindled and our craftsmanship lay idle. We will replant our trees and we will once again be the envy of Valdeor for our hand-crafted woodwork." Shouts of approval, clapping, and stomping of feet followed.

All heads turned and the crowd quieted. Lauressa swung her head around to see as Alloryn led the prisoner from the castle doors. Jeers met the former ruler. People spat at him and called him names. They acted as if they would have snatched him and killed him out of hand except for the threat of the Crestin Sword, and Stepan's warriors, quick to surround them.

"Let the prisoner pass!" Stepan commanded. The crowd made way.

During the interval, Tris placed a chair on the dais. Stepan escorted Lauressa to it, and as she sat, he took a position behind her. Other family members lined up on the dais behind them.

Alloryn pushed Bastil on his knees before Princess Lauressa and the rightful king, Stepan.

Stepan glared at the man. "You are accused here and now before a tribunal of your peers." He indicated Bastil should look at the princess.

Lauressa gazed at her enemy and felt the anger at their last meeting rise in her breast. She only had to say the word and she could have him executed this very minute.

Sweat glistened over all his face, though he sneered back at her. She saw no remorse, only fear at being caught.

Lauressa pushed down her personal feelings of anger, willing her hands to unclench beneath the folds of her gown. She drew on her years of experience in exile, longing to right the wrongs of her people for their sakes, not revenge. Faces of the oppressed, the beaten, the hopeless rose before her face. Justice belonged to them.

"I, as princess of the realm of Valdeor, and heiress of Stellin the Just, along with Stepan, his successor, and all our kin present, accuse you, Bastil, of tyranny and unlawful rule of the Forest Kingdom of Domadaria. You will be imprisoned in your former dungeon until such time that a trial can be arranged with impartial judges." The crowd erupted. "Take him away," she commanded.

More jeers and boos accompanied Bastil as soldiers led him away to prison.

"I proclaim Stepan King of the Domadarians, to be ratified when I take my throne. Long live the king!"

"Long live King Stepan!" the gathering shouted. The people lifted their voices in joyful song, but those nearest the dais grew silent as the stone on Lauressa's medallion shone forth. Soon waves of silence rippled outward as all noticed the light that grew bright as the noonday orange sun. Far beyond the castle walls in the north, a blaze shone like a huge forest fire of golden hue. Many cried out with wonder.

"Justice is served," King Stepan said in a loud voice. "A heartstone is won. See and dwell on this, for future generations will remember this day that you have seen." All stood in awe till the two lights faded away.

The Domadarian people celebrated in the city that night. The castle kitchen prepared sumptuous meals and shared them with the populace, especially the poor. Tidings of Bastil's deposing traveled by swift wings to villages and hamlets throughout the forest. All rejoiced at their rightful king's reinstatement.

Deep in the forest beside Thunder Falls, Hakal was the only witness to the gem's disappearance.

A blizzard struck the area the day after Alloryn and Talud left. It raged for eight days. The last laborer died from hypothermia. Most of the soldiers with Hakal died from a lack of food. The subzero temperatures that followed the blizzard killed the remaining few. Even the great Thunder Falls froze, spray hardening in the frigid air and coating everything it touched.

Hakal was the last man left. Weakened, he searched for firewood around the camp. He stood rooted to the spot as the citrine gem shone through the frozen falls with the light of a small sun. Then it burst like a geyser from under the ice. Knocked over by the force, drenched and freezing, he lay there and hoped the man who sent him on a fool's errand would pay for this with his life as well.

In the capital city, Feornson paced his chamber angrily, as his second-in-command, Dukaat, watched. Three stones had miraculously materialized in the palace. True, Feornson did not use the throne room where they appeared. He was a very superstitious man.

The original Feorn, the first Warlord after the fall of the royal dynasty, also avoided it and made another council room, which his grandson used as well. Even the servants feared the room. Rumors were it was haunted by the slain king.

Dukaat had been with Feornson earlier when he visited the throne room after the citrine heartstone arrived with a clap of thunder. He had seen his master blanch and seem to shrink in size as he looked at the menacing stone of justice. Dukaat, knowing Feornson since they were boys together, tried to put himself in Feornson's mind. He imagined that with the gems winking at him, Feornson must have felt even more stifled than usual, as if unseen ghosts were whispering above his head, threatening his power.

Standing beside him, he thought he heard Feornson say to himself, "Only the wind sighing through the embrasures."

Feornson assumed a posture of defiance in front of his men, but Dukaat could see him hiding his unease in the presence of the stones.

When he was back in the room he used for daily business, he ordered Dukaat to stay, dismissing everyone else except his bodyguard.

A hard look glinted in Feornson's eyes. "These mysterious stones trouble me. They stir up the citizens and give them false hope that a mere girl, even if she is of royal descent, will oust me from my throne. Me, who slew more foes than any man living." He slapped his big hand on the table, making a mug wobble and splash the maps laid on it.

"After all, I hold this realm together, not an upstart girl from the past. I won my right to rule on the battlefield."

Dukaat had never seen Feornson with such a haunted look in his eyes. He was usually calm and cunning. He saw his master grow frustrated and even fearful at the return of the heartstones. Rumors swirled around the castle that Feornson was at the end of his reign. The lesser warlords were more audacious in their attitude toward him, as were the courtiers, something that had never happened before.

"The wench must be found and stopped before I have an out and out rebellion on my hands," Feornson declared. Dukaat nodded in agreement.

"I see a pattern. At first, I thought the stones were randomly appearing, but with the third one, I notice they come from the directions: west, southwest, southeast." He stabbed his finger on the maps as he named them. "The next one will come from the east. I am sure of it. But which town or wasteland in the east is the girl? That is what you will find for me."

Feornson crossed to stand at the eastern casement and gazed across the verdant farmland beyond the rivers' confluence.

"Order someone to look through the archives. I want to know what this girl looks like, what the next stone's virtue is, and the most likely place she will search."

Feornson did not admit it, but Dukaat knew he could not read. He discounted education in any form. He believed solely in his arms to carry the day or the argument.

Unfortunately for him, this worked against him.

A while later Dukaat returned. "My lord, no archivist is left in the city," Dukaat reported to him, "And no archives are left either."

"What! No scrolls? No parchments? Nothing?" He smacked his fist on the arm of his chair. "How can this be? Is there not a room in this palace devoted to the lore of the realm?" he stormed.

"You banned all the teachers when you conquered the city," Dukaat reminded him. "They must have taken all the accumulated knowledge of the realm with them." He dared be blunt because he had a long history with Feornson, back to the days when Feornson was a minor warlord. Even then, he had dreamed of taking back the throne of his grandfather Feorn the First, the warlord who emerged victorious in the decades after the Myrkr Revolt.

Feornson rose and paced about.

"Then send spies to the east, northeast, and northwest provinces. I want any information they gather sent to my garrisons in those provinces. And make sure the captains have a full complement of soldiers stationed at each garrison. They are to follow all possible leads and detain anyone deemed suspicious." He got within inches of Dukaat's face. "I want you to personally go to the garrison in the east and lead the investigation."

"As you wish, my lord."

Feornson called scribes to write the new orders for the different garrisons. Dukaat hastened on his way when he had the orders in hand.

A great feast was in the making to honor the reinstatement of King Stepan as the ruler of the Domadarian region. The marketplace did a booming business as farmers brought their wares to Forestown. The kitchens hummed with preparations for days beforehand. Aromas of hearty bread and delicate cakes, roasting meats, and savory sides wafted through the keep courtyard, tickling Alloryn's nose and making him perpetually hungry.

Talina sent her tailor to Lauressa and Alloryn to fit them for appropriate fancy dress. Alloryn grumbled that his clothes were fine after a good scrubbing and sent the man away.

A light knock sounded at Alloryn's door a short while after that. He was surprised to see Queen Talina standing there.

"May I come in?" she inquired, when he was too slow to invite her inside.

He stepped aside, embarrassed. "Of course, Your Highness."

"I hear you refused my tailor. Remember, this is in a good cause," Talina chided him. "It is all well and fine to be ready for battle at a moment's notice, but think of this as a different battle. Lauressa must win the hearts of her people. She must also look the part of a princess of royal descent. Clean clothes do not send the same message as royal robes."

Alloryn gestured at himself in a mirror, pointing to his serviceable brown tunic, black pants tucked into black boots, and wide leather belt which held the Crestin Sword's scabbard. "All the more reason for me to fade into the background. I am a simple shepherd boy. The fancy dress I have seen at your court will not suit me." He made a face at the remembrance of fine lace and ruffles he saw noblemen wearing.

Talina smiled as if she read his thoughts. "Fear not. I do not intend to dress you as a peacock. But as Champion of Valdeor you, too, have a presence to maintain. The right clothes will gain you respect. Trust me."

He looked at her image in the mirror. Her dimpled smile jogged a distant memory of his mother, so fleeting he was not sure it was a real memory, and he could not but help smiling back at her. "Very well. I will put myself in your hands."

He reluctantly let the tailor measure him.

The afternoon of the feast, he tried on the new clothes. He was relieved to see that they had no ruffles or lace. Standing before the mirror he saw they were elegant versions of his garb. The tunic was a soft brown, edged with gold tracing. Over that was a fur-lined dark brown vest. His pants were deep forest green with a gold stripe along the leg's outside edge, tucked into gleaming black boots with tassels. The new belt was leather with a bright gold buckle. The Crestin Sword's scabbard was newly polished, the leather gleaming, and the dark tracery highlighted in black.

Alloryn was satisfied with what he saw.

He had polished the Crestin Sword until it glowed, and now he replaced it in the scabbard. The only bright color of his ensemble was the ruby in the pommel, which twinkled in the light against the dark colors.

He saw Talina in the doorway. She smiled. "You will do nicely." She held out an imperious hand. "Come, it is time to attend the feast."

He followed her through the hall to the grand staircase. He stopped short at the sight of the gowned lady standing at the head of it. He hardly recognized the vision before him as his traveling companion.

Lauressa's hair was brushed to a bright chestnut sheen and cascaded around her face and down her back in a profusion of curls. She wore a rich forest green gown that deepened her green eyes. The dress widened to a bell shape from her waist. Her creamy arms were bare from the mid-upper arm down, except for matching emerald bracelets on each wrist. She wore an emerald tiara, which sparkled in the chandelier's light.

He saw her looking over his fine clothing and he saw a slight smile on her lips at his dumbfounded admiration. He pulled himself together and joined her and Talina.

"We will greet the guests as they ascend the staircase. Alloryn, you need not make any speeches. A firm handshake will suffice. After we receive all the guests, we will process to the dining hall and take our places at the main table. Then you can relax."

Stepan joined them, and the men at arms threw open the castle doors. The chamberlain introduced each guest and family who climbed the staircase. The host and hostess greeted them and introduced the princess and her champion.

Alloryn's feet were tired after the first couple of hours, and when he thought the introductions would go on forever, the last guest shook his hand. Talina shooed them into a procession, with Stepan and her in the lead, and the guests trailing after Lauressa and Alloryn, by rank and file, into the grandly decorated dining hall.

Banners hung from every window. Garlands of leaves intertwined around columns. Candles gleamed from chandeliers twenty feet over their heads, and more candles shone from sconces around the walls.

Shields with the Domadarian coat of arms, as well as the Valdeor royal arms, were displayed on the wall above the main table.

They took their places at the head table. After all the guests were seated at the surrounding tables, Stepan stood. "Long live Princess Lauressa of Valdeor! Long may she prosper!"

The guests rose to their feet and raised their goblets, repeating the phrase.

For the next several hours servers tempted Alloryn with every kind of food imaginable, and those he never imagined. Lines of servants laid platters of roasted meats: lamb, pork, beef, sausage, duck before them. Bowls of potatoes and an assortment of vegetables, garnished and in sauces, were offered for him to sample. Sliced bread and rolls with clotted butter and several kinds of jams, as well as aromatic cheeses, were available around the table.

He ate a few bites of the dishes that interested him, or he was sure they would have to roll him away from the table when the festivities were over.

A number of different entertainers played instruments and sang ballads. Desserts were served, the wine was drunk, and the candles burnt low before the feast was over. At the end of it, Alloryn could hardly stay awake. He was glad he did not need to stand watch.

All too soon, Alloryn and Lauressa made their farewell to King Stepan and their new friends and took to the road again.

Lauressa sighed inwardly as Stepan, Talina, and their sons waved good-bye. The castle faded slowly in the distance, the griffin banner the last glimpse of it to disappear.

Seeming to sense her mood, Alloryn glanced at her. "Something troubles you, Princess?"

She turned her eyes away from the castle and met his eyes. "I wouldn't be honest if I denied I would miss the wonderful food and soft bed, but I have lived without finery for longer than I experienced it." She resolutely faced forward. "What I will miss is the easy camaraderie of family. They accepted me as I am."

As much as she cared for Alloryn, he gazed on her with reverence, putting her on a pedestal, expecting her to be perfect all the time.

With every league, the burden of her task resettled on her shoulders, like a heavy cloak weighing her down. An invisible crown of responsibility reminded her of her duty.

"For the first time in my life, I long to be a simple baker's assistant again."

The lingering glory of winning another stone dimmed with her knowledge that still more awaited finding.

They rode borrowed horses to the river dock where they boarded a ship for the northeast coast. To cross the northern border was too difficult. The Blue Range was at its highest there, with the mountains ending abruptly at the coastline.

They sailed with fair weather for two weeks. The shoreline was rocky, so the ship stayed farther out to sea. Without incident, they stopped at the Laketown Harbor, a city in its own right. The houses were built from the harbor into the hills until they were blocked by the great Lake Genesay, the largest lake in Valdeor, which lay in a valley above the town.

Laketown Harbor bustled with ships offloading the last

loads of timber from the Forest of Domadaria. A messenger traveled on the same ship with them. He carried a notice from King Stepan stopping all shipments of wood since he no longer honored the agreement made by Bastil.

"I fear there will be riots when the cheap laborers have no more lumber jobs." Lauressa leaned on the ship's deck railing. "When I take the throne, I will suggest they reopen the weaving mills. This area is the best place for growing flax and making linen. Maybe I can revitalize the industry."

As the two headed north with Trekker in the lead, the flat land became rolling hills. They eventually came to the crest of a high hill and overlooked a valley.

"This is the northeast province's boundary." Alloryn pointed below. "This is the Smoky River Valley, so called because of the frequent mists that form here mostly in the spring and autumn. Once, this was as far as I had seen of Valdeor. The cottage I was born in is a few days' ride from here."

He sat in silence, lost in his thought for a short time.

"I had forgotten the air's smell here. The tangy smell is an herb that grows near the river." As they rode toward the valley, he breathed deeply and saw her sniff the air as well. Memories came to the surface of his mind. At first, they were good memories—the bleating sheep, the smell of stew as he entered the cottage after a long day on the hills, his father's hands, always busy with work. Then bad memories replaced them with the smell of smoke as the cottages burned, the broken bodies and fear of danger touching his home. The memories threatened to overwhelm him. He clenched his teeth and fought to push away the vision of his father lying dead at the hand of marauders.

A touch of her hand on his brought him back from the past. He gazed at her, sitting on her horse beside him, and saw understanding in her eyes.

"I see the faraway longing in your face. Much has happened since you were last here, I know. I understand loss, loss of parents and childhood, and the innocent belief that the world is good. Loss of a life that was once simple."

He nodded in agreement. She summed up what he felt. He constantly witnessed her compassion for others. *She will make an amazing ruler.*

He gave his horse a slight kick to get them moving again.

The horses wound around the lazy path leading to the river. They decided to make camp for the night, even though it was afternoon. At the river edge were many deciduous trees to shelter them. Alloryn found a circle of stones where others had lit campfires many times in the past. Lauressa gathered firewood as he dealt with the horses. The area had plenty of grass for them to eat, so he hobbled them in a sheltered area and joined her.

He caught fish for their meal, and she soon had a fire started with her flint and cooked them. She broke chunks of bread and passed the cheese bought in Laketown. She put the rest back in her saddlebag.

They had a cheerful meal and Alloryn spoke of his days as a shepherd. Even Trekker seemed to recognize they were near home, as he joyously sniffed out a rabbit from its den, chased it for fun, then chased his tail in exuberance. They laughed as they watched him. Finally, he stopped, panting with his tongue hanging out in a doggy grin. Alloryn never heard Lauressa laugh before. She had a rich laugh that was infectious. His usual somber expression also lightened, and he chuckled at his dog's antics.

That night, they slept on either side of the campfire beneath the stars, which looked close enough to smother them in a black, twinkling blanket. On a night like this, they could both believe that the quest's end was near. All was peaceful, so Alloryn trusted Trekker to guard them while they slumbered.

A day's journey from them, Dukaat arrived in the northeast garrison. Word had reached here of the stone of justice two weeks ago. Patrols roamed between the sea and the Laketown district looking for the couple.

Dukaat readied himself to join in the search in the morning.

They were close. He could feel it in his bones. *No matter that the next gem's whereabouts were still unknown.*

He knew the princess and her champion must pass the Smoky River to gain the next province, so he ordered spies to watch all the most likely fording spots. Not an easy task, since the river was at its lowest till the spring melting, and fording it was easy along much of its banks.

Still, the princess and her companion would eventually seek civilization for food and supplies. They had not avoided the villages in Laketown province but were one hamlet ahead of his bands of spies. No big towns existed in this area where they could lose themselves. The northeast province mainly consisted of farms and sheep ranches.

Dukaat felt confident. *I have spread the net. Now the prey had only to step into it.*

Alloryn led the way along the Smoky River's southern side. He saw tracks that showed bands of riders had recently passed that way. He had Lauressa halt in a grove off the path while he went forth and scouted the area.

Returning half an hour later to her hiding place in a thicket, he told her, "It is unusual for traders to come here this late in the winter. I fear something else is bringing them. They have no reason to be traveling in a large group unless they mean trouble." He was almost certain the roving bands were looking for them, but he was not ready to alarm Lauressa unnecessarily.

"We must be cautious," he said. "This land is scarcely populated. No cities are in this province. Zendira is the largest, several weeks north of here, and I would call it a market town. It is not even a port."

"The warlords are alerted now. I have shown my face and my intent. They hunt for us." Lauressa, too, felt the danger looming. She knew the more stones she obtained, the more intense the search for her would be, not only by Feornson but by any man who sought power.

They left the valley behind and followed a mere track in the woods, which Alloryn thought gave them more safety. It would take longer, but it would not be as easy to follow them. They left the heavily wooded area at a place he judged would be an easy river crossing, yet far enough from the common trails that no scouts would be watching.

The river was slow-moving here, but the bottom was rocky.

He chose to have their horses walk downstream so they left no tracks to show where they left the riverbed and crossed back into the woods.

They managed to make good time despite not traveling the well-worn trails. "I hunted many a time here with my father Yarrek. Most paths I'm leading us over are deer trails." Once he spotted soldiers riding in the distance as they came to the edge of a clearing in the forest thicket. He signaled Lauressa to stop, and they waited, holding their horses still until he was sure which direction the men were traveling. Then he led them on a different path, taking a perpendicular route to the band of men through thickly wooded hills.

Alloryn sent Trekker ahead to scout the canyon before them. In a short time, Trekker bounded back with his tail and hair standing on end. He gave a low growl. Alloryn motioned Lauressa to move back around the previous bend of the trail and drew his sword. He dismounted and crept around the canyon wall. A small group of soldiers were on the march at the intersection ahead, headed perpendicular to their trail. In the middle of the band were a man and a boy tied together with a rope around their wrists.

"Let us go! Let my son, at least, go! We do not know anything."

A soldier slapped him. The captive lost his balance and pitched to the ground.

"Father!" Turning to the soldier who hit his father, the boy kicked him. "Let him be!" he sobbed.

The soldier unsheathed his dagger. That was the last thing he ever did.

Alloryn swept the Crestin Sword down on the soldier's arm

and severed it before he could pull his blade. The other soldiers grunted and pulled their weapons. Alloryn knocked the first one to the ground where Trekker attacked his throat. The other two fared equally as Alloryn blocked their attacks, kicking one man aside while engaging the other. With a few strokes, a feint left, then a plunge through the man's heart and the third man was down. The last soldier, taking his measure, looked as if he would rather run away. He was slower in his attack. They circled.

"Watch out!" the captive man warned him. "He has a knife!" But before the soldier could use it, Trekker leaped on the man's back, throwing him off balance, and Alloryn struck him.

Wiping his blade, he turned to the man and boy. With a few quick strides, he knelt and using his dagger, sliced the ropes tying the two.

"Wow! I wish I could be a warrior like you. I bet you killed lots of bad men." The hero-worship in the boy's face made him uncomfortable.

"A good warrior only fights when he has to. Those men were searching for me, else I might have chased the last one away." He helped the man stand.

"Thank you for saving my son and me. We are in your debt."

Alloryn whistled for his horse, then unslung his canteen from his saddle. While the man and boy drank, he searched the soldiers. He took their food, water, and weapons, and gave them to the former prisoners. "Take these and tell no one you saw me." They profusely thanked him again and returned the way they came. When they were out of view, Lauressa led her horse from the gully.

"I thought it better that they did not see me. I fear they may be captured again, and this way they have no knowledge of a man and woman traveling together." She looked around the scene of carnage. She chose a bow and quiver of arrows and swung them on her back.

"We best leave this place before others come searching for this patrol," Alloryn told her. They remounted and rode away from there.

"We are very close to my old home. Tomorrow afternoon we will reach it if we have no more delays."

The wooded hills were fast ending the farther the pair got from the river. Soon the trees dwindled to nothing, and the gently rolling hills were crisscrossed by shallow canyons or gullies. Alloryn navigated them around the familiar small hamlets and farmsteads. He knew these were simple folk, such as his father, and they would welcome strangers with wariness but hospitality. Nevertheless, he feared for Lauressa's life with soldiers on the hunt. He sent Trekker ahead to look for danger.

Alloryn decided unconsciously to head for home. He knew the land and the people there best. If he could trust anyone, it would be his former neighbors. And he knew the rocks and rills and hiding places for leagues around.

Alloryn chose a campsite beside a huge, felled tree. Lauressa practiced with the bow and arrows until she felt confident that she had not forgotten how to use them. She stalked off to find food for dinner and managed to kill a rabbit after several false tries. She used the meat along with herbs and a few edible tubers she had dug near the Smoky River to make a stew. He used dried branches to make a shelter from a snow squall while she cooked. He figured the fire's smoke would mingle with the snow and not be visible.

Dukaat was frustrated. A spy reported signs of a recent camp in the Smoky River Valley, but when he got there, with a dozen men, his scout soon lost the trail. That was after they had ridden for nearly a day and came across many other tracks crossing the river. The trail was confusing, and it took an hour to find two travelers' horse prints after many false starts.

Dukaat had the scout brought before him.

"What is the delay?" He glared at the local man from his superior height on his horse.

"Sir, there are too many prints. The prints are harder and harder to find. Many travelers have passed this way in the last few days." The scout scratched his beard. "I figure that the princess's companion realized a band of soldiers was searching for them, and from that point on he became cautious. The man, whoever he is, is a good woodsman, able to cover his tracks. "

"That is what you are paid for! I was told you are the best scout in the garrison. Huh!" Dukaat leaned down from the saddle, threateningly. "Death awaits you if you fail. Feornson is not a forgiving master, and neither am I."

Dukaat straightened in the saddle. "Find them!"

His voice and posture spoke of his impatience, and boded ill for anyone in his retinue that crossed him. The soldiers kept their distance, seeing his foul mood.

But as Dukaat's scout had more difficulty, he realized they were falling farther and farther behind the quarry. He hoped that the soldiers he stationed at all the major fords would have more luck.

After all, there were only two quarries against a full

regiment of soldiers hunting for them. No man could be that good to outwit so many.

How bittersweet, Alloryn thought, *coming home after so many years.* He rode the old familiar paths through the hills and passed landmarks from his childhood. Memories flickered before his mind's eye. *There is the well. Here is where I saw a wolf. This was the stump where I played king of the mountain. There stands the tree I loved to climb.*

And around the bend was the cottage where he had grown up.

I miss you, Father. Would you even recognize me now?

Seeming to sense his sober mood, Lauressa asked no questions and made no comments until they stopped the horses before the front door.

"This was your home?"

"Until I joined Justinian. I only came back once in my travels—the night my father was dying." The memories were too poignant to tell her the story. His emotions were raw as if it had happened just yesterday.

They dismounted and walked into his old house. It seemed so big to him as a child and so small to him as a man with many years of wandering behind him.

Lauressa walked around the abandoned ruin, touching a chair here, looking at a broken piece of dishware there.

Standing before the cold hearth, he could imagine it warm and inviting after a long day on the hills tending sheep.

Alloryn looked at the ladder that led to the loft where he had slept. *I can still hear Father's voice calling me for the morning meal as if it were yesterday.*

A sound came from outside, and bark and deep growl from Trekker alerted them. They ran to the door and looked out. A band of soldiers rode into the clearing and made a loose circle around the hut's perimeter.

Alloryn's heart raced as he assessed the situation. He called Trekker in. One man rounded up their horses. No escaping by horseback.

Lauressa counted six men. Beside her, Alloryn drew his sword. She knew he was a good swordsman, but even he would be hard-pressed to fight all of them. "We need to get away from here. I know a place that is more defensible a league and a half from here." He looked at her in puzzlement, but she did not give him a chance to ask how she knew of it. "You know the ruins?" He nodded.

"We need to split up. I will make a distraction, then meet you there." Her tone of voice let him know this was not a discussion.

She did not often take charge when her safety was involved, but she hoped the determined look in her eye and her swift actions would leave him no time to argue.

She wrapped scraps of material around a few arrows, doused them with leftover lamp fluid, then she lit them using her flint. When they were blazing, she sighted a horseman through the broken window and let the first arrow fly. Her second arrow set alight a dried tree branch above a second soldier. The third arrow hit a soldier in the arm and started his cloak afire. She slung the bow over her back since she had no more arrows.

In the chaos and rearing horses, Lauressa escaped through the back window. She ran into the woods, heart pounding with fear. She struggled through whipping tree branches which clawed her as she passed. For over half a league she ran as fast as she could, ignoring the stitch in her side. She pushed herself onward, although she was out of breath, struggling uphill.

She eventually found a little-used path that once was flagstone. If she had not been looking for it, she would have missed it. Winding around a craggy hill, steeper as it went, the path turned into flagstone steps. Crumbling walls and a ruined structure loomed over her on the hilltop.

Once a fine fortress when she had last visited it, she spent a moment to stare at the ruin it had become, before climbing over fallen stones to reach the main entrance. She reached the safety of the ancient keep. Three outer walls remained standing. She climbed the rock stair along one side. From here she had a commanding view of all the surrounding hills and lands stretching into the distance.

The ruins would make a good, defensible position. Of course, it would be better if a legion of soldiers were available. But Lauressa trusted Alloryn to protect her. He was strong and smart.

Here she waited, her weapons a simple dagger and her wits.

While the foes reacted to Lauressa's attack, Alloryn threw his dagger into the throat of the horse closest to him. The mount and his rider fell. He grabbed his father's wooden staff leaning against the wall by the door, using it as a weapon to unseat another rider who charged him as he raced into the clearing. He struck the downed rider with his sword. Trekker attacked and bit the leg of another horse who reared and threw his rider.

Alloryn jumped one of the riders, dragging him off his horse, then mounted the steed and rode into the hills behind his old home. He had two goals: foremost in his mind was leading the remaining soldiers far away from the direction Lauressa took; the other, namely, to survive. He knew this land as well as he knew himself, so he led them on a merry chase for most of the afternoon. He finally deemed them lost and confused in the myriad of gullies and rills that looked the same, so he doubled back toward the old ruins that Lauressa named as their meeting place.

He arrived at dusk. He did not climb the stairs as she had done but went up a long winding path with his stolen horse. He reached the courtyard, and he called her name. Trekker whined and sniffed the area until he found her. Lauressa stepped from her hiding place. He dismounted and led the horse through the tumbled stones.

"Are you all right?" he asked. When she nodded, he sighed. "Thank the One Who Fashioned All. I was worried the forces would split and follow us both."

He gazed around at the fallen fortress. "So much time has passed since I was here last. When I was a boy I used to like to let my sheep graze around the ruins while I explored them, pretending I was a king or a fierce warrior."

He barely glimpsed her secret smile before she looked serious again.

He rummaged in the stolen horse's saddlebag to see what

it might contain, embarrassed by his admission. He found a little food.

"A fire would be noticeable from this height, so we are better off eating dried food."

She led him to an area where the roof and walls still stood, allowing them to hide and shelter.

"I led the soldiers all around the hills. They should be halfway to Zendira by now." He gave a wolfish smile. "Did you have any trouble getting here?"

"No. Uphill running was difficult, but once I found the old path, I had no trouble." She broke the bread he gave her and passed half back to him.

"I cannot understand how you knew of this place."

"Really? Do you not remember whose fortress this was?" She gave a lift of her brow.

"No, I do not remember if I ever heard." He turned from scanning the horizon. "Whose was it?"

"Why, I am surprised Justinian did not tell you. This is the ancestral home of Prince Jarell's family."

He stopped chewing. "Jarell? Your fiancé? I had no idea."

"Yes. This was once a wild border country, so a king ordered a fortress built here. Jarell's family were the stewards, but in time the king gave the land to them as a minor kingdom when it became more civilized." She glanced around the rubble. "I visited here several times after our marriage was arranged. It was strong and well protected then."

Odd that Justinian had never told me this tale. His history lessons were usually most complete. Aloud he said, "All the time I lived here, it was a lifeless ruin. Occasionally my father and other shepherds used it to shelter from a sudden storm, but no one ever inhabited it. Do you know what happened?"

Lauressa split the dried fruit with him. "When Justinian rescued me from Mintala, at the death of my father, his goal was to protect me. He wanted to bring me to Prince Jarell so we could be married, and the throne and succession would be safe. But he knew my enemies would be looking for me, and the most obvious route we were likely to take led here. So Justinian chose to take me to the most unlikely places, including, eventually, the independent island continent of Hamleor."

They washed down their meal with water from the canteen.

Alloryn left the wall and began to prepare separate sleeping areas. She could sleep just inside a broken doorway, and he put his saddle and blanket within some scattered masonry that would shelter him.

Lauressa joined him with her saddlebag, continuing her story.

"After a time, Justinian decided that it was safe for him to travel, and he disguised himself and came here. He told me he could find no trace of Jarell, but this fortress had suffered many attacks.

"After many years he pieced together what happened. Hearing the palace at Mintala had fallen, my father was dead, and I was missing, Jarell left to find me. Marauders attacked the fortress in that time of chaos, but without Jarell's leadership, it eventually fell.

"Jarell searched for me for years. He was at one time caught between two warring warlords and their bands. They injured him and left him for dead on the battlefield. He owed his life to a crofter who found him and carried him to his home.

His daughter nursed Jarell back to life. They fell in love, and fearing that I must be dead, they married."

Lauressa pulled her cloak around her, moved inside the gaping jaws of a doorway, and prepared for sleep.

Alloryn sat outside, back propped against a stone, and pondered her story. *Justinian told me a part of the tale, but not all of it, and certainly not that I lived at the foot of Prince Jarell's fortress. I wonder why he did not?* He suspected a mystery here.

Dukaat simmered with anger. His men gave him a wide berth.

He had fought with the princess's champion at the old, abandoned homestead and the whelp had beaten him.

He, the mighty warrior of Feornson's army, beaten!

Who was this man who defended Princess Lauressa? Where had he gotten his training?

His surviving men had chased the man through the hills for hours and eventually lost his trail. His best scout was dead from Lauressa's arrow, so they wandered around lost for a time.

His rage boiled up every time he thought about how his quarry had been in his grasp, then slipped away.

Night fell and he decided they would have to camp until morning. He barked at his men to set up camp. No one wanted to go back to the garrison and admit a girl and a single warrior had outwitted them.

He promised himself he would personally drag that vixen and swordsman back to Feornson in chains.

*L*ong before dawn, Alloryn and Lauressa got to work because they both knew they had to get their defenses in place before the soldiers found them. If not the ones he had led on a wild goose chase, then other roving bands.

They walked around the remaining battlements and outer walls to plan their strategy. "It would take a small army to defend this place," he told Lauressa in all honesty. "We can see the enemy coming, but we cannot do much about it."

"I know it seems hopeless, but we must not give in to doubt and despair. Though I did not know the fortress had suffered such damage when I suggested we make our last stand here. Jarell once showed me a secret weapon room. I fear we have little chance that it is still stocked, since its fall so long ago, but there is that chance. So much of the building has changed with time. Let me get my bearings." She walked around, orienting herself. She stopped and pointed. "That way."

Alloryn called Trekker over from where he was sniffing for vermin. He pointed to the top of the flagstone path that led to his old home. "Guard!" The dog obediently sat and stared down the path.

Lauressa led the way past the courtyard and into the main Keep's ruins. Stone blocks littered what was once a Great Hall. Weeds grew between the stones covered in lichen.

"Help me move these blocks." She pointed to ones next to a broken fireplace. They pushed and heaved until the stones gave way. Lauressa, panting, pushed the hair out of her face. With their combined effort they freed the wall panel. She gently pushed it open to reveal a musty stairwell leading into the bowels of the fortress.

"Careful! The air might be bad. Let me test it." He made a torch with dry twigs bundled together, and she used her flint to light it. He cautiously entered the secret entrance holding the torch in front of him and descended a few steps. The torch flickered but did not go out. She followed him. The stair curved to a landing, then curved again. He brushed away cobwebs stretched from side to side. Spiders scurried away, and she tried not to imagine what else made scrabbling noises in the dark, scuttling from the light.

"Stop!" she cried.

He turned about on the stair below her.

"I think this is the right step by my count." She turned the base of a torch knob and a narrow space opened with a groan of stone grating upon stone. A gust of musty air met them.

He was amazed at her remarkable memory. *More than one hundred years passed since she was last here.*

He handed her the torch.

He pushed open the hidden door farther, and picking up a loose rock, he jammed it open. "Just in case it is rigged to close behind us."

Taking back the torch, he thrust it first into the narrow corridor. Fresh air made the flame flicker again. "At least the air is better. Must be a vent somewhere."

They proceeded cautiously. The corridor opened into a small twenty by twenty-foot room. The walls were full of weapons: pikes, axes, maces, and a few nicked swords. On closer inspection, he saw the pikes' wooden handles had rotted, as had the ax handles, and all the weapons showed rust. He was disappointed that none of them were much help in a battle. "Anyone handling them would soon find themselves wielding a broken blade." An idea formed in his mind.

He turned to tell Lauressa but found her engaged in opening a chest in the room's center. She had a neat pile of arrows at her feet, and she was using her dagger to pick a lock. As he moved closer, she managed to open it. She threw back the lid and sneezed. He peered over her shoulder. A strange weapon lay there. An iron cylinder lay packed in thick cloth, surrounded by iron balls the size of large nuts. Several small bags of leather tied up with leather strings were tucked around the odd weapon.

"Jarell showed me this odd contraption the last time I visited him. His weapons master developed a new invention. You put the ball in the cylinder, sprinkle the fire powder from the bag in with the ball, set it down, aim it, and light the wick with a flint. A clap of thunder follows and the ball blasts out. I was amazed to see it send a chunk of the hill flying." He picked it up and eagerly looked it over while she dug in a smaller chest beside the first.

She pulled out an unusual bow with a cross arm. He put down the cylinder and took the bow she handed him and an arrow from the chest.

"You put the arrow here in the middle as usual, but you hold the bow perpendicular to your body, not vertical. That is right. Jarell demonstrated that the arrow will fly farther with this arrangement. Another of his weapons master's inventions."

"A brilliant man." He paced around with excitement. With this cache of weapons, he had a glimmer of hope.

He proceeded to tell her his idea. "Let us take as many of these weapons as we can to the tower. We can use them to make the enemy believe there are more of us." They grabbed pikes first and headed back up the stairs.

He showed her how to place each pike in a battlement around the walls, spacing them till it looked like several dozen men or more crouched in position watching for the enemy. They spent the rest of the morning bringing up all the weapons. They used stones to hold the pikes in position when necessary.

Alloryn also made a few rough snares to trip the enemy on the crumbled steps leading uphill. He used a few rusted swords, breaking off the point with a battle-ax, and wedged them in areas where the enemy would pass. He put battle axes in strategic positions where he could hurl them on any invaders.

He wished he could test Jarell's special weapons and be familiar with them before using them in the coming battle, for battle he was sure there would soon be, but he would not have an opportunity.

He hated to endanger Lauressa and told her so.

"Let us take a moment to pray to the One Who Fashioned All, and to the Guardian of Valdeor, who is surely watching over us. We must put our trust in the One. At this point in our quest, we must have hope that His will be done," she advised him. And they bowed their heads and sent their combined prayers winging into the fast-approaching afternoon.

Trekker had sat at guard duty through the preparation, and now Alloryn gave him the commands, "Scout, Trekker. Guard!" The dog immediately stretched his curled muscles, shook himself all over, and raced along the path pointed out to him. It was one of the few not laid with traps.

He showed Lauressa where he wanted her. She assured him she remembered how the fire powder cylinder worked, and he left her readying it. He saw that she had her regular bow and plenty of arrows. He did not give her a sword, because she was not able to fight with it in close combat. For himself, he had the axes in strategic places, his trusty sword, as well as the new bow with a cross arm. He placed himself where he had the best view, on the opposite side of the fortress from her. He forced himself to relax, stretching his muscles, and munching on his rations. Nothing left to do but hope for a good outcome.

Dukaat and his twelve men rode toward a hulking ruin, which loomed on the horizon.

After fruitless hours of riding in circles chasing the princess's swordsman, he and the soldiers who survived the fight at the cottage had finally made their way through the woods and back to the cottage. From there it was half a day's ride back to the garrison.

Dukaat knew that his prey was nearly within his grasp. If he could stop them, he would demand of Feornson a kingdom of his own, maybe the whole eastern province. For these two upstarts were the greatest menace Feornson had ever faced.

Sure, they did not head an army, but they won the citizens' hearts and allegiance.

After a change of horse, he deployed with a fresh batch of soldiers. He ordered the new scout to locate the girl's trail.

Dukaat was smart enough to figure she would have headed straight for a meeting place. According to the new scout, she showed a little knowledge of trail craft, running where her light footprints left little passing, but still broken twigs, disturbed soil, and a few muddy footprints told the tale for those able to read it.

"An abandoned structure is on top of a hill nearby," the lead soldier, familiar with the area, told him. "My guess is that is where she was headed."

The scout nodded his agreement.

"Let us be careful not to be seen." Dukaat faced his men. He caught the eye of each, emphasizing they must obey his commands or face his wrath. "Surround the hill when we get there, but be stealthy," he sternly admonished them. "We do not want to lose them again, or Feornson will have our heads on pikes."

Dukaat nodded to the scout. "Lead on."

Dukaat could taste victory. Prince Dukaat sounded nice in his ears.

Alloryn saw a flicker that was gone as fast as he focused on it. He gave two short whistles, the prearranged signal for 'the enemy is spotted.' He stretched his tense muscles and readied an arrow. The long wait was over. The battle seemed preferable to endless watching.

The blood started pumping in his veins. His focus sharpened. His eyes sought out any further motion. Anticipation replaced boredom.

The soldiers approached from all sides.

Alloryn was not sure of the range of his new bow, although he knew what the princess thought its range to be. *Closer*, he thought, *come a little closer*.

He slowed down his breathing to steady his aim. He mentally noted the direction and speed of the wind.

Two things happened simultaneously. A soldier screamed on the path where Alloryn had buried rusted sword blades between the steps leading to the courtyard, and an animal bark was immediately followed by a shriek cut off in mid-note.

Alloryn saw a soldier flinch on the rock face below him and, sighting along the bow, he shot him. With a loud twang, the arrow burst from his bow. The soldier fell back and tumbled down the hillside. Lauressa was right, this bow had a much longer range. It should help keep the enemy at bay if he could find and shoot them fast enough.

The remaining men crept closer. Alloryn made a headshot when one man moved to look over his stone cover.

Dukaat cried out as he injured himself on the stairs, but the blade had only pierced the side of his foot. He cursed silently, but it would not stop him from winning a crown.

Dukaat slowed and crouched low as he lost three men in as many minutes.

How was this possible?! The odds were in his favor— twelve hardened soldiers against one unproven warrior and a simple girl.

Closer to the fortress, Dukaat peeked over the stairwell. He could see pikes pointing at his men from many positions along the battlements. *The two must have convinced the locals to help them.* This might not be as easy as he thought.

When he was almost to the top of the stairs, the princess's companion changed position, and Dukaat realized the man spotted him. His last sight was of a battle-ax aimed at his head.

Dukaat's last thought was anger that he would perish within sight of his outnumbered, but not outwitted, enemy.

Lauressa had the fire shooter ready, but she would use the bow while the enemy was in the arrow's range. She warmed up her arm muscles by rubbing both hands up and down her arms, then gripped and ungripped her fingers to stretch them. Jarell had taught her how to shoot arrows for fun competitions between them and his sisters. Justinian had taught her to shoot arrows hoping she would not need the skill, never knowing if it might save her life, nonetheless. She brought to mind the guidance they had both given her.

Remember to breathe, she told herself.

Lauressa sighted a quarry and shot an arrow into his upper arm. She ducked as the soldiers sent arrows back her way. Unlike Alloryn, her range was only as great as theirs. She saw a movement out of the corner of her eye, and with another arrow, sighted along her bow. She paused when she saw it was Trekker moving along the hill, half crouched as he trailed someone. She held still. She saw two men crawling on the small loose stones covering the hillside. She let loose on the one closest to her, while Trekker pounced on the other. Two fewer attackers.

She counted three soldiers. As Lauressa ran along the wall, she spotted one of them headed for Alloryn's last position. She ran back and spun the cylindrical weapon that sat on a centrally located block, lit the fuse, and ducked. With a loud bang that made her ears ring, the weapon fired a ball that collapsed part of the wall near the soldier focused on Alloryn. He fell screaming as he plunged down the hill, the blocks from the wall smashing him as he landed.

She crept around the wall, looking to see how Alloryn fared. Two more soldiers had breached the walls from different positions near Alloryn, but they must have frozen at the sound and sight of the explosion.

Lauressa saw Alloryn recover first, guessing what had caused it. Drawing the Crestin Sword, he attacked the nearest soldier in an outburst of strength and speed. He was well-matched with the big, seasoned soldier.

"You have met your better, son," she heard the soldier say as he gave blow for blow.

Lauressa peeped around the keep, her dagger in her hand. She wished she could even the playing field, as the second enemy edged up the wall to join the fight, but the fire weapon was too hot to handle. She had burnt her hand trying to lift it. She was determined to get a man to chase her and cross in front of the weapon. She went back and lit it with a long wick.

I can do this. She took a steadying breath.

She stood suddenly in the second soldier's range of vision as he climbed over the battlement, then ran for her life. He changed direction and gave her chase. As soon as she rounded the corner, she flung herself on the ground. She heard boots pounding closer. At that second, the fire-powder weapon belched a ball, which although did not hit the soldier chasing her, caused a section of the already unstable wall to totter and fall on him. A fragment of the wall fell on her as she lay hugging the flagstones, and blackness replaced her victory smile.

Alloryn parried blow for blow, saving his strength. Here was a foe who fought well. Not frenzied, not rash, this enemy measured each move. The fallen stones made for an obstacle course, not allowing free movement. Alloryn knew one false move meant tripping and losing concentration, yet he could not look away from his opponent and give him an advantage.

Alloryn fought for his life, Lauressa's life, and their quest. This gave him an incentive, and motivation to win.

Thrust, parry, circle with feet carefully placed, sliding to avoid stepping on a stone. They were both growing tired, muscles straining. Alloryn was at a disadvantage from lack of sleep. His eyes were gritty, his body felt twice his weight, but his steely determination never failed. Time seemed to stand still. Nothing existed except defeating his blade-wielding opponent.

He saw an opening in the other's guard. His blade slipped under the thrust and connected with flesh. The soldier again blocked, keeping Alloryn from scoring a deadly hit. But as the enemy changed his stance to regain his control, his foot stepped on an uneven surface. The second of an imbalance was all Alloryn needed to give the fatal wound.

"I wish you were on my side," he told the man laying on the ground. "You are a good man in a fight. Too bad you chose to follow the wrong master."

He spent no more time over his beaten opponent, but wiping the sweat from his brow, he went in search of Lauressa. He had heard the second explosion but gave it no heed during battle. Now he realized he was not hearing or seeing the princess or other enemies.

He quickly picked his way around the fallen stones of the keep and saw a new section of the wall had crumbled. The figure of a soldier crushed under it let him know Lauressa had been busy.

His grin faded when he saw her lying crumpled, as well, under the same wall. He rushed to her side, and as he stood over her, he realized that she was pinned by one stone. He pushed it off her. Blood matted her hair where the stone had bounced and struck. Luckily for her, it had not struck her head full force but had been a glancing blow.

He felt for her pulse with trepidation. He sighed with relief when it was weak but steady. He gently turned her on her back. He felt along her arms and legs for broken bones and gave another deeper sigh of relief when he knew they were unbroken. Ever so gently he carried her to the roofed area where their canteens were.

He poured water on a clean strip of cloth and washed her face. He raised the canteen to her lips when she came to and let her drink. He spoke soft words to her and laid her head gently on his rolled cloak. He left Trekker snuggled against her for warmth since she suffered from mild shock.

He found the soldiers' horses tied in the scrub bushes in the gully below and raided the saddlebags. He desperately hoped to find healing herbs for her head wound. He was dumbstruck when he found their horses among the soldiers' steeds. He found Lauressa's stash of herbs.

He had watched her use them, and combined with memories of Justinian's herbal lore, he made a poultice and put it on her wound, then covered it with a scarf wound around her head.

He built a fire and cooked a simple stew with food he found in the saddlebags. He managed to get her to swallow a little broth. She tried to smile and be brave, but he could tell she was in a lot of pain.

"I feel like I have a lump the size of a bird's egg." She gingerly felt her head.

"More like a fruit," he corrected with a tight grin.

"My arm," she cried when he lifted her to make it easier to sip from the cup.

"It is not broken, but it must be sprained or fractured."

"Do you know how to make a sling for it? I will walk you through it."

"No need. I have a lot of practice. I have broken and sprained a few things in my years of training."

She told him how to make tea from the herbs that would ease her pain. The tea would also settle her stomach, once the headaches were gone.

All day and the next he tended to her while praying no more soldiers headed to the fortress. He worried about the lack of food, the princess's injuries, and if other bands of soldiers were in the area. Keeping on the move was their only chance at safety.

The third day Lauressa looked better.

"My headache is less."

"You need another day of rest, and then we will go."

"I insist. We should get away from this place. It is too dangerous. Patrols will come looking for the soldiers when they do not return to their base."

He did not tell her that the last soldier—with whom he was evenly matched—had disappeared. His aim had not been fatal. He knew the man would report to the garrison and lead more soldiers here, but he feared she could not ride. Yet he had to give in to her for prudence's sake.

Lauressa was worried. They had lost too much time. She could tell that Alloryn was concerned too, though he would not say so. His expression was uneasy, and his movements were jerky. His gaze darted this way and that when he thought she was not looking.

She gritted her teeth when he hoisted her onto her horse. He led the animal at a walking pace, and she was glad of it because she was afraid she would fall off. The jouncing and bouncing made her head ache again until her stomach roiled and she called a stop.

One look at her pale face and he tied his own horse's reins to her pommel. He swung behind her and cradled her. She found that she liked the feel of his chest against her cheek and did not want to leave the safety of his arms, but she held her tongue. Now was not the time to indulge in her feelings for him. She leaned back against him and soon fell asleep.

She drifted in and out of consciousness for the next day and a half. They were near the border when he found a dry shelter from the light snow. He carried her in. She was partly awake.

The shelter was a rude abandoned hut. It had a straw pile for sleeping, and he laid her there. She waited as he gathered wood for the little fireplace and built a fire quickly to warm her. He disappeared with a bucket, and when he returned, he filled their canteens. She smiled gratefully when he held it to her lips and let her sip.

Then he gave the horses drinks from the bucket. A little lean-to would do for the horses, and if the hay wasn't fresh, it was clean.

"Trekker nosed out a small drove of wild pigs," Alloryn said. "I will use my new crossbow to kill a fat one. Will you be alright?"

"I will rest awhile. Do not worry. I will be fine."

When she awoke next, he had a roasted pig for their meal.

Once she was warm and fed, Lauressa was almost back to her perky self.

They stayed there a week until Lauressa claimed she could ride by herself. They proceeded on their way toward Zendira, the largest town on the eastern seaboard.

The dawn came early as they rode. The sky glowed a tawny yellow gold before them. The birds did not sing with the rising of the sun.

Lauressa felt uneasy. *Was a patrol in the area?*

Alloryn did not seem to notice. "I was unsure that we could outwit the soldiers—just the two of us. You were sure we could, even though we were badly outnumbered."

"I had to believe. The opposite was unthinkable. We made the right choices against unbeatable odds."

They soon realized that the sun was not shining, but a topaz gem, the gem of wisdom, hidden in the hills.

Confidence rose in their hearts.

A deep, yellow glow radiated over Mintala. Like a wave of wind over fields of wheat bends the stalks and makes them more pliable, wisdom rippled over the land.

The citizens showed a mixture of emotions—determination now joined charity for their neighbor, courage to stand up for what was right—and many other virtues. For wisdom encompasses all virtue.

Deciding the time was ripe, Odem began approaching those he felt were loyal to the crown. He arranged for them to meet in the upper room of Crown Imperial Inn. He asked them to bring others they knew were trustworthy.

When the evening of the meeting arrived, he was pleased with the number of men standing around the room. Merchants, landowners, innkeepers, and tradesmen united in their love of their country. He banged his mug on the table to get their attention. Forty men turned their eyes on him.

"Fellow citizens, I have gathered you here today for important work. The time has come to decide which side we stand on—tyranny or freedom. As we have all witnessed, the heartstones continue to reappear in the city. The return of the Reina of Valdeor is no myth, no children's fable, but an impending event." His gaze sought out every face, connecting with them.

"When the battle comes—and it will come—we in Mintala must take the city from the remnant Feornson will leave behind."

"Won't the battle be fought here?" a voice called out from

the back of the room.

"Feornson knows he is more vulnerable outside the city. Surely the stand will make a stand here," a man in the front row added.

"Friends," Odem spoke when the murmuring died down, "I have been in constant contact with Preedim, ruler of Winterhome, and they're making preparations for luring Feornson from the secure defenses of the city.

"Do you stand with me?"

A great hurrah was his answer.

Over the next weeks, Odem observed the citizens seeking to understand and accept their plight, for now. They suffered without complaint, knowing the time of their deliverance was near at hand.

On the crest of a mountain, with the Icemelt River far below and to the east, Lauressa looked over the land they had traversed for the last three weeks by caravan. The rolling hills went toward the far valley below. As the other wagons rolled by, she mused on how far they had come from the fortress. From Zendira, they had traveled through the Everlasting Winter range's steep foothills, the greatest mountains in Valdeor. The grandeur of the serrated massifs before them was awe-inspiring. The silence of the ages was like a weight upon her heart.

Although the air was thin here, they had not even reached the highest pass on their way to the northern city of Winterhome. It had been many years since she had visited. Once a summer palace for the kings of Mintala, then a major trade outpost for the mining of gems, now it was a thriving mini-kingdom of its own.

The day was cold, colder than Lauressa could remember, although it was early spring. She pulled her cloak tighter around herself. She was thankful they had stopped briefly in Zendira, the largest easternmost town, and bought heavy, warm clothing for the mountain passes.

Alloryn came riding on horseback from the front of the caravan to her wagon.

"What news?" Lauressa joined her wagon to the back of the caravan.

"We have several days' journey yet to go."

Alloryn never seemed to tire, Lauressa thought, as he sat as straight as ever in the saddle.

"Mentioning Eleedur the Hawk's name to these merchants was a brilliant idea."

She smiled at his compliment.

"Without them, we would not blend in, since Feornson's men are looking for a couple traveling alone." He drew his waterskin and offered it to her.

"And bandits are less likely to attack a larger force." She gave the waterskin back to him after taking a drink. She shivered as she remembered how they had had a more difficult time avoiding marauding bandits before joining the caravan.

"More lawless men are on the prowl, now that the Domadarians chased Bastil's soldiers from their land." Alloryn gazed about as if he expected men to jump out from behind the boulders and brush.

Lauressa absently pulled a handful of nuts from her pocket and ate them. "Then there were Feornson's men who must have abandoned the garrison after you killed so many of them at the fortress. Otherwise, we would have never found the garrison empty. I figure that since none of those men wanted to bear bad tidings to Feornson, who might kill them, they too probably roam the land, living on what they could steal from farmsteads and travelers." She offered some of the nuts to Alloryn.

In doing so, her cloak fell away and disclosed her trousered leg.

Lauressa felt self-conscious in front of Alloryn. She looked down at her manly garb. She was growing to like its comfort, but she still felt exposed. She hid her long hair under her hat, making her look like a teen boy. She did not want any undue attention when they were a few stones away from the quest's end—not with bands of soldiers searching for them.

Alloryn had shortened his name to Al for the trip's duration. She went by the male name Lorn, though most of the time she forgot to answer when called by it.

Alloryn must have sensed her sudden tenseness, so he distracted her thoughts.

"The lead merchant told me that after weeks of traveling, the caravan is nearing the second to last pass before the valley where Winterhome nestles between mountains. Winterhome is the jewel of the north, both literally and figuratively. The beautiful city rests in a wide valley, its many spires reaching for the heavens. You would be amazed to see the citizens skate or ski the streets, as horses are few."

"I know in my time the city was a bustling center, trading with all the other provinces for food, and cloth, and goods of all kinds."

"The city was also wealthy since great mines were found in the nearby mountains. Miners dug gems of all colors from deep in the earth: emeralds, rubies, and the most brilliant of diamonds."

Lauressa lowered her voice. "Legend claimed the diamond heartstone was mined here." She touched it under her clothing.

"Their most famous silversmith fashioned my medallion."

"I did not know that."

They rode in companionable silence after that.

The caravan thinly stretched out negotiating the steep, treacherous Upilon Pass when armed bandits suddenly blocked the way forward and back. Even Alloryn was unprepared. Nets dropped from the heights above onto them before he could draw his sword. They subdued and tied the whole party. Trekker alone managed to escape notice and disappeared.

The mountain men made the travelers walk before them, while they lead the horses pulling the wagons loaded with merchandise. A canyon bend widened, and they left the main trail. They made them walk all day, stopping briefly, allowing them a little to drink.

"We do not want you to die before you make the camp. Oh, no. You will wish you were dead when you break your backs working the mines." One captor laughed.

The break was short.

"Get up, you lazy dogs, and no talking." Not that they could, for the air was thin in this high mountain pass, and all felt weak. They saved their strength.

Soon they left the canyon and descended a steep path to a rough camp in a hidden valley surrounded by mighty mountains. Here they saw tired, dirty men and a few boys leaving the mines.

A big man rode up and looked them over. "Not too bad a lot." He wheeled his horse around them, inspecting them. "Get them chained together. Might as well have them relieve the regular crew as was next. They be fresher than the old lot that just finished their shift."

He addressed the prisoners directly. "I am Warlord Uthryn, and you are my prisoners. You will have the minimum clothing and food you need to do your work. Escape is impossible. You will freeze before you reach the city, which is several days' walk from here." He looked at them with a menacing smile. "Do not try to retake your horses. They are the food that will help you survive."

Meanwhile, Uthryn's crew chained the two dozen prisoners together and removed their warm cloaks and leather vests.

"Put them to work."

Lauressa shivered in the cold but kept her head down. She pulled her hat down lower over her ears. She hoped her disguise would hold.

The mine was a gaping hole in the mountainside. The rounded mount above the hole and the two ventilation shafts further up the hill gave the impression of walking into the mouth of a skull. Torches lit the tunnels. Rough-hewn walls and floor led them deeper under the mountain. After forty-five minutes they came to the tunnel end, which widened into a work area. Veins of gems glittered in the dim light. Warlord Uthryn's men pointed to pickaxes. Guards with long pikes stationed themselves at the cavern's exit, blocking the way back up the tunnel.

'Al' picked up an ax and they went to work. The smaller prisoners, including 'Lorn', used shovels to put the dirt and rubble in a wheel cart. The work was grueling. The ax strikes reverberated in the tight quarters with each blow into hard mountain stone. Lorn favored her right arm, although the shallow fracture healed since the fight in the fortress nearly six weeks ago.

Hours passed in mind-numbing labor. They were beyond exhaustion when their shift was finally over. Their captors escorted the prisoners to the rough huts above. There they chewed meager portions of food and gulped lukewarm tea, before they fell into dreamless sleep huddled in a mass on the floor for warmth.

Night and day had no meaning in the mine. As the days passed, hope seemed forlorn. Lauressa strove to keep believing there was a reason for their suffering. Toiling in a forsaken mine deep in the mountains was not what she imagined would be their next test. They were essentially slaves, with no compensation for their back-breaking labor. She understood why the surly, forsaken mountains towering above this valley were named the Mountains of No Hope.

Alloryn saw no way to overcome this hopeless situation. Lauressa was wasting away. The food was barely enough to keep them alive, and although she was no weakling, she was unused to such hard labor. On top of that, the bitter cold sapped whatever strength they had left.

Rescue was impossible. No one knew where they were, no one was even expecting them in the city. No one would miss the members of the caravan, as they lived a nomadic life with few family ties. Warlord Uthryn had the perfect setup.

Alloryn wondered what had happened to Trekker. He kept thinking he would see the dog around the camp but had not. A scrap of paper under the wolfhound's collar and a simple command could have sent the dog on a rescue mission. Alloryn would have to come up with an alternative plan.

He spent his time planning a way of escape, and when he did, he did not think Lauressa would like it. He shared it with her that night after the others fell asleep.

"Our only hope is for me to escape and go for help alone." He spoke so only she could hear.

"No. It is too risky. We must stay together."

"I know it does not sound like a good plan. I knew you would say we should not split up, but honestly, I see no other way. I must leave while I still have the strength to make it to Winterhome."

Before she could protest, he went on. "I will take the first opportunity I see to sneak away."

"Alloryn—"

"Trust me. I can bring help."

"Maybe if we bring all the prisoners into our confidence—"

"They are too weak after their prolonged stay here. The guards have the only weapons. It would be a slaughter."

By the weak firelight, he saw denial on her face, followed by concern, and then finally acceptance as he finished speaking. She knew he was right.

"I fear nothing I can say will dissuade you, by the determination in your face. You are right, it is not a good plan, but it seems like the only plan," she reluctantly agreed. She was too weak to travel so far on foot. "I always have hope in you, and hope in us as a team."

"We should not speak of it again, lest we are overheard," he cautioned.

She was silent, but when he thought she must be asleep, her voice floated out of the darkness, a mere whisper. "We must have faith. Greater than hope, we must believe that all this serves a purpose. Like the back of a woven tapestry that has many hanging threads, which make a whole pattern on the front when finished, though we cannot see it from our perspective, the One Who Fashioned All knows what the tapestry looks like when finished. We must have faith in Him."

She reached out and held his hand until they both fell asleep. He knew her well enough to understand she needed the comfort of his touch because she did not know if he would be there when she awoke.

Alloryn managed to hide some dried food in his pockets for the next few days. Better to go hungry now and have a little for later. Uthryn slaughtered some of the horses in the weeks since his men captured them, but a few horses remained. Alloryn hated to think of the others starving if he stole a horse, but without one his chances of survival were almost nothing. Winterhome was too far a walk with no food or water without a horse.

Several days after he determined to leave, Alloryn saw his chance. His shift began to enter the mine, ready to relieve the previous shift when a terrible rumble belched from the mountain entrance. In a very short time, the men above ground learned that a support beam collapsed below with a group of miners still inside. While chaos reigned and men shouted, Alloryn and the other prisoners used pickaxes to dig out the trapped miners. Once he and the strongest men shuffled with their chains to the cave-in area, instead of digging rock from the collapsed tunnel, he used his pick to break the chains connecting him to the next man in line. This was not noticed, since the choking dust clouds and uncertain light hid what he did.

The men worked hard, digging to reach their companions on the other side of the cave-in. He waited till the guards were distracted, then slipped his arm under a coughing miner who crawled from the rubble. Alloryn escorted him until they reached tunnel's end. There he gave the miner into the helping hands of the crowd, and, in the turmoil, slipped away.

He managed to sneak around to the corral to the horses with no one noticing what he did. Choosing the healthiest one he could find, he led it around a rock outcropping before mounting. He headed back to the canyon and the main trail to the city.

The snow was falling, lightly at first, then increasingly heavy with bigger flakes, as the day wore on. Lauressa helped the injured captives rescued from the cave-in. Some men had only scrapes, and others had broken limbs. The worst injuries were those who were nearest to the collapsed beam. Three men were dead.

Warlord Uthryn was more concerned with the blocked tunnel access. "We have the richest vein yet found, and now fifteen feet of rubble blocks the way. Get these men up and dig it out. Now!" he ordered the overseer.

"All you uninjured men, back with you in the tunnels." The overseer stopped at Lauressa's kneeling form.

"I am a healer. Please let me help these men," she begged.

The overseer studied her a few moments and grunted. "You seem too scrawny to make much difference below. Very well. But if they are not on their feet when Warlord Uthryn comes back, he will see them dead."

She saw him stride away, but he cast a surreptitious glance back her way. He looked at her oddly. But she soon forgot it as she used her healing skills on those who received the greatest injuries.

Lauressa checked over the injured miners that night before tumbling into bed. Fortunately, most of the men's injuries were not too serious as they had not been directly under the roof where it collapsed.

No one seemed to have noticed Alloryn missing except for her and the man chained to him, and he would not raise the alarm. As work resumed clearing the tunnel, she put shovel loads of rubble into a cart that others rolled and dumped outside. She prayed for Alloryn's safety and for the rescuers she hoped would come back with him.

As she straightened her back, easing the cramped muscles as she walked out of the tunnel into the waning light after her shift, she looked at the mountaintops surrounding the valley. She thought she caught a glimmer of deep reddish-purple. She wiped the sweat from her eyes.

The sun did not set in the north, the direction she was facing. She looked around and saw no one else paying attention.

Was a storm coming? She shivered in anticipation. The wind picked up. A blizzard in the high country would be especially dangerous for Alloryn.

She picked up her pace but nearly stumbled when she felt a warm glow from the medallion. Cupping her hands to shield it from view, she stared at the amethyst stone shining.

Hope rose in her heart as a warm tide bubbled up within her.

She stared at the mountain crest before her. The purple gem of hope flashed in the mountain before dark clouds covered it.

Alloryn's horse struggled through the snowdrifts. The snow was still swirling, but the canyon blocked the worst of the keening wind. The wind was like a wild fury trying to penetrate every corner of his being as they left the canyon for the mountain pass. The high screeching deafened him. He had no idea how he and the horse would find their way in the blinding snow, but he could not stop or they would certainly die.

They pressed on for a time, but he realized it was futile. He had to find shelter until the storm passed. His only choice was to go back to the canyon and take shelter there. He spent another hour backtracking, as he missed the turnoff the first time. He had to lead the horse on foot, feeling his way along the ice-crusted walls till he came on the opening.

He was exhausted, as was the horse. They could find no more than a rock outcrop to give them a little protection from the blizzard, but the canyon walls partially blocked the wind. He feared they would be frozen and dead by dawn, but he remembered Lauressa's whispered words to have hope, and so he sent up a silent prayer. At that moment the snow lessened, and he saw a cleft in the rock with an overhang.

He dragged himself into it. He was able to lead the horse beside him where it would aid in keeping him warm. Amazingly there was a small pile of wood for warmth. He lit a smoldering fire with the damp wood and thanked the One Who Fashioned All for hearing his humble prayers. He heated snow for water. For the first time since he left Lauressa, he had hope, and perhaps faith.

The snow stopped sometime in the early morning. After heating a little snow to make a weak tea to drink, Alloryn mounted the horse. But although he could see where he headed, the drifts were deep in areas, and he had no choice but to dismount and lead the horse until they left the canyon.

The winds had sculpted the snow in fantastical shapes and curves, and the trail was passable till they reached the main pass. There the horse made heavy work of plowing through the snow that was as high as Alloryn's boot as he sat on the horse. He eventually had to lead the horse again, shouldering through the snow the best he could.

He did not stop to eat, but munched on dried food, just enough to keep up his energy. Last night was a welcome respite, but he did not think he would be so lucky again. He had to push on while he the strength to do it.

After several days of riding, the horse finally collapsed dead. Alloryn hated to use the beast so hard, but many lives hung in the balance. He trudged on alone, tiny in a huge universe of white. He put one weary foot in front of the other, heart throbbing, and head aching with the lack of food and water. Sometimes he counted his steps, sometimes he imagined his father walked beside him. Sometimes he heard Lauressa's voice telling him, *Hurry, Alloryn, hurry. I am counting on you. We all are.*

He thought he saw a glimpse of her disappearing around

the ledge before him and tried to hurry to catch her. Rounding the corner, the world dropped away to an icy death. He caught his breath and leaned against the cliff looming beside him. He momentarily rested his weary body and blistered feet. But he was afraid if he stopped too long, he would never be able to start again.

The cold was mind-numbing, but after a while, he felt that spring had finally come for good. He wanted to yank off his cloak and soak in the sudden warmth. He did not know it was an illusion. He fell to the ground. He was near death by exposure when he saw several men on horses appear in the snow before him.

He thought he was hallucinating, till a warm tongue licked him and a dog's whine filled his ears. Hope surged in his heart. Then he drifted into the blackness that he had tried so hard to fight.

In the capital city, hope also dawned. The stones' appearance was not the startling sight it once was. The populace openly rejoiced with the coming of the fifth heartstone. Odem saw how hope filled the air. People acted as if good would prevail again. They walked around with smiles on their face and greeted neighbors cheerily.

Feornson's soldiers were the sullen ones now.

Odem's growing network of spies kept him informed at what went on within the palace.

"No word from Dukaat," reported the cook's assistant. He and Odem sat in a dim booth at the back of the Crown Imperial Tavern. "We heard from the soldiers' talk he was sent to intercept Princess Lauressa and her companions."

"The Warlord seems mighty worried, rumor has it." Odem leaned forward, his hands around his mug of ale, a frown on his face.

"Feornson is in a permanently bad mood," the cook's assistant agreed. He scraped his spoon around his bowl, eating every last bite of the stew. "Feornson snaps and barks at those around them, which works itself down the ranks. No one wants to be the one to serve him or bring him messages for fear of his taking out his anger on them. All the soldiers and servants fear him in his state of mind."

What Feornson did not know was that as his retainers, warriors, and soldiers became more dissatisfied with him, a few joined the citizens in the underground movement. Odem sat back and grinned fiercely at the thought.

Odem was more confident they would be ready to take back the city when the time was ripe.

Open rebellion had not broken out yet, because wisdom had come first, but it brewed below the surface of everyday life. Now was not the time, not until the princess declared war on Feornson.

But soon, very soon.

*T*he day after the cave-in, as Lauressa bent over the most injured miners, before her shift, the overseer came to where she was. He roughly grabbed her arm and yanked her to her feet. She hung back in alarm, but he overpowered her and dragged her from the cabin.

Uthryn stood outside the door. "What have we here?"

"He calls himself a healer, but I think he is a woman in disguise. Look at the soft hands." He thrust her hands out, palm up. Then he lifted her chin, as she stared at him defiantly. "And no facial hair, even after weeks of captivity."

And with that, he tore off her hat and her long chestnut hair billowed around her face and shoulders.

The men gathered around gasped.

Uthryn stepped close to her, so close she could smell what he last ate. She drew back as far as she could against the overseer behind her. The minor warlord put a hand to her neck and caressed her. He felt the hidden chain. With a quick flick of his hand, he yanked the medallion free for all to see.

Uthryn's leer disappeared, and he stiffened at the sight.

Oblivious, the overseer prodded, "A reward for finding her for you, O great lord?"

"Bring her to my cabin." A frown etched between his brows. The men snickered around him.

They grew silent and fell back at the sight of his menacing scowl. "No one is to touch her—" his glare focused on the overseer who stared covetously at the revealed medallion twinkling, "—nor any of her belongings."

They marched her to the warlord's private cabin tucked against the mountainside. Uthryn shut the door in the face of the curious onlookers. He narrowed his eyes and looked her over when they were alone, not as a man looks at a pretty girl, but as if he was assessing the worth of a precious gem dug from his mines.

Her gaze darted around the cabin, looking for any weapon close at hand to defend herself. She longed for Alloryn to storm through the door, sword in hand, ready to defend her honor, but he was a day's journey away. She would have to rely on herself.

At least no one has noticed Alloryn missing. Help will come. I only hope it is not too late.

Her attention returned to the present situation as Uthryn rubbed his hands together. "Yonder fools see a woman in camp after months of loneliness. I see more wealth than a month's digging when I hand you over to Feornson."

Lauressa sucked in her breath, trembling at his words.

"You see, I know who you are, Your Highness. I do occasionally travel beyond these mountains, and I have heard the strange tales of magic stones. I will be satisfied with plain gold, the gold I will get when I ransom you. Fear not for your virtue. You are the most valuable untouched."

The light streamed in briefly from outside as he opened the cabin door before she was shut in with the darkness and her thoughts. She heard him bark out orders and set guards before the door. She sank on a chair and covered her face.

Her worst fear just came true.

A bounty hunter tied Lauressa's hands together and the rope that bound them he tied to his horse's pommel. She sat as dignified as she could on her mount despite it.

"If yer try to escape, yer can walk the whole way behind my horse, girl," he threatened.

The weary hours passed slowly. They traveled south through the Upilon Pass, where the caravan had been ambushed. The tree line came in view below them.

A great cliff loomed up, named Shiprock, which rose along the path, like the brow of a ship parting the waves of trees. He diverged from the main way. Her captor led her to the cliff's base, then down a barely discernible trail leading behind the rock outcrop. Branches reached for her, snagging her hair. But she bit her tongue rather than let a sound escape. She would not give him the pleasure of jeering at her, although tears stung her eyes as some of her hair was ripped out.

The trail wound along Shiprock's edge. She held tightly to the pommel as the horse picked its way down the steep slope. She was thankful when it widened at the cliff base, weaving among the forest hills and dales.

Without the wind, she was less chilly among the trees, but snow still lay on the ground. The woods were still, with no animal or bird noises. Yet there were a few tracks of deer and smaller creatures that passed this way occasionally.

Many hours passed before the man stopped. Lauressa slid off her mount before he could lay his foul hands on her, yet her weariness caused her to stumble. She bumped into her horse and managed to stay upright. He untied her from the pommel but did not release her hands. He tied the rope around himself.

"Do not want yer escaping. Ye've quite a bounty on yer head. And I mean to collect it."

He allowed her to go to the tether's end to do her business behind a bush, affording a little privacy. Her face burned with shame at his nearness.

He made a small fire. She was glad of the return of her warm clothing in the chill evening air. She paced back and forth, stretching her legs and cramped muscles while he heated food over the flame. They ate in silence.

He let her sleep as far as the rope would allow her to go. She waited until she heard him snore, then she spent over an hour trying to slip her slim wrists through the knotted hemp. When that did not work, she tried to gnaw at the rope, but it was hopeless.

Eventually, she put herself into the hands of the One Who Fashioned All Things and prayed for Him to allow her to escape. Exhausted, she fell into a troubled sleep.

A week they spent traveling, through the forest and down the Everlasting Winter Range's southern spur. On the last day, a storm whipped up and drenched them with wind and rain. They rounded a mountain pass in the late morning and looked across a treeless plain below. A long lake stretched into the distance.

But one feature drew their gaze. High on a hill, in the center of the plain, sat a mighty fortress. Its dark granite walls jutted from the black volcanic cliff it rested on, like one continuous growth from the earth. One road led to it.

Lauressa recognized it and her heart sank.

Feornang, the stronghold of Feornson's clan.

Her imagination saw it as a black bird of prey, waiting to get its claws into her.

Any hope that Alloryn might rescue her before their arrival evaporated.

As they neared the fortress in the early afternoon, she saw the drawbridge was up and the portcullis was down. Soldiers watched from the crenellations. The smirking, jeering soldiers made Lauressa cringe inside, but she showed no fear in front of them, keeping her gaze straight ahead. The drawbridge lowered after her captor identified himself to the watchman. The horses' hooves made a heavy sound as they clopped across.

They beat out a sound of doom.

The rain slashed at her, driving strands of hair across her face. The portcullis screeched and groaned as it lifted in the air.

O Father Who Fashioned All Things, why have you brought me here? The medallion pressed against her bosom as her answer.

Light spilled from the massive front door of the keep. Her captor led her horse to the steps leading to it. She managed to slip off before he could help her. He slit her bonds with a knife, and she rubbed her raw wrists.

The bounty hunter left to receive his reward as guards surrounded her.

A servant scurried down the steps. "This way, Your

Exaltedness," he wheezed. The bright light after the storm's darkness dazzled her eyes. She faced a huge fireplace, ablaze. Instruments of war hung all around the hall, in between moth-eaten tapestries. She could see the servant better in the firelight of the Great Hall. He was a wizened old man, toothless and bent.

"I am Omek. Welcome to your new home." His eyes twinkled slyly. "A room stands ready for you, quite the finest in the castle, except for my master's." He led her up a massive stone stair, escorted by two guards. At the top, he led her through a cold corridor hung with many shields. He opened a door with a flourish. Warm air rushed to meet her. The furnishing was oversized and dark, but the fire was welcome.

"I will send a servant with hot water so you may bathe. Unfortunately, my master is not here at the moment, so you will forgive me if I send your dinner to your room." He smirked and pretended to be solicitous for her comfort.

She sighed with relief when he left. She heard the door lock click behind him. She did not doubt that this room was her prison, but at least she would have a bath, the first in many weeks. She would find a way to escape, but for now, she would face one thing at a time.

Two young men brought in a bath and several others filled it with hot water. She was glad to see they also deposited her saddlebag. She rooted in it and found a yarrow salve to soothe her chafed wrists. As soon as the door clicked behind them, she sank in the water and washed away the grime and dust of travel. She put on a fresh dress from her saddlebag. There was no use trying to pass as a boy anymore.

She rubbed on the salve and peered out the single window. The drop to the courtyard was dizzying.

The same servants removed the bath and delivered her dinner. The simple stew's aroma stirred hunger within her. She savored each bite, dipping in her piece of bread at the last to scrape the bowl clean.

Finished, she sat before the fire. She would have to plan an escape. She would start by saying she needed exercise. The better she knew the castle's layout, the better the chance of leaving it when the time came. She pushed away despairing thoughts of the futileness of trying to escape into an unknown wilderness, alone. She knew Alloryn would seek her, but she could not wait for him. He did not know where she was, and even if he figured where she was, he did not have an army to lead against the fortress.

She must find a way to leave before Feornson came.

She clutched her medallion. *I won the virtue of hope stone. Now I must continue to practice hope.*

Her days settled into a routine. She was allowed to stretch her legs, under a guard, of course, twice a day, morn and eve. She ignored the soldiers' leers and jests as she roamed around the inner courtyard. She had more knowledge of her prison than before, but not the lay of the land beyond the walls.

Today she would try a new strategy. The guard who accompanied her on her daily exercise was disinterested, rather than vigilant. The others, used to the sight of her, paid her little mind.

She turned and directly spoke to him. "Can we not vary the walk? I have seen nothing but black stone walls for two weeks. I long for the sight of a tree, grass, anything green."

He looked at her as if a stone had spoken. After a moment, he led her toward a stone stair that climbed to the battlements.

She followed eagerly, then modified her pace. No need to seem anxious. She slowed to a casual stroll.

The slippery steps needed all her attention. She placed her right hand against the wall, for the left was a sheer drop to the courtyard with no handholds. Her calves ached, then she was on the catwalk among the crenellations. Her guard spoke to the men stationed nearby, paying her no mind. She soon saw why.

Three hundred feet below her was the lake. The fortress stood on a bluff beneath her. She held to the stone edge and looked away from the dizzying drop. The plain spread out in the other direction then sloped to the steep mountains she traveled to get here. A formidable barrier encircled the fortress from the rest of the world. Snow covered the valley floor, not deep, but deep enough that anyone escaping would leave an easy trail to follow.

Escape seemed impossible.

O, Alloryn, where are you?

As she gazed as far as she could, movement caught her eye. An entourage came from around the lake edge. A horn sounded from the riders below and an answering horn blew its notes from the wall where she stood.

As they came closer, she saw a large, wide-shouldered man on the leading horse. He did not wear a helm, and his shoulder-length hair blew in the crisp breeze. He had a red, braided beard and rode the biggest horse she ever saw.

Her heart sank, and her knees trembled. She guessed he was Feornson, the bear returning to his lair.

Later that evening, Lauressa followed the old servant and

guards with great trepidation to the dining hall where Feornson sat, but outwardly she showed her usual calm demeanor. She called upon her regal heritage and wrapped it around herself like a cloak.

"Princess Lauressa, we meet at last. Please, join me." Feornson gestured to another seat from where he sat at the head of the table.

She straightened her spine and would not even look at him. The old servant grasped her arm in his claw and forcibly led her to the table. He was surprisingly strong. He roughly pushed her in a chair.

"I thought you might have better manners. No matter. You will learn."

"I have nothing to say to you." She stared at a wall sconce over his left shoulder.

"But we must discuss our wedding plans."

Her eyes snapped involuntarily to his face.

He was tall, his presence filled the room. His red beard came to a neat point. He wore a black leather vest over his shirt. His face wore a permanent frown over thick eyebrows. But his eyes held her—deep and intense with the force of his will.

"A true marriage consists of the consent of both parties. You will never have my consent. And if you marry me under duress, it will not be valid under the law." She sat ramrod straight and projected regal disapproval.

"You forget, I am the law of the land. Who will dispute me? Stepan does not have an army equal to mine. I know he backs you. But I would not count on Xander if I were you. He knows not to cross me. And he likes to be on the winning side." Feornson took a swig of ale and wiped his mouth with the back of his hand.

"Although both men would like to see their sons on the throne, they were too weak to force you when they had the chance. I have no scruples doing so." He sat back in his chair and placed his hands over his stomach, burping.

"You have no chance of escape this time, Your Highness."

She looked at him with loathing but did not argue back.

"I sent for a priest, so we shall soon have all we need."

Lauressa's heart raced and sweat formed on the palms of her hands. She found it hard to breathe normally, such a heavy weight was on her heart. She shivered in despair at his words.

"But one thing lacks. You have to tell me where the last heartstone resides. With it, our subjects will accept my rule. Tell me where it is."

"I do not know where the stone of faith is, and if I did, I would not tell you."

"Surely you know I can send you to the dungeon and have my torturer squeeze it out of you? Must we resort to such means?"

He changed tactics when he sensed she was intractable. He gave what she assumed he thought was a tender smile. "Let us be friends. We can rule jointly. The stone is a symbol that would soothe the masses."

When she did not reply, he became angry, showing his true self. He smashed his fist down on the table, making the crockware jump. "Omek! Omek, come in here this instant!"

The old servant, who had been the first to greet her, opened the door and shuffled across to his master.

"Show the high and mighty princess her new room in the dungeon." He turned to her. "Sleep on my proposal, if you can stomach the cries of the doomed in my dungeons." He flung out a meaty fist. "Away with her!"

Lauressa yanked her arm from the manservant and walked with a straight spine to the Great Hall. Two sentries took his place and marched her down steep steps, Omek holding a torch to light their way.

Her ability to escape dwindled with every step.

The procession wound around a spiral staircase, the torch flickering, casting weird shadows. The guards followed right behind Lauressa, preventing any escape. They traversed three flights, then reached a heavy, wooden door. At a knock, a soldier opened it. His gaze raked over the new prisoner.

"Our master's orders are she is to be kept unharmed," the servant Omek told the prison warden. Then he and his light disappeared back up the staircase, the upper-level guards following.

"Now the master imprisons pretty maids. 'Tis better to do the master's will than to be sent here," the jailer admonished her.

He led her past cell doors through a dank hallway carved from stone. The place smelled of must and mold and human occupation. Water seeped through the walls. Cries and moans met her ears. At last, the warden opened an unoccupied cell, grabbed her elbow, and thrust her in.

She saw a small, square cell with some old, moldy straw on the floor before he closed the door, and his lantern retreated the way they came. She stumbled across the room and sank on the cold, hard floor. She put her head on her drawn-up knees. Her courage fled, and hope with it. She gave in freely to the tears and sobs that she held back before her captors. Her hope for escape vanished in such a place. She doubted she could ask for exercise in the fresh air anymore.

Did Alloryn even know where she was? Even if he did, he could not penetrate Feornang, no matter how good a swordsman he was.

After a while, she dried her tears and lifted her heart in prayer to the All-Seeing Father. *You know how hopeless my situation is. How truly dependent I am on You. Please guide Alloryn to rescue me. Let not your enemy Feornson prevail. Thy will be done.*

Peace descended upon her. She determined to think of a plan. She would pray for inspiration. She would be ready to play her part when the time came. Maybe she could not climb out a window, but she would not depend solely on others to come to her aid. She would seize any opportunity to free herself. But for now, she would be patient and have faith. She would not believe she lived this long to die in a dirty dungeon.

In the wee night hours, Lauressa formed a plan—not the best plan—but maybe it would buy her time. By now Alloryn had reached Winterhome. He needed time to raise an army to defeat Feornson. The Winterhome province was a notorious enemy of the Warlord. If Alloryn could raise an army, Feornson would leave and meet them on the battlefield, and she knew her champion could best him. His faithfulness would not let him fail her. Her job was to delay her marriage to the Warlord. She prayed her plan might work and drifted asleep.

She awoke hungry. She waited for hours before she heard footsteps coming along the hall. Light shone around the edges of her door. She held her breath, wondering if Feornson sent his servant for her answer. Instead, the jailer opened the door, put down a tray, and pushed it in with his boot. She eagerly scuttled across the floor and pulled the bread and jug of water toward her as the door swung shut, and with it, the light disappeared. She ate and drank by feel alone.

When done, she stood, and briskly brushed off any lingering crumbs, afraid of attracting bugs or rodents onto her clothing. She extended her arms and blindly walked till she was against the far wall. She made multiple trips around her cell until she wore herself out, then she again crouched against the cold wall.

Later the same day—at least she guessed it was the same day—she heard Omek's voice outside her cell. She squared her shoulders, ready to do battle. Then remembering that she should look afraid, she slouched, as if she was willing to comply with Feornson's will.

The torchlight blinded her after the total darkness. A cackle greeted her. "O, how the mighty have fallen! Are you ready to heed my master and yours?"

With her hand before her face, she squinted at the hunched man. "I am if it means I can leave this foul place!"

"Come. But do not try my master's patience." He led her back up the spiral staircase to the Great Hall.

Feornson sat before the fire in a wooden chair with a high back and carved armrests in the shape of bear claws. In his black clothes, beard unbraided and bushy, he looked like a bear himself. As she approached him, his gaze slowly took in her bedraggled appearance. "Are you ready to see reason, girl?"

She nodded "yes" and hung her head. She suppressed her

desire to tell him what she thought, and forced her hands to unclench, and held them behind her back where they would not betray her true feelings.

"Then tell me where the next stone is."

"Warlord Uthryn did not send me to you with a map." It was not a lie, though the whole truth was that she had never had a map. But Feornson was not to know that. "But I know where a map is, and men who can read it."

"I have no use for maps. I want that stone."

"I know where all the other stones were found. With this map, I can see the pattern of dispersal and pinpoint the next stone of virtue."

"Where is this map?"

"In the former Warlord Bastil's archives, in the Forestown castle."

"In the Domadarian Forest? Why that is weeks away. That will never do."

She tried another tactic. "But it is such an excellent map, exactly to scale, with exquisite detail. Towns, big and small, mountain passes, river fords. Why it would help in planning your army's movement in putting down a rebellion, should anyone question your right to rule after we are married." She figured he did not have such a tool, and it might tempt him and buy her time.

He scrunched his brow as he considered it. She held her breath.

"This had better not be a tactic to delay me." He wagged his finger at her. "Very well, I'll send my courier for it."

She hoped Feornson would not get a chance to use this information against her or her army in the future. But that was a risk she was willing to take.

Anything to give Alloryn time to find and rescue her.

17 WINTERHOME

Alloryn awoke in a soft bed. He was in a beautiful room full of fine furniture and lush fabric. He sat up. Trekker was on the floor by his bed. The dog thumped his tail.

A man in Winterhome livery of royal blue got up from his place in a nearby chair gave him a drink of water, then went to the door and spoke to someone outside. He came back to the bed and said, "I have sent for food, and alerted my master that you are awake."

After the servant fed him a bowl of soup, Alloryn drifted to sleep again. He felt as weak as a newborn.

He awoke to a man dressed in rich silks standing by the doorway. After dismissing the servant, the man came to sit by Alloryn's bed. "So you are back with the living. Fear not, you are among friends. I am Preedim, Prince of Winterhome."

"I am Alloryn. How did I get here? The last thing I remember was falling in the snow when the spring thaw came."

"That was no spring thaw. When one is nearly frozen, he experiences an odd sensation of being suddenly warm. Many die from removing their outer clothes when this happens.

Fortunately for you, your dog made it to the city. His sudden appearance, alone on the trails, alerted my men that something untoward had happened. Did you get separated from a group or were you traveling alone?"

"I came with a caravan of merchants. We were near the Upilon Pass when ruffians set upon us and forced us to work in the Mountains of No Hope mines."

Alloryn hesitated to say more. Could he trust the prince, or was he in league with the Warlord Uthryn?

"Many bandits live and raid unsuspecting wayfarers in these mountains. I try to stamp them out, but they are mountain men who know the canyons and valleys better than my men do. I will send scouts to try to find your caravan."

Alloryn asked if he could come along. "We will see," was the answer. "You are far from recovered."

He pushed himself to sit up and even tried standing when Preedim left. But he sat back on the edge of his bed, fighting waves of dizziness.

All he could do was wait. Lauressa's rescue was out of his hands. How could he claim the title of a champion when he failed her and left her behind? His job was protecting her. He would put all his effort into a quick recovery. But waiting was very hard when he was itching to act and fight.

After a few more days of gaining his strength, Alloryn received the doctor's approval to leave his room. He commanded Trekker to stay behind. He explored and found the Great Hall. A contingent of men was readying themselves for the rescue.

Preedim spotted him and called him over. "My men are prepared to go back to where they first found your dog on patrol, and where your dog found you, and scour the area for the bandits you spoke of."

"They are dangerous. Their leader claims to be a warlord named Uthryn. Have you heard of him?"

Preedim had an odd look on his face at the news. The whole room became silent, as all the men froze at the warlord's name.

"Yes, I have. I hoped he was dead." Preedim's posture stiffened. "He is my brother."

Alloryn stared.

"I wrested this province away from him a decade ago. He was cruel, sacrificing men to the mines at an alarming rate to get rich. I hoped he had died in our last encounter." He paced around the hall when he finished speaking. No one dared to interrupt his thoughts.

He stopped in front of Alloryn. "You need to tell us everything you know of where you were held. How many men he has, where he posted the sentries, anything that will help us defeat him."

"I can do that." Alloryn smiled a grim smile. But he left Lauressa's presence a secret.

Alloryn joined Preedim's handpicked force. Soon they would rescue the princess, or Uthryn would pay with his life.

From his vantage point on the mountainside, Alloryn could see the camp he left nearly two weeks. One hundred soldiers, wearing white to blend in with the snow, scattered behind rocks around the valley.

The plan was simple. After stationing the main force above

the camp, Preedim himself led a small band of men through the canyon. Alloryn and the others waited for Warlord Uthryn's men to capture Preedim and his men and bring them into the camp. They would wait for the prince's signal, then attack.

Uthryn's scouts led the captured party to the main camp.

Warlord Uthryn rode up to gloat over the new additions to his workforce. He jerked his horse to a sudden stop when the lead man threw off his hood and stared at him.

"Preedim! Why, by all that is holy, I caught the fox leaving his lair. On a little hunting trip? It looks like you are the hunted this time." He guffawed with mirth at his joke.

Alloryn motioned to the men around him. Preedim lowering his hood was the signal for which they waited. With all watching the two brothers, it was time for them to descend into the valley.

"I thought you were dead," Preedim answered.

"I am harder to kill than you think, little brother. But we will see how you fare in the mines." The big man taunted him.

As Uthryn's men reached to pull Preedim off his horse, he drew his hidden blade and struck the nearest bandit. Unknown to Uthryn, Preedim's men had disarmed the six bandits that tried to capture them in the canyon and taken their place. Wearing the bandits' garb, they had kept their heads down till now, pretending to lead Preedim and his men into the valley.

Now they and the so-called 'prisoners' drew their swords, revealing the mail worn beneath their cloaks, and fought Uthryn's men. Preedim rode his horse straight into Uthryn's and engaged his brother in a deadly battle.

White-clad soldiers crept behind the sentries, grabbed them by the neck, and silenced them forever. Alloryn crouched close to the ground, headed to the main housing. Dozens of others following his lead took strategic positions around the camp.

He wanted to make sure Lauressa was safe before the fighting began. He did not want her to be a hostage again. But she was not in the buildings, which meant she was underground in the mines. He would have to reach her before the guards in the tunnels learned what was happening on the surface. He headed that way.

Alloryn flattened himself against the entrance to the mine. One guard lay on the ground at his feet, never knowing what had hit him. The white-clad soldiers joined the fray behind him. He knew he must disable the guards inside the mine before they became aware of the surface fight. He feared they would take hostages, Lauressa included. He bent and removed the guard's outer garment and put it on, shedding his white cloak now that it had served its purpose to shield his form in the snow.

He stepped into the mine tunnel, taking a lantern to guide his steps. He pulled the shade over the lantern light so that the light went downward, not illuminating his face. He gripped a pike in his hand, rather than his sword since that was the guards' weapon of choice.

His footfalls echoed in the eerie silence. After he walked a quarter of a league, he heard the pickaxes' regular rhythm in the distance. He dimmed the light, and sure enough, there was a glow ahead, so he snuffed out the lantern and set it along the wall.

Around the next bend, he came across a guard who was taking a drink from a pail. Alloryn walked right up behind him, his feet as silent as a cat. At the last second, the man sensed his presence, but before he could fully turn around, Alloryn struck his temple with the pike. He dragged the body back around the corner.

Taking the pail and dipper, he boldly walked across the wide man-made cavern toward the pair of guards watching over a group of men. The guards paid him no mind, assuming he was one of them.

"Here, Sam. I could use a long pull of that water," one said when they finally spotted him.

Before he was close enough for them to see his unfamiliar face, he swung the pail and let it sail toward one guard. While using the pike as a staff, he hit the second man in the wrist as he brought his pike up. Spinning on his heel, he stabbed the first man with the pike tip, leveraged the other end and knocked the second man under his chin with the handle.

The fight was over so fast that the men laboring in the mine barely realized that their guards were under attack. Someone shouted, and they all turned around, stunned to see they were free.

Alloryn rallied a dozen men, who joined him, to go further into the mine to rescue the other captives. Two strong men grabbed the guards' whips, and two more took their pikes. The majority held deadly pickaxes, and the rest had shovels. They went into the deeper tunnels leading to the main dig site, grim and determined.

The number and strength of Warlord Uthryn's men were not what kept the captives from escaping, but the impassable mountains, trackless lands, and unpredictable snows.

Preedim's men easily outnumbered Uthryn's hirelings, but they fought back with cunning and strength. These were mountain men and miners, used to harsh conditions, able to wield an ax, pike, and mace. They did have one weakness, though—they depended on slave labor for so long that they were not as hale as they once had been when they mined the mountains themselves for the gems. The soldiers of Winterhome soon overcame their foes, who eventually surrendered.

Prisoners shuffled out of the bare cabins and cheered the Winterhome contingent.

All stood around, starving captives, veteran soldiers, and hardened slavers, as the two mighty leaders clashed in their midst. Word soon circled that they witnessed brother fighting brother.

Preedim and Uthryn were well matched. Uthryn was bigger, but Preedim was more agile.

Uthryn unseated his brother from his horse. Rolling over, Preedim gained his feet quickly, but Uthryn's horse nearly trampled him. With mere seconds, he managed to escape. He grabbed a mace from the battleground and flung it as his brother's head. Uthryn ducked, but the glancing blow unbalanced him, and he hit the ground.

Men gasped and moved out of the way.

The brothers fought on foot, lunging and ducking, Uthryn with a sword and Preedim with a sword in one hand and a pike in the other, oblivious of the crowd watching them.

No one could be sure of the outcome of the match.

Alloryn and his band of freed prisoners tackled all the guards they met. They hid behind boulders in the area of the recent collapsed roof, overlooking the group of twelve guards in the last tunnel. Fifty captives worked with pickaxes on a new vein of diamonds. Closer to them, another twenty used shovels to put the dirt in handcarts. Ten men wheeled the handcarts to a flatbed cart. Beasts of burden were ready to pull it to the surface when it was full.

Alloryn saw a slim figure near the handcarts. He crawled backward from his position, took a pail, and used the same ruse he did earlier. He boldly stepped from the shadows and walked with the water pail toward the nearest group of guards, who hailed him, jokingly.

Alloryn reached the group, but unfortunately, the overseer was among them. Recognizing Alloryn, he raised his pike and stepped to meet him. "You, there. Stop!" he cried. At that moment, well-aimed rocks flew through the air, many hitting their targets. The freed prisoners then jumped up from their hiding places, lobbing more rocks, lifting their weapons, racing to engage the stunned enemy.

In an instant, all pandemonium broke loose. Seeing their freedom at hand, the mine workers joined those coming to their rescue. Ninety plus men soon overcame Uthryn's twelve, who seeing the odds, soon surrendered.

"Come!" Alloryn called to the slim shape, but when he grasped an arm, a stranger's face looked back at him. The boy mirrored his surprise. Alloryn gasped and looked around.

All were free now, but there was no sign of Lauressa.

A dire foreboding filled his heart.

Alloryn climbed aboard the cart's seat and took the reins.

They tied the last guard up, and he whipped the unsuspecting beasts, who leaped forward. "Everyone aboard!" Many of the men climbed on the half-filled flatbed. They rode out of the mine, ready to fight for freedom. The rest forced the guards on foot in front of them, poking them with the pikes if they did not keep pace.

Reaching the surface, Alloryn saw Preedim lose his pike to Uthryn's slashing sword. As Uthryn came closer to his brother to strike the finishing blow, Preedim slipped under his guard, held Uthryn's sword arm, and put his sword to Uthryn's panting throat. Uthryn slipped a deadly looking dagger from under his left sleeve and thrust it into Preedim's side. But Preedim moved at the last second.

Alloryn was ready to join the combat. *But this fight belongs to them.* With reluctance, he held himself still and watched.

Preedim slashed the arm with the dagger, while Uthryn's right sword hand tried to force Preedim's sword from his throat. While his concentration was thus employed, Preedim stepped back a half step and kicked Uthryn's shin. The bigger man lost his grip, Preedim twisted their locked hilts and spun away. He slashed Uthryn's back, who fell on his dagger.

Preedim stood for a long moment and stared as his dead brother. Then dropping his sword point to the ground, he glanced around and saw his men had taken the camp.

Preedim's men and those Alloryn freed from the tunnels joined forces and buried their dead. The enemy they heaped up for the carrion to pick over.

Troops stashed a load of diamond ore on the flatbed in the tunnels for later retrieval. Then they readied the long cart, used to bring the ore out, as a transport to bring the injured to Winterhome.

"My friend, why the long face? We have won this round." Preedim chided as he joined Alloryn, who was leaning against the cart.

"The Princess is not here."

"Princess?" Preedim's open expression showed surprise, then he frowned at him. "Do not tell me you are referring to Princess Lauressa?" His voice grew serious.

One look at Alloryn's face and Alloryn saw Preedim knew the truth.

"I have heard recent tales. Then you are her champion?" Preedim did not wait for an answer but crossed his arms over his chest. "I think you have been less than honest with me."

Alloryn straightened. "I was about to tell you before we left Winterhome when you said you were Uthryn's brother. Her disguise is all that stands between her and capture." He rubbed a tired hand across his brow. "But no need for secrecy now. The rescued men I spoke with say Uthryn discovered her identity. She is beyond our reach in Feornson's stronghold by now. If only I had not left her. If only I was able to take her with me."

Preedim paced with his hands behind his back. "You did your best to bring aid to her, and the others enslaved. Do not be hard on yourself. No man can predict the future. 'If only I had done this or that' will draw you into a well of regret."

"I must go after her. Maybe I can still catch them."

"'Tis better if you come back with us to Winterhome. You must have a plan before you race off to her rescue." The prince stopped in front of him. "A single man cannot stand against the fortress of Feornang, just as you could not vanquish this group without our help."

Alloryn did not like it, but he agreed with Preedim's assessment. He needed a plan.

ishing with all his heart that he could leave on his own and rescue Lauressa, Alloryn leaned on the balustrade of a balcony in Winterhome and watched the preparation for war below.

He had trained for this moment! Was not one man better than an army when it came to sneaking into a castle or fortress, as he did in Forestown? Yet retrieving Lauressa was one battle in this war. Reports came in daily that an army converged on Feornang. *Would not stopping this army before they were ready serve the princess's plan?* He had to choose between love and duty. A hard choice.

"You alone must decide if you will rescue the princess or join my army to battle Feornson on his turf. I do not envy you," Preedim said as he joined him.

"Lauressa was taken nearly three weeks ago. If only I had stayed, she may not have been discovered." His knuckles whitened as he gripped the rail.

"'If' is a path that leads you on a downward spiral. Do not blame yourself. It leads nowhere, it saps your confidence, and makes you second guess all your further decisions." Preedim bowed his head. "I share in the blame. If only I had defeated Uthryn years ago, this would not have happened. But it has. And we both share in the knowledge that our decisions have brought us to this point. The question is, what will you do now?"

Heart's desire, or head's reason? Love or duty?

Alloryn thought of what Estrell—or Justinian, as Lauressa referred to him—would have told him. What Lauressa herself would tell him. His heart and his gut warred. He knew what he had to do, which was not what he wanted to do.

He made his decision. Lauressa and Justinian's voices urging him on the right path quieted in his mind. He felt at peace. He turned away from the balcony and gripped his sword hilt. "I will join you and your army at Feornson's doorstep, Sire, if you will have me. You have been right all along, but I let my pride get in the way. I cannot do this alone."

"Good man." Preedim gestured for Alloryn to follow him. "Come, I have called together my generals and allies. Time to discuss strategy." He led the way through the palace.

The newly convened war council met in the palace's Great Hall. As Preedim preceded to call for order, the chief of the house guards burst in. "Your Highness," the man interrupted, "new messengers have arrived with important news." He ushered in a breathless man with dirty boots.

"Another army is gathering, Your Highness." A gasp of concern went around the room. Before any ventured to ask who else was assembling to fight them, the man continued. "I saw a host of many men from different provinces gathering in the plains west of here. Fierce men were wearing horned helmets and other men wearing bright robes of southerners. The two hosts met, and after seeming deliberations, camped together."

Talk erupted around the room as he finished his report.

"Send my best spies to ascertain who they are and what side they are on," the prince ordered his second-in-command.

Not long afterward the same house guard escorted in another messenger. "Sire, more bad news."

"Speak, man, and let us hear the worst," the prince commanded the new messenger.

"Your Highness, I saw several bands of men in the southeastern plains heading this way. They are within a day's journey of each other, and several days from here. The forest men in green march, carrying longbows. Others carrying farm implements come from the east. I do not know what to make of it, but Winterhome seems to be their destination."

More voices raised in concern, and demands for assembling the army quickly, drowned the messenger's last words.

Alloryn pulled the two messengers aside for a hurried conversation. Preedim called for silence, and Alloryn beckoned to him before the others burst into speech. "Sire, I believe there may be no need for concern. We traveled this land from end to end over a year. Princess Lauressa made many allies. Let us see what tidings your spies can bring us if these are enemies at all."

Waiting for the hosts to arrive made Alloryn restless, and the walls seemed to press in on him. He strode around the inner courtyard when his gaze alit on a teenager, a few years younger than himself, fighting in the training yard. He fought with a curved scimitar. Alloryn stopped to watch. The young man showed a superior technique. He was easily winning the fight with the older swordsman.

They stopped and the younger man looked his way and spoke. "I have not seen you before. I see you carry a sword. Are you another challenger?" He wiped the sweat from his brow with a towel, then waved his servant away. "No one beats me in a fight, although men love to try. It gets old after a while."

Alloryn did not like his tone. He longed to teach this braggart a lesson. "Aye, I will fight you." Unbuckling his scabbard, he laid it down and hefted a wooden sword.

"What? Are you so poor a fighter that you fear to use a real sword against me?"

Alloryn felt his hackles rise. "You need to be taught a lesson." He clasped the wooden sword tightly in anger and strode to meet his opponent.

They slowly circled each other.

"I will teach you a lesson, easterner." And with a cry, the young man was upon him. He was strong and nimble. In no time, Alloryn found himself leaving behind the thought of quickly besting this boy. Here was a worthy opponent.

Swords clashed, both men panting, putting everything they had into it. Lunge, duck, parry, circle around the enemy. A complicated dance between the two swordmasters soon attracted the idle men standing around the courtyard to watch the contest.

Alloryn was not even aware of the crowd, so intent was he on trying to keep the upper hand. The younger man pinked him, and he was so surprised at the trickle of blood that he nearly stopped fighting.

"Call craven?" the teen taunted.

"Never."

"Your Highness," the chamberlain came hurriedly. "Your father, Prince Xander, wishes to speak with you. Now."

"Till we meet next time, easterner." And the young prince strode away.

Alloryn stared after him. *Wait. He was a prince? Why did he not make that clear earlier? My reputation would have been ruined had I injured him. Not that he did not deserve it, the cock robin.*

The prince's first contender clapped a hand on Alloryn's back. "You gave him a better workout than I. But beware, Prince Gensard does not like to lose. I have never seen his match, until today."

Alone, he did not feel cheered by the words. *I feel like a failure. It's my fault Feornson captured Lauressa. And now I let a young prince nearly beat me. He probably would have if the chamberlain had not stopped us. Who is the Champion of Valdeor? Not me, not now.*

One of Preedim's generals called to him from the door to the palace. "Prince Preedim desires your presence."

"What news?" Alloryn walked with him down the palace halls.

"A letter has come from his spy in the capital. He wants all to gather for an important announcement."

Preedim acknowledged them with a grim smile on his face before addressing the assembled war council. "We have news that Feornson is no longer in Mintala. He is holed up in his fortress, Feornang, two weeks' march from here."

Restlessness ramped up to keen anticipation for Alloryn. The moment drew ever nearer to face his enemy.

Tense days of waiting ended as emissaries came from all corners of Valdeor carrying the white flags of truce. In the plains south of the city they erected a tent. Prince Preedim met with the leaders who agreed to come weaponless to the first meeting.

Alloryn headed for the royal tent. As he neared it, Gensard stepped in his path. The prince looked him over from head to foot. Although his clothes were clean thanks to the palace servants, he could not match the prince's finery. Even Gensard's boots reflected like a mirror.

"This is official business. Yokels are not welcome." Gensard flourished his dagger.

Alloryn clenched his teeth and looked at him with half-closed eyes. But before they could continue their interrupted fight, Eleedur, the caravan leader, stepped between them. "Alloryn, my friend. It is good to see you." His grin turned somber. "Fear not, we will rescue your princess. That is why we have come. Together we will storm Mintala and defeat Feornson. The Guardians of Valdeor are on our side."

Gensard gave Alloryn an odd look and opened his mouth to say something more. He changed his mind, frowned, and joined his father, Prince Xander of Samarantha as he went into the meeting.

Entering the tent, Alloryn looked for Preedim and found many familiar faces turned toward him. Besides Eleedur there were King Stepan and his twin sons, the fierce Marjek Red Horns, and Rappallo. Alloryn greeted Nathum the nomad and clapped a friendly hand on Talud's shoulder.

Seeing so many friends was overwhelming. "My friends,

you are a welcome sight. What can I say other than thank you?"

"You helped us in our direst need." Nathum grasped his hand and spoke for them all. "We can repay you no less." The others agreed loudly.

After introductions all around, Prince Preedim addressed those gathered. "It is time to have a council of war, my friends. You have arrived at a crucial hour in our history. The latest report says Feornson is gathering his forces. We must have a plan to defeat him." And they sat to discuss the freeing of Valdeor from tyranny.

After two days of deliberation, there followed a week of preparation. The armies merged into one fighting host, with many units. Each unit brought their fighting style, so the war council devised a plan utilizing their unique talents to the best advantage. The Domadarians were the best archers, so they would be the leading edge. The fearless Winterhome soldiers were the best trained, so they would be the main army, front and center, led by Preedim's son Everard. The desert nomads and the Samaranthans would be the left and right flanks. The farmers would be the rear guard.

Several fierce Nyrmidions had the job of sailing down the Icemelt River, which flowed into the heart of Mintala. They would secure the city, and Rappallo and his men would go with them, as their faces were well known, and they could reassure the good inhabitants of the city that they were not under attack.

Preedim would ride with the main army as the supreme commander. Stepan would lead the Domadarian forces with Talud as his second. Tris would ride with Alloryn, who would lead the scouts.

The princess's allies, combined into one army, were on the march. They rode for two days from the plain before Winterhome in the Everlasting Mountains into its southern foothills.

Alloryn hated to leave Trekker behind, but a battle between armies was no place for his dog, as much of a fighter as he was. The base camp guards could use him on their patrols, so Alloryn turned over his leash to them. Giving the dog one last rub, he told him to obey.

In the evening, he walked among the men assigned to him and listened to snippets of their chatter.

"Try this salve to help the blisters."

"My dog would not drink your coffee."

"Did you see those Nyrmidions before they left? Gave me the chills, they did."

"Me, too. I have heard they put prisoners in cages high in the air—"

"At last, I can see how well the old man taught you to wield a sword," a voice spoke directly beside Alloryn. He spun around and was amazed to find Rodrek, with whom he had played swordsman, among his contingent.

"Roddy! By my sword, I never expected to see you again." Alloryn clapped him on the back.

"That I can believe. Do you remember how you were so anxious back then to learn swordsmanship? And look at you now." Roddy grinned.

"A boy has dreams," he answered, "and little does he understand the reality of fighting—the death and destruction."

Alloryn pulled his gaze back to his friend. "But you never

wanted a part of it. So, what brings you here?"

"You left after building our house, but you put the desire to fight in my heart. After Granny died, I could not go back to the dull existence of a farmer, so I sold the land and went roving." Rodrek patted the sword hilt at his hip. "I learned to wield a sword quite well if I say so myself."

"Ah, humble as ever, I see." He grew serious as a line of men with bows slung over their shoulders passed by. "We will both soon be put to the test."

Rodrek put his hand in his pocket and pulled out an apple. As he fell in step with Alloryn, he said, "So, you found your princess after all. What is she, about one hundred and fifty years old?" He grinned. "Is she cranky? Did she order you around? 'Alloryn, slow down. I cannot keep up with a mountain goat. Alloryn, fetch me a shawl, I am cold. Alloryn, my gums cannot chew this jerky. Make me a nice bowl of soup.'" Rodrek parodied a girl's high-pitched voice. "My Gran got real crotchety near the end." He bit into the apple.

"No, she is nothing like that. She has not aged in one hundred years. She is kind, and brave, and never complains," Alloryn rubbed his hand through his hair. "I left her behind. I thought I could save her on my own. And now she is lost to me."

"Oh, so that is how it is. She must be a beauty," Rodrek gave a cheeky grin between bites.

"It is not like that," Alloryn faced Rodrek, his hands on his hips. "I am responsible for her. I failed."

"You always were too hard on yourself." Rodrek tossed the apple core away and wiped his hands on his pants. "But if she were old and ugly, you would not be fretting so much, now would you?" He threw out an arm and swept it around, "After all, here is an army to find and champion her."

Alloryn felt the heat rise from his neck to his forehead. Rodrek's penetrating gaze saw through him. "All right, it is that way, for me at least." He crossed his arms over his chest. "But she is a princess, and I am nothing but a sword-wielding shepherd. She does not think of me that way."

Rodrek's teasing grin faded.

Despair pressed down on Alloryn's heart. "Rest well. Ride by my side from now on."

Alloryn made his way to his assigned tent. He rounded a corner, and he came face to face with an old opponent—the man Alloryn thought he had slain at Jarell's ruined fortress. So he drew the Crestin Sword and confronted the man.

The man threw his hands into the air to show he was unarmed. Recognition dawned in his eyes. "I remember what you said to me that day. You said I was on the wrong side, and so I've come to remedy that."

"How do I know I can trust you?"

"I was conscripted against my will. They threatened my wife. Now she is dead, and they have no hold over me. My name is Beckar and I wish to serve the right side."

Alloryn knew he might be a spy, but the soldier's words and demeanor seemed sincere. He lowered his sword and would have liked to welcome him.

He brought Beckar before the council. Talud and the others tried to dissuade Alloryn from taking him along.

"The man might easily be a spy planted in our midst." Talud gripped his sword.

"We can take no chances of losing this all-important battle." Preedim folded his arms. "He must be imprisoned. It would be easy for him to slip away and tell Feornson our strength and numbers."

Alloryn had to agree, but he watched, saddened, as they took Beckar as a prisoner. He promised himself he would look into the case after he met Feornson on the battleground.

As two men led Beckar away, Preedim placed a hand on Alloryn's shoulder. "I am sorry, my friend. Too much is at stake."

On bended knee, a weary scout knelt before Feornson. "My lord, the Winterhome soldiers are on the move south toward our location."

Feornson motioned for the man to stand. The scout bowed again and scurried off, no doubt, toward the kitchen.

Feornson gave the command to assemble his host on the plain before his fortress in the Everlasting Winter Mountain's foothills. He figured the advantage was his because the Winterhome soldiers fought in mountain passes, where their bottled-up enemy could not fight back in great numbers. Here in the open fields, there was no place to hide, no ability to sneak up on his host. The mountains ringing his valley were too high and treacherous to cross, except for the main pass. The lake on the opposite side from the entrance lapped the cliff's base and was easy to guard.

The fortress itself commanded a sweeping view. The cliff it was too high to climb, or so he thought, and even if someone could, it was too exposed. Feornang set on top of a volcanic plug with one trail leading to the front gates—unlike Bastil's castle— with lookouts able to see all around the steep sides. No one could sneak into his domain.

It had better positioning than Mintala, with its gentle hills rolling in every direction. The city could withstand a siege, but not as long as his fortress could.

The battleground was his choosing and therefore gave him the advantage. He smiled the fanged smile of a wolf smelling prey.

But the Valdeoran hosts' greatest advantage was the element of surprise. They marched to meet the enemy in greater force than Feornson ever imagined possible.

The Domadarians lined the hill's crest, on an early morning, looking over the army massed before them. The enemy spied them, and the alarm called men to arms. Feornson stormed from his tent, belting on his sword, and grabbing a mace from his servant. He smelled the cooking fires, heard the horses anxiously stomping their hooves, saw his men scurrying to form the battle lines, and he was satisfied. He enjoyed battle when it came and the slaying of his enemies. He mounted and gave the order to advance.

As his cavalry rode toward the archers, the forest men let loose their swift flying arrows. The first to fall was on Feornson's side.

The invading army's main formation surged from behind the archers into the fray. Led by Red Horns, half the Nyrmidion force swiftly rode into the center of Feornson's host, the equally determined Winterhome warriors following after. The front lines broke. Feornson's men had no stomach to fight the fierce warriors of the Isles, whose reputation for cruelty and mighty arms was known throughout Valdeor. Feornson himself checked at the sight, but giving a war cry, rode his horse up and down the lines, and tried to whip his men into fighting.

The Nyrmidions, seeing the enemy, went into a frenzy. With strange cries, they slashed everything standing in their way. Feornson's army scattered before them. What they left in their wake, the well-organized Winterhome soldiers mopped up. Although the front line broke, Feornson's main army withstood the onslaught.

After the battle raged fiercely for a time, more Valdeoran units flanked the valley. Feornson's spies, thinking the one small army was approaching from the main pass, in the north, had not been vigilant in reconnaissance in other directions.

Feornson found his men in a pincer movement.

Days before the archers came, units had split from the main allied host. Now they marched over a newly blasted mountain pass from the east to the blare of battle horns. Samaranthans used the black dust they called fire powder to blast through a canyon blocking passage to the valley surrounding Feornang.

Any organization the Warlord's army once had disassembled in the dust in the all-out, one-on-one combat. Swords clashed and mace hit on shield. The main host of Samaranthans rode in from the eastern flank with their pikes and speared the enemy. The nomads came from the western flank using their curved scimitars to great advantage. Alloryn led his men to box in the Warlord Feornson's army.

Alloryn longed to go face to face with Feornson, but in the swirling mass of men, he was hard to find. Alloryn eventually spotted him and hacked his way to his greatest enemy's side. Marjek Red Horns and Feornson were exchanging blows. On sighting Alloryn, the Nyrmidion leader gave a wolfish grin and shouted, "He is all yours, friend." He pulled away, though he had his men circle the two foes, not allowing Feornson's men to come to his aid.

So in the bigger battle's midst, the champion and the warlord faced off.

Feornson rode with a mace in one hand and a battle-ax in the other. Alloryn held a pike he retrieved from a fallen comrade in one hand and the Crestin Sword in his right hand.

Feornson goaded his horse into Alloryn's. Alloryn used his pike to jab at the incoming horse. By sheer will, Feornson turned the horse away from the deadly point and swung to his other side. The battle-ax rang against the great sword. Vibrations echoed throughout Alloryn's body while he held the other off, but the blade held true. Feornson's left hand wielded a mace, which he blocked by swinging the pike above his opponent's head. The mace wrapped around the pike and pulled it from Alloryn's hand. Feornson chortled with battle lust.

Alloryn used his left hand, grabbed the Winterhome shield off his back, and put it before him. With the mace coming at him again, he ducked under the shield and slashed at his opponent's thigh with the sword. He did not make full contact, but Feornson had a long, red scratch down his leg.

The horses reared and circled. Both men swung at the same time. Mace hit shield, then sword hit ax. Back and forth, they traded blows. Their focus on each other, the battle faded from around them.

Sweat poured down Alloryn's face, but he could not stop to wipe it, though it stung his eyes.

Feornson stood in his stirrups, yelled a war cry, and

smashed the shield. The spikes caught the edge of it and yanked it from Alloryn's grasp. The mace's follow-through bit into his horse's face. The beast screamed and fell. Alloryn jumped at the last possible second and rolled out of reach.

He knew he was at a disadvantage on the ground. As the mace swung for him again, he aimed not for the ball, but the chain attaching it to the haft, remembering as he did so what the archivists had said of the Crestin Sword's ability to break metal. The chain snapped and the spiked metal ball went sailing wide. He slipped a short sword from under his tunic with his left hand, ducked the next blow of the ax, and swiped at Feornson's injured leg on the next pass. The short sword slipped under the leather on his opponent's leg and sunk to the bone. Feornson lost his seat and fell, dropping the ax in the process. But the man seemed inhuman, leaping to his feet, pulling his longsword, and attacking in a two-handed hold.

"You were there when I slew that old man. Justinian felt the bite of my sword, as will you."

That day flashed before Alloryn's mind. His loss and anger welled up, like a pot on the boil, and overflowed from where he kept it deep inside. It gave him the extra incentive to best this tyrant. He lunged from the overhead position and met the low guard defense. He pushed the Crestin blade till their wrists locked.

As Feornson gave a mighty push to break the lock, Alloryn spun out of his way and swung his sword down in an arc, breaking his enemy's sword above the hilt. Feornson stilled for an instant, then with teeth bared he moved to cut Alloryn with the jagged sword, but he was too slow. Alloryn used all his pent-up anger to slice the fearsome warlord under the rib cage. With a great cry, Feornson toppled over like a mighty oak. Without thought, Alloryn used the Crestin Sword's sharp point to pierce his enemy's heart.

His limbs heavy, Alloryn contemplated his slain enemy. Triumph flared briefly in his heart, but above all, he felt overwhelming relief. As the battle raged around him, it was no time to indulge his feelings. He could sort them out another time.

He glanced around for the nearest enemy to engage, shrugging off his weariness.

Meanwhile, in Mintala, the other half of the Nyrmidion force and the merchants with them, led by Rappallo, soon sailed into the center of town on their swift boats. A woman with a basket on her head screamed at the sight of the pirate ship sailing down the river and the horned men aboard. People looked up from what they were doing, and then raced away crying alarm. Shop owners ran into the street to see what the commotion was and quickly ran back in, locking the doors behind them.

The ship drifted gracefully as people fled from the sight of it, like rats before a flood. The Nyrmidions landed at the palace dock and overwhelmed the small force left to guard the city. When they breached the palace walls, a formidable and well-organized force met them. Rappallo ordered his men and the Nyrmidions to stop. These looked like civilians, without a uniformed soldier leading them.

"I come in the name of Princess Lauressa." Rappallo jumped on a cart to shout over the crowd. "Who is in charge? Let me speak to him."

The mob quieted down, and one man stepped forward. He had a square jaw and look of a soldier.

"I am Odem, leader of the freedom fighters in Mintala. Who are you?"

"I am Rappallo, and I have been sent by Preedim to secure the city for the return of its rightful ruler. Warlord Feornson is even now surrounded by the Winterhome army, allied with men from all over Valdeor, fighting for freedom from oppression."

A mighty cheer went up at his words.

"And the Champion of Valdeor will soon bring Princess Lauressa to Mintala. Here she will be crowned Reina."

"Welcome, friend. My men and I have taken the palace." Odem turned and addressed all who were gathered, "Let us bring the good news to all the inhabitants of the city. We are free men!"

Another cheer erupted.

"And peace and prosperity will once again settle like a blanket over the land."

The hosts gathered the wounded when the battle was over and the last enemy defeated. Stepan was thankful that his son Tris only lost an arm and not his life.

Then came the sad task of honoring the dead. Among those who fell were their good friends Eleedur the Hawk, and Nathum the nomad. Alloryn's throat closed with grief when they announced their names to the gathered council. The months they traveled with Eleedur made his passing especially hard. He would sorely miss his friendship and words of wisdom.

Preedim ordered the Winterhome soldiers to encase the

two fallen leaders in ice, in the age-old tradition of his people.

"The princess will see they have a state funeral in the capital city," Alloryn promised, "alongside my mentor and great friend, Justinian."

19 *Storm Feornang*

After the field was won, Alloryn went back to the camp in the hills. In the distance, he could see the mighty Feornang fortress like a black bat perched on a barren hill above a lake.

Could Lauressa see the earlier battle? Did she see him defeat Feornson? Was she thinking of him as he was thinking of her?

He sighed in frustration. Yes, Feornson was dead, but the castle was still well guarded, Lauressa still a prisoner in its depths, held by the former warlord's loyal followers. She was still an important pawn in the politics of the land.

How to rescue her? How to get inside the castle? Climbing it, as he and Talud did the Domadarian fortress, was not an option here.

During the meeting with princes, leaders, and generals, he raised the issue. "We have fought the battle and won, but it is nothing if we do not have the princess. No one else can win people's hearts and loyalty. Are there any here or among your men who have entered Feornang, or know of its layout?"

The members murmured among themselves.

"Feornang has been impenetrable, for as long as I have heard," answered Preedim. Men nodded agreement. "But we will inquire of our followers."

When he was walking around the encampment the next morning, deep in thought, Alloryn remembered the soldier detained as a possible traitor. He found Rodrek eating and told him of his plan. Rodrek insisted on coming with him, and Alloryn was glad to have his friend's support.

They headed to the area where they held the prisoner. Alloryn said a word to the guard, and they entered the tent. Beckar was shackled to a post. During the recent battle, no one could be spared to guard a lone prisoner.

The man raised his head as Alloryn came before him. "You said you wanted to serve the right side in this war. The fighting is over, but we have not won the war, not until the princess is rescued. Help me now, and I will set you free."

The man's face changed from sullen to hopeful. "I was born in a village along the lake. My great-grandfather worked on an escape route from the fortress. A story passed through my family of a secret entrance to the castle."

"Do you know where this secret entrance is?" Rodrek asked, staring at the man as if he was trying to see inside his mind.

"I found it once when my brother and I dared each other to enter. I have not traveled there in years, but I know I could find it again."

"I will trust you because I have little choice of finding another with your knowledge." Alloryn pulled out a key to unlock the shackles. "But if you betray me, I will finish our earlier fight. And this time I will kill you." Alloryn unchained him.

They brought him to Alloryn's tent. He did not know how the other leaders would react to his plan, so decided not to inform them. He sent Rodrek to find Talud.

When they returned together, he outlined his plan to sneak into the fortress and rescue Lauressa.

"Do you think four of us are enough?" Talud asked.

"A contingent of soldiers would most likely draw attention, while a few of us can hide once inside."

"I suggest we tell my father." When Alloryn made a move to interrupt him, Talud continued, "Wait! Hear me out. He can use his men to create a diversion."

Alloryn pondered the suggestion as he paced around his tent. They all watched him. This was his decision because he was Lauressa's sworn champion. He stopped and faced them. "You can brief your father on our plan and ask for his help." Turning to Beckar, his ex-foe, he said, "Have you been inside Feornang?"

"Yes. A few times. I was stationed at the eastern garrison, but I traveled with Dukaat to deliver messages to Feornson on several occasions. I have a general knowledge of the keep and the way to the dungeons."

"Good. I need you to draw us the fortress' inside layout— as much as you can remember of where to find prisoners." Alloryn rubbed his hand through his hair. "And anything at all of the number of guards, when they change shifts, where the armory is, and any other useful information you can give us."

Alloryn held the gaze of each man in the small group— Rodrek looked eager, Talud frowned, and Beckar was hopeful—

and saw their trust in him and their determination. "We leave before the first light."

Alloryn and his three allies hid among rock cairns on a hill overlooking the fortress below. It looked impenetrable. Feornang perched like a black raven on a hill with three sides facing a plain and the fourth side facing a vast lake. Feornson's remaining army encamped before it, a multitude of tents and fires blocking the main entrance. Their mission looked hopeless.

As if reading his mind, Talud spoke. "All paths leading to the fortress are watched. I see no way to gain entrance. We cannot hope to get past the army, so what good is a secret entrance? Beckar tricked us to gain his freedom."

"Noble prince, I have not. If your royal father will engage the enemy here, where they feel they are strongest in the plains beneath us, we will sneak around the back of the fortress."

"Will they not see us coming? There is no cover on the lake!" Rodrek said.

"Tonight, there will be no moon till the mid of night. I grew up in a fishing village on the shores of this lake. I can navigate us through the waters in the dark. The secret entrance is in a crevice hidden on the cliff-side shore. No one could find it unless they knew it was there."

"Then we will camp here and wait." Alloryn motioned them to move back behind the cairn.

They spied on the enemy messengers moving in and out of the main entrance all day. Men in clusters sat with nothing to do. The chaos showed a weakened enemy.

But the war was far from won. Princess Lauressa was in the power of Feornson's generals, and eventually one of them would ascend above the others. With Feornson dead, their enemy was an unknown quantity. Forced marriage was the easiest road to power. Someone might also know and use the secret escape route to flee with the captive princess and gain supremacy over all the other generals and minor warlords. And Alloryn knew that time was running out.

Beckar quietly told them all he remembered of the fortress on his several visits, pointing on the map he had drawn, which the others memorized.

Finally, as the afternoon shadows deepened, the band of four left their hiding place. Beckar led them through the hills away from the plain, along the metal-colored lake's northwestern corner. His companions stood at the wood's edge as he bartered for the use of a fishing boat in a small hamlet. He closed the deal, then sailed in the craft to the meeting place in an enclosed inlet, where the others climbed aboard.

They waited until the sunset and the darkness descended. They rowed quietly from the inlet and into the lake's greater swells. Sounds reached them over the water of a battle. Stepan was doing his part by encircling the encampment in the twilight and engaging the enemy.

As they grew closer to the black volcanic mound on which the fortress perched, the sound of waves and weird whistles drowned the sounds of battle. A stiffening breeze made choppy waves that broke against the rocks and crevices. What had looked small in the distance soon became a formidable cliff wall with razor-sharp projections jutting from it.

Beckar was a skilled navigator and easily landed them on

a small strip of beach.

"It is best to secure the line, even though there is no tide. Storms blow up without warning, even on a fine night like tonight." He spoke in his regular voice, the wind and water masking anyone above from hearing the rescuers.

Nearly an hour of scrambling over volcanic rock formations, and many grazed shins later, Beckar led them into a crevice. They lit a lamp and followed him into the narrow space. The way was precarious. Alloryn thought they would get stuck in the ever-narrowing space when it suddenly widened. The sound of the waves receded as they climbed a staircase cut into the rock, but the wind became more focused in the tiny space, open to the sky. It grew in intensity, deafening them with its howling the higher they went. He fought to keep it from whipping him off his step. He thought the wind would defeat them, but Beckar led them into a tunnel away from the fury.

They caught their breath. Rodrek held the lantern high as Beckar stopped before an iron door.

"This door was not here when I visited many years ago. I do not know how to open the lock." They all stared at the big lock barring their way. They were several hours into their mission now, and to admit defeat was a heavy burden.

"Stand aside." Alloryn would not give up hope at this important juncture in the quest. Lauressa always had hope, no matter how impossible the odds were throughout their sojourn together. They had made it this far. Surely the journey could not end at a locked door.

He drew the Crestin Sword from its scabbard. He was not sure it could withstand the iron lock without shattering. But now that Feornson was dead, maybe the sword had fulfilled its destiny. He would sacrifice it rather than Lauressa.

He swung the sword down with the full weight of his arm and body behind it. His aim was perfect. Bright sparks dazzled their eyes, and when he stepped back, the split lock hung open. Fearfully he looked at his sword. Golden red light played along it, as it did that long ago day he first held it. But it showed no sign of damage. He let out the breath he did not realize he had been holding.

Beyond the iron door, the tunnel continued. Their footsteps echoed in the tight space. The lava walls reminded Alloryn of the cave in the Lost Mountains. But the stakes were greater, and the treasure was dearer to him than precious stones.

They reached another door, this one unlocked. Rodrek blew out the lamp's flame. The band drew their swords. They held their breath and listened. No sound reached them. Talud took the lead and opened the door inch by inch. They found themselves in a storage room. They spread out and Beckar found the next door. Again, they listened and heard nothing. They went through the door and found themselves in a wine cellar, which led to the kitchen area.

"I have been here before for refreshment while Dukaat received our orders from Feornson. Prisoners are held in several places within the castle walls, either the dungeons or the twin towers," Beckar told the others.

"We should split up. Two should go into the dungeons, while the other two search the tower rooms." Alloryn pointed. "Talud, you and Beckar go below, while Rodrek and I will go above. We will meet here no later than an hour before dawn to make our escape."

They crossed the dark and empty kitchen and the teams separated. Leaving the nether regions by the stairs to the main dining hall, Alloryn heard voices as they came to the top step. He and Rodrek made quick work and overcame two bored guards, taking their helms and cloaks to use as a disguise. They put the unconscious men in a small, unused room under the main staircase. Hearing the tramp of feet as they closed the door, they positioned themselves with their helms closed, masking their faces. Three other soldiers passed by without glancing at them.

As soon as the footsteps faded, they went up the grand staircase. A hall led in either direction with many doors opening from it, with the towers at the far ends. As much as Alloryn wished to split up further so as not to waste time while both of them checked a separate tower, he knew that two swords were better than one in a fight where they were sure to be greatly outnumbered. So he strode to the right without pause, Rodrek in step with him.

They heard nothing from behind the doors. The door to the tower remained locked, but that posed no problem, as the key hung on a hook beside the door. No, the problem was the guard posted there. They had to improvise.

"Halt! What business do you have here?"

"We have orders to take the prisoner to the dungeon where the torturer awaits," Alloryn said.

Rodrek stamped madly in the dark corner. "Rats! I cannot stand them!"

The guard snapped his head toward the commotion and involuntarily stepped away from the imaginary rats. Alloryn used the pommel of his sword to knock him sharply below the chin and caught him before he fell and possibly alerted anyone behind the many silent doors.

Rodrek grinned at his acting. "Aren't you glad I am with you?"

Alloryn shook his head.

"What?" Rodrek asked. "I did not see you coming up with anything better."

Rodrek removed the key, unlocked the door, and Alloryn dragged the guard inside. They found themselves in a little room at the bottom of a spiral stairwell.

"A guard implies a prisoner worth watching. Princess Lauressa is probably up there." Alloryn's heart beat faster at the prospect. He hoped Rodrek could not hear it.

"Do I have time to comb my hair?" Rodrek spit on his hands and rubbed them on his hair. At Alloryn's frown, he added, "What? After months with you, she might like someone less serious. You are not the only one coming to her rescue."

Alloryn was not sure if his friend was ribbing him or not.

He spared a moment to glance out a slitted window on the scene below the front gate. Cries of men met his ears, yet there was not a full-scale battle waged. As he looked, though, an arrow hit a tent and sent it aflame. Seconds later, from another quarter, the same thing happened. He realized that Stepan was harassing the soldiers in the dark. He gave a tight smile. That type of diversion could last all night.

Alloryn and Rodrek took the steps two at a time. On each level, there was a small, lightly furnished room. They were unoccupied. At last, they reached the top floor with a heavy wooden door blocking their way. Rodrek used the key again to open it. Inside they found an aged man laying on a rough bed of straw.

He shaded his eyes from the torch. "What are you doing here? I have nothing to tell your master, no matter if you drag me back to the dungeons."

Before Rodrek could say a word, Alloryn pulled him back out of the doorway.

Rodrek protested. "Should we not free him? An enemy of Feornson may be a friend of ours."

"Or a worse enemy! I heard rumors that Feornson imprisoned his uncle so he could assume command of the provinces. We cannot risk the princess's life for his." Before Rodrek could disagree, Alloryn continued, "I will tell Preedim and Stepan of his plight. But none of us will leave here alive if we do not accomplish our goal."

His friend reluctantly agreed with him.

Retracing their steps, they were soon at the tower's base. They had left the top floor door unlocked, but made sure the door to the tower was secure, and the unconscious guard safely locked away inside it.

Half the night was spent, and they still had no clue where Lauressa was.

Alloryn noticed shields of conquered enemies hanging on the hall walls. Stopping, he took one, and finding it in good shape, slung it over his shoulder. Rodrek followed his example.

They walked noiselessly through the long hall toward the other tower. No guard stood firm at this door, making Alloryn's heart sink. Soldiers would surely guard Lauressa's cell. Rodrek looked a question at him, and he nodded to proceed anyway. The same key unlocked this door as well. The layout was identical. They heard voices above them, and from what they could hear, a dice game was in progress. The sound invigorated Alloryn. Lauressa would rate more than one guard because of her importance. Hope flowed into his soul.

He signaled that he would go alone, and Rodrek would follow and join the fight. He crept up the stairs, then swiftly propelled himself into the room. He caught the men unawares, their swords still buckled on and their shields set along the wall. Alloryn fought the first soldier to react, then Rodrek appeared. When his foe was down, he raced up the spiral staircase as fast as he could. He left Rodrek to finish off the other, having no fear of the outcome.

Finding that Rodrek still had the key, and not wanting to waste time getting it from him, Alloryn once again used the Crestin Sword in his impatience to break a lock on the door at the top level.

The half-asleep princess leaped up at the crashing of her prison door opening.

"Alloryn!"

In one stride he was beside her. "Lauressa! Are you hurt?"

"Thank the All-Seeing God!" She threw her arms around him, her usual formality forgotten. "I am feeling wonderful now."

Relief made his limbs weak. Emotions crashed inside him, but he had no time to analyze them.

"Sweetheart, we must go." The endearment slipped out without his noticing. "Can you walk?"

"If you give me your arm. I am fine. I was allowed to walk regularly around the keep, so I am fit."

Rodrek met them when they were halfway down the stairs. He grasped her other hand to help her navigate the steep steps only lit by a torch below at the guards' station.

At the bottom of the spiral staircase, in the full light, Lauressa appeared thinner and paler than the last time Alloryn had seen her, but she smiled bravely at her rescuers.

"I am Rodrek, at your service, Your Highness." He made a flourishing bow. "Alloryn's oldest friend."

Alloryn let go of Lauressa and slowly eased the door open, looking down the hall for any activity.

As Rodrek joined him, he whispered to Alloryn, "I see why you are so reluctant to share her."

"This is not the time—" Alloryn hissed back, then stopped at the devious twinkle in Rodrek's eye.

After regaining the hallway, the three of them heard sounds below in the Great Hall. Creeping to the grand staircase's top rail, they saw their companions engaged in fighting a couple of guardsmen. Signaling Lauressa to stay unseen, Alloryn and Rodrek raced to help Talud and Beckar. The four of them soon dispatched the enemy soldiers.

A cry from above and the four looked back toward the stairs. The old man from the first tower had a knife at Lauressa's throat. Alloryn had his foot on the first tread when the captor said, "Another step and you will see her blood."

All four companions froze.

Still holding her, the gray-haired warrior made her walk toward the others. "I have no desire to hurt her, but now having tasted freedom, I command you to take me with you."

Under his breath, where his allies could hear, Beckar hissed, "Trust him not. He is Feornson's uncle, the Warlord Judlaw."

Alloryn's last suspicion that Beckar could be a traitor

evaporated.

Judlaw stopped halfway down and challenged them. In the tower room's poor lighting he had looked frail. Standing above them, they could see the straight stance of a warrior. He had grizzled whiskers and thick jowls, and the bowlegged look of one who was more at home on a horse. His eyes were his dominant feature with an imperative will behind them, a fierce look that penetrated one's thoughts, seeking any weakness.

"She is the prisoner you were looking for earlier." He glanced at each one in turn and nodded at their silence. "I will not harm her if you agree to let me join you. This cursed fortress has been my prison far too long."

Alloryn hoped Judlaw did not know who Lauressa was.

"You will not harm my sweetheart?" Alloryn asked. "You swear?"

"No, no. I merely want you to let me go with you. See, I have removed the knife." Judlaw lowered it from her throat but kept it at the ready. "Lead on and we will follow at a safe distance behind. No tricks, though, or I will hurt her."

Alloryn had to be satisfied with the warlord's promise for now, but he did not trust him one tiny bit.

I practice an act of kindness, and this is my reward?

Help me defeat him, O Guardian of Light, he prayed as they retraced their steps into the bowels of the kitchen.

Have faith, was the answer that came to him.

So easy to say, so hard to practice.

He heard Justinian's words echo through his mind as they made the way through the storage rooms. "You will find many enemies on your journey, but you will find allies too." Yes, they had made many friends, friends that fought beside him recently in battle. Yet friends surrounded him on this venture, too.

He sought out the eyes of each of his companions as they retraced their steps to the kitchen. Talud, Rodrek, and even Beckar gave slight nods of their heads, indicating they were ready to act when the time came.

Once he would have attempted this rescue alone, but now he knew he was stronger with trusted friends, and their combined swords would win the day. He did have faith in them.

Rain joined the earlier wind and the way down the outer staircase became slippery. As they began the descent of the outer winding staircase in the early morning light, Lauressa seemingly tripped on the treacherous lava steps, yanking Judlaw off balance. Judlaw reached out with one hand to steady himself on the rock wall, and in the process, he dropped the knife, which went clattering over the edge into the rough waves below. Alloryn was in the lead, too far away to take advantage of the situation, but Beckar, closest to the warlord, leaped the steps between them to fight him.

Judlaw flung himself between the princess and Beckar, and the two of them wrestled bare-handed for supremacy. Although the seasoned warrior was cunning and desperate, Beckar was younger and determined. The toll of prison food, lack of exercise, and length of time of imprisonment dictated what happened next. Beckar forced the prisoner close to the abyss, both men gripping the other's throat, teetering on the edge. Beckar, with the stronger grip, overcame the old warlord, who let go of him. But as he fell, his hand gripped Beckar's ankle, and the next moment they both went over into the pounding surf below.

The helpless friends drew in their breath, gasps coming

from four throats simultaneously. They strained to see a head bob up from the waves, but it was not to be. Beckar made the ultimate sacrifice to rescue the princess.

The four remaining froze, their perilous situation forgotten, their gazes strained as they stared at the one spot with diminishing hope until they heard a roar greater than the waves. A bright light erupted from the spot they last saw Beckar, like a beacon searching the sky above. The last heartstone exploded skyward as they watched with hearts stopped. It flew directly over them, its sapphire brilliance washing them with wonder.

They won the heartstone of faith at a great price.

Alloryn moved as if in a dream. He could never after recall traversing the stairs or joining the others in rowing back to shore.

As they walked to the allies' tent city, he told Beckar's story to Lauressa. "He was a good man. He proved that. I should have been better prepared, and he need not have died."

She put a hand on his arm, and he looked down at her. "I am partly to blame. If I had not pretended to trip on the stairs, Beckar would not have had the chance to take down Judlaw."

They walked in silence, both pondering the part they played in the death of an enemy turned friend.

Trekker was the first to greet them as they arrived back at camp. He barked and whined and nearly tripped them with his playful darts around their legs.

Lauressa leaned down to rub the dog's belly while he made moaning sounds of pleasure.

She stood, turning her face to her three rescuers. "Beckar died a hero's death. You say he had no family left. Then we will remember him in the chronicles of our quest, and future generations will know his courage and sacrifice today."

She looked back at the brooding fortress. "It matters not how a man begins his life, but how he ends it."

20 QUEST COMPLETE

*I*n the war's aftermath, many of the victors returned to Winterhome to recover and let the wounded heal. Alloryn and Lauressa stayed amongst them until the mountain passes were open.

One night, several weeks later, a hint of spring was in the air. A smell of new earth and a touch of a warm breeze drew many outside. Lauressa searched for Alloryn. She found him standing on a balcony overlooking the city below dressed in festive streamers and banners since her coming. They had hardly spent any time together while Preedim and his wife Ariata wined and dined them.

The royal couple fostered their son Everard's attentions to Lauressa. He was handsome and accomplished, and eligible. Although he seemed attracted to her, she was in love with Alloryn. She could admit it to herself now. There was but one stone to win, and that was love. She was not sure if her task was to win the love of a man, or the love of her people, though she reasoned it was probably the latter.

She thought she detected a gleam of jealousy in Alloryn's

eyes at times, like when Everard took her on a tour of the city by skis or paid her compliments at dinner, but she was not sure. Alloryn did not wear his heart openly.

"I have enjoyed the celebrations and this time to rest, but I think it is time we discuss our next move." She leaned her hands on the balcony.

She could not resist teasing him. "You look rested. I see the ladies are all agog, hanging on your every word as you relate your adventures."

"I care for none but you," Alloryn spoke bluntly.

"I do not know if this is the right time to speak to you of my feelings," he continued, "but I fear if I do not let you know them now, you will not consider my suit for your hand. It has been grievously hard to watch my rival flatter and woo you. And if not him, there are princes Tris and Talud, and that cocky Gensard, standing in line behind Everard."

"I turned Gensard down—twice. His father took him back to Samarantha, or I fear Gensard would have challenged you to a duel."

Taking her shoulders gently in both hands, he turned to face her. "Do not torment me. I need to know if you love me as I love you."

"I needed to keep my feelings locked inside. Until we came this far, I did not want emotion distracting us." She touched his cheek. "Of course I love you. Not because you are my champion, not because you are the heir of Jarell, but for yourself." She put her hand on his arm and gazed at him earnestly.

She saw happiness turn into puzzlement on his face as her words penetrated.

"Jarell's heir?" His breath caught in his throat. He looked

more shocked than if she threw cold water over him. "You mean I am of royal blood?"

She nodded and smiled. "Of course. Your parentage is from the union of Jarell and the girl who nursed him. Justinian tested the heirs of the house of Jarell to find the one who could win the Crestin Sword from the Kratigula, who he would train to be the Champion of Valdeor. That is why you were chosen to fight the beast."

Alloryn recalled the past when he won the sword. "I remember now—Justinian said I was descended from noble warrior's blood."

The old ruins where he had played as a child took on new significance. He pictured them in the moonlight, imagining how stately the fortress must have been, and saw in his mind's eye the kings and princes and their courtiers walking the cobblestones. His childish make-believe that he was a prince was the truth. A shepherd boy's dream of becoming a warrior had come true.

A glow started in his heart, and soon flooded his whole body, as he realized that he had a right to ask Lauressa for her hand in marriage. He made up his mind long ago that he would serve her the rest of her life, no matter the cost to his happiness, his own heart's desire. Lauressa would not relegate him to be her chief bodyguard, as he had feared, watching over her and her heirs while she was happily married to another. He was the direct descendant of her fiancé, after all.

He could not remember the flowery speech he rehearsed often in his head. "I love you and want you for my wife," was the best he could do.

He swept her in his arms and kissed her as he had longed to do, practically since they had met. She entwined her arms around his neck and kissed him back.

They exchanged endearments and lost track of time.

At this moment Everard turned the corner and saw them. One look told him all he wanted to know. Stunned, he discreetly slipped away unnoticed, to brood over a glass of ale in a local tavern with his loss of a princess to a humble, ordinary man.

At the head of her army, Princess Lauressa, with the Champion of Valdeor by her side, rode in style through the streets of Mintala. People thronged the roads and waved from balconies above. Young men jostled each other from the rooftops. The citizens reached out to touch her garments, cheering. She smiled and waved to all.

She and her entourage rode along the thoroughfares headed for the now-empty palace. Tears gathered at the sight of her lost home. How long she had been away. How many memories it brought back as she gazed on it. Here her mother had carried her as a small child. Here her father had sat in judgment. Here she had first met Jarell. And here Justinian had snatched her from harm.

A hand closed over hers and she looked over at Alloryn riding beside her. "Welcome home, sweetheart."

He helped her dismount before the palace's throne room doors. The impressive corner tower loomed above them. In the embrasures far above the plaza, the heartstones twinkled in the late morning light.

With Alloryn at her side, and Trekker sitting at their feet, Lauressa smiled at the citizens lining the street and touched the children's heads who ran up to her, flowers spilling from their arms. As she mounted the double set of stairs with her hand on Alloryn's arm, she turned around at the top to wave again to the crowd.

Tears rolled down her cheeks as she looked at the multitude gathered to welcome her, a stranger. Love for them surged up in her heart and overflowed through her every fiber.

O, thank you, All-Seeing Father for bringing me home and blessing me with so many friends and loved ones. Please keep me and them in Your loving care.

Odem and his men opened the doors to the palace hall.

At that moment, the final stone blazed white-hot in the center of Mintala's throne room. The black blood, congealed on the stone with the murder of King Arness, burnt away and the diamond of charity beneath burned bright. The brilliant light was like a torch spewing forth flame toward the ceiling, causing the other heartstones to radiate their light into the sky. As a beacon afar, the sky lit with a glorious rainbow of colors.

Awed, they contemplated what the light meant.

The Quest was complete.

It was a few moments before noon as they entered the throne room, along with Preedim of Winterhome, and Stepan of Domadaria, and their sons. Behind them, as many people as were able crowded into the room. A hush fell over the crowd as the sun reached its zenith.

Lauressa approached the now-clear diamond center stone

before the throne. As she did, the stones in her medallion burst into light. The sunlight passed through the heartstones above, flooding the room with the colors of the rainbow. The room was aswirl with light beams, which converged on the diamond. A mighty burst of light from the center stone had all present throwing their hands up before the mini-sun.

In a rapture, Lauressa saw a being of light before her. She bowed in profound respect as it spoke. "Child, you have accomplished the quest I gave you a century ago," his voice boomed like thunder, echoing around the room. "You gained the virtues a great ruler needs and suffered much to obtain them. Use the wisdom you have acquired to rule well. Your line will reign for a thousand years if you pass on what you have learned."

The light dimmed and Princess Lauressa came to herself. The stones ceased to shine. No one showed any sign of having shared the vision until she caught the look on Alloryn's face as they exchanged glances. The Guardian included them both in the prophecy.

Lauressa ordered the body of Justinian exhumed and brought by wagon to the gates of Mintala. There Alloryn and Lauressa met it on horseback.

Tears rolled unchecked down her cheeks. Justinian had been a father and a friend during her long exile. Bells tolled mournfully throughout the city announcing a funeral procession. Lauressa glanced at Alloryn and saw his eyes brimming with tears, manfully trying to restrain himself. The sad sound of the bells reverberated deep in her soul.

Men at arms, women, and children joined the procession, which grew as they wound through the city streets. The high priest and a retinue of clerics met the wooden coffin at the gate of the royal burial ground.

Lauressa would have liked to give Justinian a state funeral, with the body lying in state for all to revere, as she had done with the ice-encased Eleedur and Nathum the previous week, but since he died over a year past, she and Alloryn decided a solemn graveside service would suffice. Justinian would have preferred it.

But they spared no expense in the marble edifice erected over his tomb, which portrayed a warrior in full battle regalia with the Gildran royal house of arms emblazoned on his shield. He would never be forgotten in the land, as she ordered bards to write and sing tales of his deeds, and the archivists to record the story in the royal archive, as dictated by herself, whom he had watched over, and by the champion he had forged.

The people of Mintala and the whole land rejoiced. They arranged a great feast for a month hence when Lauressa would be crowned Reina of Valdeor. The bishop, the chief of the priests, would perform the ceremony. The whole city was in a flurry till that time. The bakers baked a towering cake, the seamstresses made beautiful gowns, the citizens cleaned the streets and their houses, strung festive banners, flowers, and lights from the windows. The inns were full of those who traveled to see the great ceremony. Alloryn felt excitement in the air everywhere he went.

He was unused to the attention he received every time he

left the palace on an errand. Adults would turn their heads and whisper. Children would point and follow him around. Being the princess's champion meant being in the public eye, a new burden for Alloryn.

What would being married to her be like? Even more in the spotlight. How does she do it?

Lauressa seemingly took it all in stride. Of course, she was born to it and trained to be a ruler. Still, he found it wearisome.

Lauressa promised to restore the great bells throughout the city's towers that Feornson had melted to make weapons. Forges worked night and day melting captured armor, swords, maces, and pike tips. Alloryn grew used to the smell of hot metal, sulfur, and woodsmoke permeating the air around the blacksmith shops. The bells were re-forged and hung in time for the celebration day.

Alloryn suffered through fittings for finer clothes than he had worn to the feast in Forestown. This time, understanding the importance of his position, he did not protest. And he was proud to discover his tunic had the crest of Prince Jarell's house embroidered on it. It made him feel less of an impostor among the nobility.

Finally, the great day arrived. The mild summer day was heavy with the smell of new flowers and new growth. The solemn procession wound from the church to the palace. Rows of chanting priests came first, then the bishop in splendor. Next were children carrying candles and behind them younger children throwing flower petals. The leaders who had helped bring Lauressa to this point followed the children, dressed in their finest: King Stepan and his wife Talina and sons Tris and Talud in rich forest green with crowns on their heads; Prince

Preedim and his wife Ariata and son Prince Everard dressed in deep red with silver embroidered snowflakes; fierce Marjek and his wife Irda and son in stark black with blood-red sashes. Prince Xander had sent an emissary in his place, miffed that his oldest son, Prince Gensard, was not to be her consort. Next came Rappallo, the caravan leader, with a short cape over his crisp trousers and high, polished boots, followed by Rodrek, now chief of the guard in fancy livery.

At the procession's end, in the place of honor, Lauressa rode a white horse, and Alloryn confidently rode beside her on a black charger, with Trekker trotting alongside them.

Alloryn proudly looked over at his beloved dressed in regal splendor. Lauressa wore a pure white gown embroidered with floral designs in gold thread, covered with a sweeping crimson cape. Her hair flowed in chestnut curls down her back. She displayed her medallion for all to see.

Alloryn felt he had come a long way from the shepherd boy playing warrior as he contemplated what the crowd saw as they gazed upon him. He wore a rich magenta mantle, with gold tracings on the edge, and a rampant lion on his tunic—the symbol of Jarell's house—over his black trousers. The Crestin Sword hung at his side, now a badge of honor.

He rode straight in the saddle with his heart singing, for today, after the ceremony, Lauressa would announce their coming nuptials.

The coronation procession entered the enormous church festooned with greenery and fluttering ribbons, and crowds of people filled every seat, and in both tiers above. All wore their finest clothing of bright colors, which made the inside of the church look like a kaleidoscope image. The children left their places in the procession's front and joined the crowd. The bishop and priests processed to the church front, below the altar, while the nobles filled in the front pews.

When all was silent, the great trumpets sounded, and the triumphal march began. Rodrek and Rappallo held Alloryn's deep red mantle, a sign of his princely heritage, as he strode to the front.

Alloryn caught the eyes of many friends and allies as he took his place. Nods, smiles, and even winks made him relax his tense muscles. He realized he would never enjoy ceremonies. Give him a practice ring and a good opponent, and he would be happy.

A sigh escaped the audience, and Alloryn turned his attention to the main aisle.

Lauressa, bareheaded, in her white gown, followed with three ladies-in-waiting—Talina, Irda, and Ariata. She reached the front, and the women received her symbolic fifteen-foot gold mantle from the pages, draped it over her shoulders, and spread it gracefully behind her.

The bishop intoned, "With the putting on of this royal mantle, may the One Who Fashioned All infuse you with knowledge, wisdom, and majesty from His power on high. May He clothe you with the robe of righteousness and the garment of salvation."

He then led her to the throne from the palace, positioned before the altar, facing the assemblage. Her ladies-in-waiting settled her mantle around her, as her gaze sought out Alloryn, who gave her a secret smile from his place in the front row with the other nobles. He was awestruck at all the pageantry, yet the tiny quirk of her lips and twinkle of her eye let him know that her heart was his.

A priest passed a purple pillow with a golden globe and scepter upon it to the bishop. He reached for the globe first and placed it in Lauressa's right hand, saying, "Remember the whole world is subject to the One Who Fashioned All as you rule the land of Valdeor by His goodwill."

He removed the globe from her hand and replaced it with the golden scepter. "Receive the royal scepter, symbol of kingly power and justice. Execute justice, but forget not mercy. Punish the wicked. Protect the just given to your care."

He placed the scepter back on the pillow, and bowing, the priest removed it. Another priest took his place carrying a purple cushion with a tiara on it. The tiara was finely wrought gold encircled with gems of ruby, sapphire, amethyst, citrine, topaz, emerald, and a diamond. The bishop carefully lifted it above his head. He stepped forward and cried, "Behold the Reina of the north." He turned to the right. "Behold the Reina of the east." Again, he turned and spoke, "Behold the Reina of the south." And finally, "Behold the Reina of the west."

Turning back to Lauressa, he placed the tiara above her head and pronounced the blessing. "I crown you with the crown of glory and righteousness. That having the right faith and bearing fruits of virtue, you may hence obtain a crown of an everlasting kingdom by the gift of Him whose kingdom endureth forever." He placed the tiara on her head and stepped aside.

At his final words, Stepan, Preedim, Marjek, and their families, put their crowns on, which they had removed upon entering the church. Then the audience made a deep obeisance as the music swelled to a crescendo. Trumpets blared, and the bells rang far above their heads. Bells answered across the city, and throughout Valdeor at the appointed time, so all the inhabitants knew the moment their Reina was crowned.

Alloryn put a simple gold circle on his head that was his new right as a prince. His heart swelled within his chest as the music soared toward the sky. He felt he could not contain his joy, as it threatened to burst its bounds.

The Quest was finished, but the best was yet to come as Reina Lauressa and he, Prince Alloryn, would soon spend their lives together in a peace-filled kingdom.

The End

ACKNOWLEDGEMENTS

I thank my talented sister, Susan Peek, for pushing me to write the story she knew I had in me, my editor, Ansley Blackstock, for all her good advice, and my understanding husband Tom for encouraging me to keep at it.